Riches and Prosperity

Other Books by R. A. Stokes

The Nehemiah Project

Riches and Prosperity

By R. A. Stokes

MountainFirePress

To Jesus Christ, my Lord and Savior: Thank You, Lord, for putting this story on my heart. May this book serve to further Your kingdom and glorify Your name.

To Mary Jo—my wife, companion, and friend: Thank you for your many years of love, friendship, and support.

Blessed is the man that walketh not in the counsel of the ungodly, nor standeth in the way of sinners, nor sitteth in the seat of the scornful.

But his delight is in the law of the LORD; and in his law doth he meditate day and night.

And he shall be like a tree planted by the rivers of water, that bringeth forth his fruit in his season; his leaf also shall not wither; and whatsoever he doeth shall prosper.

(Psalm 1:1–3)

Prologue

*R*iches and Prosperity takes you into the lives of a group of people in success-driven, prosperity-minded America in the days before the return of the Lord. The Christian walk is filled with valleys and mountaintops, twists and turns along the pathway, times of great victories and times of failure and defeat.

Riches and Prosperity is a story about the struggles of Christian believers, some with a history of commitment, some with little fruit to bear, some new to the faith.

In the story of *The Nehemiah Project*, Benjamin Sharon, a Messianic Jew, and a group of Christian pastors join together in prayer to seek God's face for an outpouring of the Holy Spirit in their city—in spite of seemingly insurmountable challenges. *Riches and Prosperity* is not a sequel in the truest sense of the term in that the story does not pick up immediately following the events of *The Nehemiah Project* but rather picks up a number of years after *The Nehemiah Project*, moving past events in time not unnoteworthy but simply not yet chronicled.

The story begins during the early part of the Trump presidency, before COVID-19, before the Afghanistan withdrawal, before Russia's invasion of Ukraine, before the Dobbs decision overturning *Roe v. Wade.*

Much can be written about the success-driven, prosperity-minded church in the days before the Lord's return. Events have changed, battles have intensified, but the struggles of man remain.

Chapter One

Over twelve years had gone by since the first body of Christ prayer assembly in Mountain Fire, New Mexico. In spite of significant challenges, Benjamin Sharon and the pastoral group had faithfully obeyed the Lord's call and had labored together for the advancement of the gospel in their community. In the early years, there were community prayer gatherings every three to four months, which included believers from every part of the state gathering to seek God's face for revival in their midst. A massive evangelistic effort throughout the city and surrounding reservation lands followed the early prayer assemblies.

As the years passed, the pastors continued to meet for prayer each week, but with life's circumstances changing, the group had also changed, with some leaving the area, others joining.

Compton Atherton had retired from the ministry and moved back to Ohio. Justin and Jacob Randall were gone. Nathanial Allan was gone. Alfred Yazzie was a faithful participant in the meetings as were Thomas Begaye, Juan Gutierrez, and Jonathan Nelson.

And Alexander Joseph, the patriarch of the group who had so faithfully sought revival over the course of his life, who had cherished the teaching and preaching of God's Word, was now in the presence of Jesus.

The funeral was attended by parishioners from every life-giving church in Mountain Fire, as well as from churches throughout the state.

Among the congregation, there was sadness in losing a friend, a Christian brother, a co-laborer in Christ and His work in the kingdom. And certainly family members from Michigan and other parts of the country—a son and daughter, grandchildren, great-grandchildren, two younger siblings, and nephews and nieces—were grieving over the loss of their beloved "Papa," "Dad," "Alex," "Alexander," the cherished patriarchal saint of the Joseph family for now part of four generations, but fittingly, the emotion most present in the assembly was that of joy. No one who knew Alexander and who also knew Jesus as Lord and Savior questioned the faith of a man who had so earnestly and graciously exemplified the Christian life. There were no "good works" that had saved Alexander from the sting of death, but Alexander had trusted Jesus. And for all who knew him, there was a firm belief that God had granted him a saving faith and prepared his homecoming: "We are confident, I say, and willing rather to be absent from the body, and to be present with the Lord" (2 Corinthians 5:8).

A large wooden cross hung elegantly on the front wall of the sanctuary, prominently displayed to each parishioner entering the beautifully adorned worship area. Banners hung on each side of the theater-style, arch-shaped church sanctuary—scroll-like banners with beautiful portraits of Jesus, pictures of Jesus blessing children, touching a blind man's eyes, standing at a closed door knocking, seated with His disciples in the upper room, and standing with Mary Magdalene in the garden following His glorious resurrection. Other banners held divine titles:

> "Yeshua Hamashiach
> Jesus the Messiah,"

> "Elohay Selichot
> God of Forgiveness,"

> "HaShalush HaKadosh
> Holy Trinity,"

and

> "Elohim Kedoshim
> Holy God."

Each banner was adorned with colorful embroidery, polished rounded wood frames, and tassels hanging gracefully from the corners.

An ornately decorated room, arranged like a small orchestra, symphonious with the white cross on the church steeple, elegantly pointed to a place of future glory.

It was to this house of worship that family, friends, former students, and notably, members of the body of Christ throughout the state and from churches as far away as Michigan had come, to honor the passing of a true patriarch and Christian revivalist, to a place adorned with proclamations in the foyer, the hallways, every classroom and office, the chapel, the upper room, and the sanctuary that Jesus Christ is Lord and King!

This was the church that Benjamin Sharon pastored, a beautifully adorned theater-style house of worship seating up to seven hundred parishioners between the main floor and balcony.

It was here at Faith Gospel Tabernacle that Benjamin began the funeral service for Alexander Joseph.

"Good morning! Greetings to each of you in the precious name of Jesus Christ, Yeshua Hamashiach, the very God and Creator of the universe, the Author and Finisher of our faith. The One that the psalmist references in reverence and honor by saying, 'Cause me to hear thy lovingkindness in the morning; for in thee do I trust: cause me to know the way wherein I should walk; for I lift up my soul unto thee.'

"What a blessing it is to be in the Lord's house today to celebrate the kingship and lordship of Yeshua, Jesus, in the life of our dear brother, Alexander Joseph. I'm honored and privileged that the Lord has allowed me to preside over this service and grateful that He has put a message on my heart to share with you. And certainly, I'd like to say thank you to each of you for being here this morning.

"The title of my message is 'A Life of Readiness, A Life of Preparation,' in honor of Alexander and the life he so well lived as a servant of our Lord.

"A small honorarium to a man who so nobly exemplified the Christian walk for each of us. In honor of his ministry; in honor of his professional work in teaching the tenets of revival; in honor of his commitment to sharing the gospel message to a lost and dying world; in honor of his prayer life; in honor of the legacy he left to each of you who are family and to all of us who knew him as friend.

"Before we begin, please bow with me in prayer. Yeshua, Lord Jesus, Redeemer, Lord, and King! We come to you in the mighty name of Jesus to honor Alexander Joseph, who we know has entered Your presence after trusting You as Lord and Savior. The Bible tells us, 'For God so loved the world, that he gave his only begotten Son, that whosoever believeth in him should not perish, but have everlasting life.' Lord Jesus, You know that Alexander believed in You. And we rest in the certainty from Your Word, the Holy Scriptures, that he is with You this very day, this very hour, this very moment. I ask You to speak to our hearts this morning as I deliver this eulogy to those who have come to honor Alexander's passing into Your presence. Please speak to our hearts, dear God. In Jesus' precious name, amen.

"It occurs to me that we're all at various stages of our Christian walk," Benjamin began his message, "and we're all learning different lessons at any given point in our lives. And we recognize that the lessons God is teaching us are sometimes juxtaposed or overlapping or layered, and the stages of our Christian walk are oftentimes occurring simultaneously.

"For example, you may be a great soul winner, and I qualify that by saying, 'the Lord through you,' yet still be learning lessons of faith in your everyday walk with the Lord. Or you may be a person with a great deal of faith but still need to be more active in the work of the kingdom.

"So in answering the question, Lord, what am I supposed to do with my life and how do I get to that place where You want me to be? I thought that we would examine a number of scriptural passages this morning that give us direction as to the type of life that Yeshua, Jesus, would have us live.

"The first passage I believe the Lord would direct us to is from the Gospel of Matthew. In Matthew 22:37 we read, 'Jesus said unto him, Thou shalt love the Lord thy God with all thy heart, and with all thy soul, and with all thy mind.' This is the Scripture passage in which Jesus gives us the greatest commandment. And that is that we're to love God with all of our hearts. The Bible tells us we were created in God's image. We were made to worship Him. We are His creation. He desires our love, our affection, our emotions. He desires our obedience. Jesus said if we love Him, we will obey Him. That means obeying not just His commandments but His calling for our lives.

"And we're to love Him with grateful hearts. Hearts and minds thankful, first and foremost, for His amazing salvation. For His blessings each day. For His protection in our lives.

"And even as we strive to love God with all of our heart, soul, mind, and strength, we're to walk justly with Him. Micah 6:8 so eloquently tells us that God has shown us what is good and what He requires of us. And that is that we're 'to do justly,' we're 'to love mercy,' and we're 'to walk humbly' with Him.

"Doing justly and loving mercy involves our attitude toward God and also our attitude toward our fellow man. Even as we live in a fallen world, we, as a chosen people, redeemed by the precious blood of Jesus, are to love our neighbor as ourselves. Jesus tells us that this is the second greatest commandment.

"And in loving God and in loving our neighbor, we're to be a praying people. Scripture is very clear about the prayer life we're to have as individual believers and also as a local church. The Bible says we're to 'pray without ceasing,' and 'in every thing by prayer and supplication with thanksgiving let your requests be made known unto God.' The Word of God tells us that 'the effectual fervent prayer of a righteous man availeth much.' The book of Revelation describes the prayers of God's people as golden vials filled with incense. Imagine what a wonderful fragrance those prayers are to Almighty God.

"We see from these passages that we're to live our lives in a state of prayer. That our prayer life is to be reverential, attuned to Him, earnest, focused, and vital.

"I'm reminded of John Hyde, the renowned and distinguished saint known as 'Praying Hyde,' who our brother Alexander spoke about in a pastoral devotion not long ago. John Hyde was referred to as 'Praying Hyde' because of the hours that he spent in prayer, because of the fervor and intensity in which he prayed, and because of the tremendous results that accompanied his prayer life.

"The story is told by a former missionary from England, the late Dr. Wilbur Chapman, who had written to a friend about lessons he had learned concerning prayer. Dr. Chapman wrote, and I read:

" 'I have learned some great lessons concerning prayer. At one of our missions in England the audiences were exceedingly small. But I received a note saying that an American missionary . . . was going to pray God's blessing down upon our work. He was known as "Praying Hyde." Almost instantly the tide turned. The hall became packed, and at my first invitation, fifty men accepted Christ as their Savior. As we were leaving I said, "Mr. Hyde, I want you to pray for me." '

"And then, and I read from the story,
Dr. Chapman went on to say, 'He came to my room, turned the key in the door, and dropped on

his knees, and waited five minutes without a single syllable coming from his lips. I could hear my own heart thumping and his beating. I felt the hot tears running down my face. I knew I was with God. Then, with upturned face, down which the tears were streaming, he said "O God!" Then for five minutes at least he was still again; and then, when he knew that he was talking with God . . . there came up from the depth of his heart such petitions for men as I had never heard before. I rose from my knees to know what real prayer was. We believe that prayer is mighty, and we believe it as we never did before . . .

" 'It was a season of prayer with John Hyde that made me realize what real prayer was. I owe to him more than I owe to any man for showing me what a prayer-life is, and what a real consecrated life is . . . Jesus Christ became a new Ideal to me, and I had a glimpse of his prayer-life; and I had a longing which has remained to this day to be a real praying man.'

"And we're to be a caring people. In James we read that true religion is taking care of widows and orphans. As Alexander so frequently pointed out, most of the great moves of God throughout the centuries were outreach-oriented, having great social ramifications that included the establishment of orphanages and hospitals and shelters for those in need. In fact, the entire advancement of Western civilization—and all of the liberties and material blessings that we oftentimes take for granted—came about largely and greatly from the influence of Christianity.

"We see this concern for those in need in great revivals such as the Great Awakening and the Welsh Revival, and of course modern-day missions work is all about helping the disenfranchised, the poor, the hungry; about sharing Jesus and providing material needs to those less fortunate than we are. We understand that institutional outreach is comprised of individuals who are willing to be of service.

"Turn with me if you would to Matthew chapter 25, verses 31–46 (TLB). Jesus said,

" 'But when I, the Messiah, shall come in my glory, and all the angels with me, then I shall sit upon my throne of glory. And all the nations shall be gathered before me. And I will separate the people as a shepherd separates the sheep from the goats, and place the sheep at my right hand, and the goats at my left.

" 'Then I, the King, shall say to those at my right, "Come, blessed of my Father, into the Kingdom prepared for you from the founding of the world. For I was hungry and you fed me; I was thirsty and you gave me water; I was a stranger and you invited me into your homes; naked and you clothed me; sick and in prison, and you visited me."

" 'Then these righteous ones will reply, "Sir, when did we ever see you hungry and feed you?

Or thirsty and give you anything to drink? Or a stranger, and help you? Or naked, and clothe you? When did we ever see you sick or in prison, and visit you?"

" 'And I, the King, will tell them, "When you did it to these my brothers, you were doing it to me!" Then I will turn to those on my left and say, "Away with you, you cursed ones, into the eternal fire prepared for the devil and his demons. For I was hungry and you wouldn't feed me; thirsty, and you wouldn't give me anything to drink; a stranger, and you refused me hospitality; naked, and you wouldn't clothe me; sick, and in prison, and you didn't visit me."

" 'Then they will reply, "Lord, when did we ever see you hungry or thirsty or a stranger or naked or sick or in prison, and not help you?"

" 'And I will answer, "When you refused to help the least of these my brothers, you were refusing help to me."

" 'And they shall go away into eternal punishment; but the righteous into everlasting life.'

"And so we see that Christianity is not a self-centered type of lifestyle, but rather, its arms reach out in love and help and power and influence far beyond the confines of these church walls.

"These church walls are where we come to get refreshed. To draw near to God, pleading with Him to draw near to us. Taking in His Word, enjoying the fellowship of His saints.

"But then, once refreshed, filled with the Holy Spirit, equipped for the battle, we're to go forth from these church walls, ministering to a lost and dying world.

"Young people, or people like me who are not so young." Benjamin paused and smiled at the gathering. "Let me say that it's a wonderful thing when God calls you to a foreign land to share the gospel of Jesus Christ. What a blessing it is when God gives you the privilege of serving those in great need.

"And yet all of us here today are called to be disciples, and I remind you and encourage you not to neglect the harvest field that is right here in Mountain Fire, New Mexico, and the surrounding Navajo Nation lands.

"Why do you think that work teams come here every summer, from all over the country by the way, to minister at various church camps in the area? It's because they've identified this area as a mission field. An area with great needs. And truly it is a field white unto harvest.

"And then we're to use the talents that God has given us. In Ephesians 4:11 we read that there are five offices of the Holy Spirit: those offices are apostle, prophet, evangelist, pastor, and teacher.

"We read on in verse 12, 'Why is it that he gives us these special abilities to do certain things best? It is that God's people will be equipped to do better work for him, building up the Church, the body of Christ, to a position of strength and maturity' (TLB).

"And as we use these talents, as we go about the Lord's work for the kingdom, we're to trust God and have faith.

"Our beloved brother, Alexander, was a man of great faith, and we celebrate that faith as we join together to honor his life in the Lord.

"So, what is true faith as it relates to our Christian walk? We live in a society where many would say they believe in God but have never been what the Bible refers to as 'born again.'

"Yeshua said you must be born again to enter the kingdom of heaven. He was speaking of a new birth. Not a physical birth but a spiritual birth.

"Just prior to Jesus beginning His earthly ministry, John the Baptist preached repentance, saying, 'Turn from your sins . . . turn to God . . . for the Kingdom of Heaven is coming soon' (Matthew 3:2 TLB).

"Jesus preached repentance, warning of the broad road that led to destruction, that led to hell for all of eternity. It was understood that those who would inherit eternal life, those that would receive this new birth, would come to a place of repentance.

"And so true faith means a surrendered life to Jesus. A life that no longer belongs to us.

"In James we read, 'Are there still some among you who hold that "only believing" is enough? Believing in one God? Well, remember that the demons believe this too—so strongly that they tremble in terror! Fool! When will you ever learn that "believing" is useless without *doing* what God wants you to? Faith that does not result in good deeds is not real faith' (James 2:19–20 TLB).

"What James is saying, under the inspiration of the Holy Spirit, is that it's simply not enough to believe intellectually that God exists. The devils believe He exists, so much so that they tremble in terror.

"So, in other words, faith is not merely a cerebral exercise, but rather, it's a commitment that says, 'I have counted the cost and I am going forward on the narrow road that leads to life. It doesn't matter what anyone thinks. I'm going to live my life for Jesus.'

"And so, first of all, we're to trust Him for our salvation and trust Him with our very lives. And then we're to be a people of faith that look not at our circumstances but rather at Jesus our deliverer.

"In the Gospel of Luke, we read about a Roman army captain who had a slave who was sick and near death. The army captain was considered a friend of the Jews and had even helped them by paying for the building of a synagogue. So the captain sent a group of Jewish elders to Jesus to request that Jesus come and heal his slave.

"We read that 'Jesus went with them; but just before arriving at the house, the captain sent some friends to say, "Sir, don't inconvenience yourself by coming to my home, for I am not worthy of any such honor or even to come and meet you. Just speak a word from where you are, and my servant boy will be healed! I know, because I am under the authority of my superior officers, and I have authority over my men. I only need to say 'Go!' and they go; or 'Come!' and they come; and to my slave, 'Do this or that,' and he does it. So just say, 'Be healed!' and my servant will be well again!" ' (Luke 7:6–8 TLB).

"The Bible tells us that Jesus was amazed by the army captain's faith and that when the captain's friends returned to the home, they found that the slave had been completely healed.

"The army captain had a true faith in God. A faith that was confident that God would provide.

"The Bible also tells us that we're to be doers not just hearers of the Word. As a result, our labors should be with eternal rewards in mind. Are we about the work of the kingdom? Jesus told His disciples that the fields are white unto harvest.

"In Proverbs 11:30, we read that 'the fruit of the righteous is a tree of life; and he that winneth souls is wise.' Jesus was very clear that before His return the gospel would go forth to all the ends of the earth. He instructed His disciples to go forth with the gospel message, saying, 'You are to go into all the world and preach the Good News to everyone, everywhere. Those who believe and are baptized will be saved. But those who refuse to believe will be condemned' (Mark 16:15–16 TLB).

"The apostle Paul, under the anointing of the Holy Spirit, so eloquently compels us to share our faith, first by stating, 'For whosoever shall call upon the name of the Lord shall be saved,' and then by asking a series of rhetorical questions: 'How then shall they call on him in whom they have not believed? and how shall they believe in him of whom they have not heard? and how shall they hear without a preacher? and how shall they preach, except they be sent?' And then he summarizes and says, 'As it is written, How beautiful are the feet of them that preach the gospel of peace, and bring glad tidings of good things!' (Romans 10:13–15).

"We see a sense of urgency in Paul's writings as well, as we read in 2 Timothy 4:1–2: 'And so I solemnly urge you before God and before Christ Jesus—who will someday judge the living and the dead when he appears to set up his Kingdom—to preach the Word of God urgently at all times, whenever you get the chance, in season and out, when it is convenient and when it is not. Correct and rebuke your people when they need it, encourage them to do right, and all the time be feeding them patiently with God's Word' (TLB).

"Jesus, the master soul winner said, 'Do you think the work of harvesting will not begin until the summer ends four months from now? Look around you! Vast fields of human souls are ripening all around us, and are ready now for reaping. The reapers will be paid good wages and will be gathering eternal souls into the granaries of heaven! What joys await the sower and the reaper, both together!' (John 4:35–36 TLB).

"The urgency of the gospel message is captured in 2 Corinthians 5:11, where we read, 'Knowing therefore the terror of the Lord, we persuade men.'

"And then Jesus said that we're to be perfect even as our Father in heaven is perfect. This is a very difficult passage of Scripture. As we examine this verse, let us remember that Jesus told us to live one day at a time. We were created to live one day at a time in the presence of Jesus. God desires that we live each day, each hour, each moment, in a state of prayer, in a state of communion with Him, in a state of being perfect, even as our Father in heaven is perfect.

"And finally, we're to love. The Bible says, 'Give, and it shall be given unto you; good measure, pressed down, and shaken together, and running over, shall men give into your bosom. For with the same measure that ye mete withal it shall be measured to you again' (Luke 6:38). God is not a respecter of persons. It doesn't matter if we've been part of a particular church for fifteen years or for six weeks. Our fellowship should never be about cliques, about our own inner circle of friends, but rather about loving one another, regardless of our economic or social status.

"If Stephen, as he was being stoned in his dying moments, would beseech God to not hold that sin against the angry mob who was killing him—who are we, brothers and sisters, to build walls around those who so desperately need Jesus?

"If our Lord and Savior Jesus, Yeshua, in His final moments on the cruel cross of Calvary, would cry out, 'Father, forgive them; for they know not what they do,' who are we to set boundaries for our love?

"And yet we are so easily offended. But the Bible tells us in 1 Corinthians 13, 'Love is very patient and kind, never jealous or envious, never boastful or proud, never haughty or selfish or rude. Love does not demand its own way. It is not irritable or touchy. It does not hold grudges and will hardly even notice when others do it wrong. It is never glad about injustice, but rejoices whenever truth wins out. If you love someone, you will be loyal to him no matter what the cost. You will always believe in him, always expect the best of him, and always stand your ground in defending him' (vv. 4–7 TLB). The Bible says that 'love goes on forever' (v. 8).

"And then this beautiful, eloquent passage of Scripture ends by saying, 'There are three things that remain— faith, hope, and love—and the greatest of these is love' (1 Corinthians 13:13 TLB).

"In closing, do you want to know what God wants you to do? Then ask Him. He doesn't begrudge you that guidance. He will gladly tell you. As you seek Him, He will help you to love Him more and more. He will walk with you, even as He instructs you to walk justly. He will teach you to pray and direct you to take care of those around you who are in need. He will show you the talents He has given you and He will increase your faith. He will help you to be doers of the Word and to go forth with the gospel message. And finally, He will help you to understand the beauty of living in His presence moment by moment, living a life of faith, a life of preparation, living in a state of readiness, being great givers, a people filled with His love.

"Our brother, Alexander, embraced these tenets of the Christian faith. Alex was not a perfect man. None of us are. The Bible says that 'All have sinned and come short of the glory of God.' But Alexander accepted the salvation that Yeshua alone can give. Alex would often say, along with Paul, 'Jesus is my righteousness.' Alexander loved the Lord Jesus, earnestly sought His will in this life, and looked forward to the words of His Savior, 'Well done, thou good and faithful servant.' "

Chapter Two

After fifteen years of pastoring Jesus Saves Pentecostal, and as many years ministering to the East Indian motel owners in Mountain Fire, Nathanial Allan resigned his pastorship and had been ministering overseas for the past three years. He was part of an international relief effort in Haiti when the news of Alexander's passing came.

Benjamin,

With both a heavy heart and a heart filled with joy, I read your note to the pastors about Alexander going home to be with the Lord. A heavy heart because he meant so much to me, personally (and to all of us, I know), but a joyful heart knowing he has gone home. In my mind's eye I can see him now, bowed down or lying prostrate before the throne, sitting humbly at the feet of Jesus, grateful that the Lord allowed him to be a servant of the Most High God.

Amy and I give our heartfelt condolences to Grace Marie and the rest of Alexander's family. Please greet each of the men for me. I miss our times together and the labor we shared in Him.

My love to each of you. All glory to our Savior, Jesus, who we all embrace as Lord and King!

Warmly in Christ,

Nathanial

Compton Atherton always joked that he had been trying to leave Mountain Fire ever since he arrived and that once he did leave, he would probably never return. Compton beamed when he saw Benjamin in the foyer. The men warmly embraced. "So good to see you, my friend," Benjamin said. "I was hoping you would be able to come."

"I guess I always knew I'd be back but of course didn't know the circumstances. Alexander was a pillar in the community. I count it a great honor to have known him. You know, Benjamin, Alex and I spoke in December, just before Christmas. The note he wrote to me in the Christmas card he sent was so moving I went straight to the phone and called him. He sounded great. We had a wonderful conversation . . ." Compton's voice choked. "He was a true friend. He loved the Lord deeply."

"Yes, he did. And your dear wife, Elizabeth. How is she feeling?"

"Beth is much better, thank you, but not well enough to travel. She sends her love. We so much appreciate your prayers for her. They mean so much to us both."

David Janssen still pastored Elim Lutheran Church, his wife, Elisha, still rang the church bell twice weekly, and David still met with the pastors for prayer, although his attendance was no longer weekly.

The day before the funeral service, Jacob Randall and Justin Randall boarded a flight from Des Moines to Albuquerque with a stop at Sky Harbor in Phoenix. They arrived at Albuquerque International Sunport airport, rented a car, and proceeded to drive to Mountain Fire. It was a gorgeous New Mexico morning, the sun shining brightly in a cloudless sea of azure sky. Neither spoke much on the two-hour drive, gazing off into the distance at rock formations, foothills, high-desert terrain spotted with piñon and juniper trees, and abandoned homes along old highway Route 66—trailers, adobe structures, shelters for denizens from another time. They passed by once-familiar road signs and exits to Casa Blanca, Paraje, and Cubero, continuing on through a winding cliff gorge, and then past the stucco, earth tone colored pueblos on the sloped mound of Laguna Pueblo—rustic dwellings encircling the San José de la Laguna Mission, its white adobe-shaped architecture settled majestically on a hill in the midst of the surrounding mesas and foothills of Mount Taylor, its symmetrical face forming a stately crown with two side-by-side belfries fashioning eyes below a large cross prominently resting at the pinnacle of the church. They continued on past Mount Taylor near Grants and argued playfully about which of them had braved the hike to the peak with the most energy. Jacob, the former high school wrestling star, won the debate. They passed the exit to Blue Water Lake and then, further on, the exit at Thoreau, where Justin would take Highway 371 north when he and his family went to Pagosa Springs. They passed a dilapidated Whiting Brothers sign near the Continental Divide and a refinery near Jamestown.

The trip brought back unforgettable memories of their years in New Mexico, wonderful years of ministry at their church and with the local body of Christ during the prayer assemblies and evangelistic work.

The men entered the foyer together and saw Benjamin, David Janssen, Jack Broholm, Compton Atherton, Gary Smith, Alfred Yazzie, and Robert Thompson gathered in the hall near the entryway to the sanctuary.

"Jacob, Justin, my friends!" Benjamin called out. "It is so good to see you both!" Hearty hugs and handshakes intersected the circle as the men embraced, each brimming with excitement, welcoming two more old friends back to celebrate the life of the group's patriarch.

Questions and answers ensued.

"Yep, still pastoring the EFCA church south of Decorah," Jacob said. "I expect that to be my last stop, unless, of course, the Lord says otherwise."

"You may remember, the church isn't large enough to support a full-time music director, so I've been teaching music at a small community college and touring with a gospel ensemble. I'm never gone more than one night. Home for Katie." Justin smiled.

"Benjamin, you look great! How have you been? Are you still running?" Justin asked.

"I feel great. I am still running. I'm afraid if I stop, I won't be able to get going again." The men laughed heartily, happy to once more be together.

"I am blessed, my friends," Benjamin said. "So good to see you both."

"Indeed, we are all blessed!" Compton joyfully exclaimed.

"Brothers, I'm reminded. Join hands!" Justin reached and took Jacob's hand to his left and David Janssen's hand to his right. He raised each hand toward heaven and began singing.

> "Bless the Lord, O my soul,
> and all that is within me, bless His Holy name!
> Bless the Lord, O my soul,
> and all that is within me, bless His Holy name!"

An impressive mix of tenor, baritone, and bass voices ascended on the final refrain:

> "He has done great things,
> He has done great things,
> He has done great things,
> Bless His holy name!"

"It is so good to be back together!" Benjamin exclaimed. "How long will you be here?"

"We fly out early Monday morning," Jacob said, Justin nodding in agreement.

"Compton?"

"Monday afternoon. One twenty."

"So good to see you all," Benjamin said. "Albeit different circumstances would have been preferable to all of us. Alex would be honored to know that you were here."

And so the men were joined together once more, if not in physical presence, certainly in Christian spirit, united with a simultaneous sadness and joy in the passing of a beloved saint who had left this life behind but entered the rapture and grandeur of eternal life in heaven.

Chapter Three

Across town at the Abundant Blessings Word of Faith Sunday morning church service, Reverend Parker was finishing his message to a packed auditorium. "You have an unfulfilled destiny," he exclaimed to the shouts of many in the auditorium.

Parker was a youthful looking, handsome man, about six two, with curly goldish-brown locks that hung halfway down his forehead and just above his earlobes. His presence loomed largely on the two mural-sized screens, one to the left, one to the right, on each side of the stage.

"You may think you're walking in blessing, but the best is yet to come!"

Affirmations erupted throughout the auditorium. "Preach it, Reverend!" a man cried out.

"I can feel a wave of blessing blowing through this room. I sense abundance settling on each man, woman, and child. The blessing is yours for the taking, friends. Turn to your neighbor and say, 'You deserve the blessing.' "

Voices resounded through the building as Reverend

Parker paced the platform. Ushers passed attractive velvet offering bags with oak-colored handles down the aisles as the service began to close. "Be abundant givers, friends, just as abundant blessing is coming to you," Reverend Parker cried out.

Jack Broholm worked his way through the crowd toward the stage and waited patiently as a group of churchgoers stood talking and shaking hands with Reverend Parker. One after the other, they were greeted, hugged, acknowledged with a nod, or made to feel welcome as Reverend Parker, now down from the platform at the base of the auditorium, pressed against the crowd, turning from side to side, touching arms, touching shoulders several feet away, smiling broadly as he interacted with each member of the gathering.

"Reverend Parker, may I have a word with you?" Jack said after about five minutes, unsure if he was heard, but the reverend seemed to catch his eye and Broholm continued. "Reverend Parker, my name is Jack Broholm. I normally attend Faith Gospel Tabernacle. A group of pastors and several laymen meet each week for prayer. I wanted to invite you to join us next Thursday."

Moments after Jack's invitation, Reverend Parker was interrupted by a woman who quickly tugged at his arm, leading him through the mingling crowd toward the exit. "I'm so sorry, friends, but when the wife says I need to go, I need to go." Parker glanced at Jack, raised his eyebrows, smiled, shrugged, and lifted his hands as if to say, "What can I do?"

Jack turned and walked toward the rear of the church toward the doors he had entered, weaving his way through the still-crowded assembly. As he left the building, Jack bumped into a young lady who crossed suddenly into his path in an effort to catch up with her husband just ahead of her.

"Excuse me, I'm sorry," Jack said, leaning back, giving space for her to pass.

"No, no, it's my fault. I'm in too big of a hurry some days." She smiled warmly. "Andréa Veronique," she said, extending her hand. "My apologies."

"Jack Broholm. Glad to meet you. You look familiar . . ." Jack squinted as the morning sun lit on the small group as they exited the foyer. "You're running for office, aren't you?"

"Yes," she replied. "I must have made an impression. A good impression, I hope." Andréa Veronique smiled and laughed.

"I saw you on a local station the other night," Jack said. "The debate with Congressman Ross. Now I remember. I thought you came across well."

"Thank you very much. I appreciate that. Mr. Broholm, this is my husband, Stuart."

Jack turned slightly and acknowledged a man who had just placed his left hand on Andréa Veronique's shoulder. The men shook hands. "How long have the two of you been attending this church?" Jack asked.

"Actually, it's our first time," Stuart said. "We enjoyed the service."

"We thought it was a good way to get connected to some of my future constituents. Hopefully, future constituents," Andréa Veronique said lightheartedly.

"I normally attend Faith Gospel Tabernacle, but I was hoping to have an opportunity to meet the pastor and spend a few minutes with him. It was kind of hard with the crowd. He's very popular."

"We've heard good things about him. He sounds like a good family man," Stuart said. "We've been in Mountain Fire for a couple of years, three and a half actually, but haven't really settled into . . ."

"We've been looking for the right church," Andréa Veronique interjected. "As Stuart mentioned, we liked the service. I think we'll be back."

"Where are the two of you from?" Jack asked.

"I grew up in Wilmette, Illinois. Went to school in Evanston," Andréa Veronique replied.

"A little further north, Highland Park. We met when we were sophomores in college," Stuart said.

"Really! How interesting. My daughter went to Moody."

"Moody Bible Institute. Very impressive," Andréa Veronique said.

"After college we were in Galena for ten years, so Illinois most of our adult lives," she offered.

"Beautiful area," Jack said. "I spent some time on a houseboat on the Mississippi one summer. When I was much younger," Jack added with a chuckle. "I always enjoyed that part of the country. Why did you leave Galena?"

"Other than the snow?" Andréa Veronique laughed. "And the ten below?"

"I understand, believe me," Jack said, nodding in agreement. "I was in Madison before Chicago."

"Where is your daughter now?" Stuart asked.

"She's involved in missions work, church planting. Right now, she's in Peru. She's doing very well. We couldn't be prouder of her."

"And you?" Stuart asked. "How long have you been here?"

"Thirty years . . . seems like a lifetime," Jack said and then laughed. "It's home at this point. I love the Midwest, but New Mexico has a special charm. It grows on you."

The three had been walking slowly through the parking lot when Andréa Veronique and Stuart suddenly stopped momentarily and then shifted directions. "Looks like our car is over here," Stuart said. "We need to drive around and pick up the girls from their Sunday school class. Very nice meeting you, Mr. Broholm."

"No mister needed; Jack is fine. I'm not that old," Jack said and chuckled. "Nice to meet you guys. All the best with your campaign, Andréa."

"Thank you, Mr. Broholm . . . Jack, I'm sorry. Very nice to talk to you."

"Nice to talk with each of you. We'll probably cross paths again. Small world for sure," Jack said.

"You know who to vote for." Andréa Veronique smiled and waved to Jack as they parted.

Jack continued through the parking lot to his car. He

had hoped to have the chance to introduce himself, get to know Reverend Parker, converse a bit, and then invite him to the weekly prayer meeting. It didn't work out. The prosperity message, although expected, left Jack uncomfortable. The emphasis seemed misplaced. The Abundant Blessings Word of Faith church wasn't the only church in Mountain Fire that preached some level of prosperity, but today's service seemed all about blessing, nothing about surrender. The church's statement of faith was orthodox in itself yet less than a half page in length. What the statement covered was sound, but much in the realm of church doctrine was not addressed.

Jack reflected on last Thursday's pastoral prayer meeting and the discussion that followed their time of prayer.

"He bought the house on Sagebrush Lane. The two-story adobe at the end of the cul-de-sac. It has a very nice view of the arroyo and a spectacular view of the foothills in the distance," one of the men noted.

"Wow," David Janssen said, pulling his head back in a rapid jolt. "How much did that go for? Some of the homes on that block are four or five hundred, aren't they?"

"It was listed for $450,000," replied Juan Gutierrez, the pastor of a small nondenominational church north of Mountain Fire. Juan lived in an attractive trailer park with lamppost-lined streets interspersed with small pine trees and poplars. "I've been looking for something a little bigger, which is how I know about the listing," Juan clarified.

"Well, it wasn't seven figures," Alfred Yazzie said lightheartedly.

"In fairness, there are no mansions in Mountain Fire," one of the men interjected.

"We live in a wonderful church parish, and the Lord has blessed my family in more ways than I can count. But if we were to leave the church, guess what? We leave the parish behind as well. The synod has graciously provided for our physical needs, and I thank God for that! But we could never in our wildest dreams buy a house on Sagebrush Lane," David Janssen said, with more than a hint of dismay.

The men were divided. Most of the group lived in what would generally be described as nice residential neighborhoods in Mountain Fire. Some of the long-tenured pastors had homes that were paid for, most of the men had mortgages, several lived in a trailer park, and a couple of them rented apartments.

"We need to support him. He's one of us," one of the pastors said.

Jack winced. He wasn't so sure. And yet, where was the line of affluence drawn? Was a $400,000 home in a nice suburb of Phoenix any more prosperous than a $250,000 home in Mountain Fire? Lord, help me not to be judgmental, Jack thought.

Before adjourning the weekly prayer meeting, one of the pastors led the men in a prayer for the new church and Jack agreed to attend the service on Sunday and introduce himself to the pastor. He was glad he had gone, but it wasn't the outcome he'd been hoping for. Maybe he'd try again in the coming weeks, he thought.

Chapter Four

Organizing and leading the local body of Christ prayer assemblies, a responsibility under the Lord that Benjamin cherished and labored faithfully in, had drawn attention far beyond the scope of churches in Mountain Fire and the surrounding area. Indeed, the prayer meetings had grown to include congregants from Farmington, Albuquerque, Santa Fe, Carlsbad, Ruidoso—small towns and large cities alike—and had garnered attention from other prayer ministries throughout the country including Messianic Jewish organizations that became aware of Benjamin's Jewish upbringing and dramatic conversion to Christianity. Invitations to share his testimony, speak about the prayer assemblies, and preach sermons on prayer came far more frequently than his schedule would allow considering his primary responsibility was pastoring Faith Gospel Tabernacle. This was the calling God had given him a number of years before, and attending to the needs of his congregation was always of foremost concern. The needs and hurts surrounding him were momentous. An associate pastor, Gabriel Joshua, also a Messianic believer, had been hired and filled the pulpit in Benjamin's absence, but with a wide range of added ministerial work as a result of the prayer assemblies, Benjamin's schedule was filled to the brim. It was this circle of engagement that perpetuated even greater invitations for ministry and provided the backdrop for his sabbatical.

His speaking engagements would take him from Madrid to Luxembourg to Wittenberg, and then on to Tiberias for a special baptismal service at the Sea of Galilee and a special dedication at the Western Wall in Jerusalem. He would spend ten weeks in Israel and, if circumstances permitted, meet with a group of Aramaic Christian believers in Lebanon and a group of Jordanian Christians at Petra. He would fly from Tel Aviv back to New York, spend several weeks in Brooklyn, and then return to Mountain Fire.

His intelligence work in Israel so many years before was seldom thought about and known by only a handful of close friends. His acceptance among the Arab community in Mountain Fire was remarkable considering his unwavering support for Zionism.

Doctrinal challenges among the group remained, but there were no discernible disagreements to the statements of faith found in the Nicene Creed and the Apostles' Creed.

All adhered to the infallibility of Scripture, the inerrancy of the Word of God. The deity of Christ, the triune

God, the virgin birth, the death of Jesus on the cross of Calvary, His literal resurrection from the grave, the eternal nature of man's soul, the need to be born again by the Spirit of God, salvation by grace through faith—not of works—and an eternal heaven and hell were all nonnegotiable biblical truths that each of the men taught, preached, and steadfastly believed. Old Testament stories of the serpent in the garden, the flood, Noah's ark, the crossing of the Red Sea, Moses leading the Israelites through the desert for forty years, David defeating Goliath, and Jonah in the belly of the whale were not metaphorical teachings but rather literal events, providentially ordained by God and passed on to His people by the Holy Spirit's divine revelation to the prophets.

Differences persisted on the interpretation of certain passages, with some translations more esteemed than others, but the complete authority and perfection of original Scripture was never in dispute. Eschatology viewpoints varied among the men and certainly among the church bodies within the area churches. Most of the group held firmly to a last-days theology, believing that Israel's status as a nation in 1948 was the beginning of Jesus' statement, "Even so, when you see all these things, you know that it is near, right at the door. Truly I tell you, this generation will certainly not pass away until all these things have happened" (Matthew 24:33–34 NIV).

All felt the Lord was returning soon, perhaps in their individual lifetimes—certainly not hundreds of years from now. Too many signs pointed to the return of Jesus.

With those agreements acknowledged, doctrinal positions on the rapture, the millennium, infant baptism, Arminianism, and Calvinism persisted. Within the full orthodoxy of church teaching, some doctrinal challenges might have arrived if examining the complete catechism of the Westminster Confession of Faith, though largely the entire creed would have been accepted and embraced.

Only two of the men were Sabbatarians in the strictest meaning of the term.

Opinions on the "music wars" and varied preaching styles were as different as the cultural and ministry backgrounds of the men themselves.

David Janssen decried the "name it and claim it" prosperity teaching that he viewed as heresy and had no tolerance for sermons filled with anecdotal stories and an occasional Scripture verse rather than scriptural exhortation and admonishment with a brief testimonial story to help support the text.

"Churches today are filled with humor-laden, light-hearted, feel-good messages filled with uplifting stories but little mention of sin and repentance. Sell your cotton candy at the state fair; don't bring it to the pulpit!" he would say with conviction.

David often shared the story of a preacher he once heard who spent the first fifteen minutes of his message telling stories about the family cat. The congregation was in an uproar with cries of "c'mon" and "don't I know it" and "preach it, brother!"

"Painful," David said, describing the scene.

"Quit fooling around! Preach the Word!" he would admonish, not singling out anyone in particular, but if his message settled on a pastor in need of this exhortation, then so be it.

"There is a life-and-death earnestness to the gospel message of the Bible. In the Bible you don't hear levity. You hear an earnest call to serve God, the Creator of heaven and earth." He bemoaned topical sermons, entreating a serious exegesis of the Word of God and reciting verses from the Psalms in his Sunday morning liturgy.

David frequently weighed in on the music wars—the ongoing debate involving contemporary Christian music. Regarding the praise and worship songs at some churches, he would say, "Here comes the blastoff. Get ready for a high-intensity, bass-driven, lyric-repetitive twenty-five-minute concert. If you still have your senses afterward, you might be able to concentrate on the sermon."

David loved the liturgy, the reverentially recited creeds, the beauty of ornately designed stained glass windows, and the splendor and erudition of the great hymns of the faith.

David was a hymnologist, teaching an adult Sunday school class on traditional hymns from eminent forebearers of the faith. In his private devotions he studied Isaac Watts, Fanny Crosby, Charles Wesley, John Newton, and the reformer Martin Luther—theologians, evangelists, and composers who had written great hymns filled with sublime lyrics, profound theology, and musical accompaniments of grandeur.

His conviction for doctrinal positions, illuminated for the common man during and after the Protestant Reformation, "borne from the Word of God," he would say, was unshakable. He often felt critical and knew he came across as judgmental but believed he was called to defend truth whatever the cost.

Gary Smith still pastored Faith Bible Church, though many of the pastoral duties had been turned over to Alfred Yazzie, a former parishioner of Faith Gospel Tabernacle. Alfred worked diligently to support the Faith Bible Church–affiliated missions group on the reservation and, with Gary's mentoring and Benjamin's encouragement, earned a pastoral degree and then an associate pastor role. Gary still had the prison ministry, preaching each Sunday morning at the local jail. Emily Smith managed Living Water Christian Bookstore and was president of the Mountain Fire Right to Life chapter.

"I will be leaving early next week on a three-month sabbatical," Benjamin announced to the men at Thursday's pastoral prayer meeting. "The church is in good hands with Pastor Joshua. Jack, keep Gabriel in line," Benjamin said and then shook Pastor Joshua's shoulder playfully.

Jack Broholm smiled at Gabriel Joshua. "I think Gabe will keep me in line."

"You are coming back?" Gabriel asked. "You didn't bring me to Mountain Fire to abandon me, I hope."

"The East Coast will never be the same for you, my

friend. Whether I'm here or not, Mountain Fire is your new home as long as Yeshua has you here." Benjamin smiled at the men. "But yes, Lord willing, I am coming back. Three months seems like a long time to me, but I'm sure the days will go by quickly. I'll be back before you know it. Pastor Joshua will probably say, 'I thought you just left yesterday. You're back already?' "

"I don't think so, Benjamin," Gabriel replied. "You will be missed."

"I covet your prayers. I have an exciting trip planned—that Yeshua planned—an itinerary many months in the making. I have the honor to teach and preach at a number of exciting venues, some new, some familiar from times past. I'll be seeing old friends and also meeting up with believers who I have only corresponded with by phone or email. Pray each day that Yeshua will go before me, protect me, and guard my steps."

"We will pray for you every day," Gabriel said, as a chorus of affirmations followed.

"Let's gather around Benjamin and pray right now," Gary Smith said.

The men crowded around Benjamin, laying hands on his shoulders, arms, and back, one pastor placing his hand on Benjamin's head and praying, "Lord Jesus, we lift up Benjamin before You. Anoint our brother by the power of the Holy Spirit, we ask. Keep him from the enemy's attacks. Protect him from the schemes and devices of the Evil One, we pray. Lord, the psalmist tells us that Your Word is a lamp unto my feet and a light unto my path.

Illuminate the path before our brother and bring him back safely to us in Your time. In Jesus' name we pray, amen."

Jack Broholm and Robert Thompson were among the group of men who committed to praying for Benjamin Sharon that day. Neither of the men foresaw the trials that they and others close to them would endure in the coming days. Neither understood the level of prayer that they also would need in the days and weeks that lay ahead.

Chapter Five

Andréa Veronique approached the podium, stopped at the lectern, and flashed an endearing smile at the audience. She had a striking appearance, like someone you might see on the cover of a fashion magazine or the celebrated presence of a leading actress on a screen set or, perhaps most notably, the appearance of a young CEO for a Fortune 500 company—very professional, very confident, very poised. None of these images detracted from her demeanor of an aspiring politician with a focused agenda.

"We have far too much homelessness on our streets," she said after a brief introduction. "Drugs and alcohol have ravaged Mountain Fire and many other communities across the state. For too long, establishment politicians statewide have accepted the status quo. I refuse to do that!"

A short time later she finished her speech with the words rising on a crescendo, "I commit to you, real change!"

Andréa Veronique raised her fist as the crowd erupted in cheers. As she descended the steps from the podium, a man approached her and extended his hand. "Nice speech, Mrs. Veronique. My name is Arthur Cousins. Great comments, fresh perspective! Or may I call you Andréa?" The man was well-dressed and wore a black wool homburg hat. He had a neatly cropped mustache and beard. His spectacles belied his age.

"Actually, Veronique is my middle name. Mattheson is my last name. Spelled like the German composer. My husband is Stuart Mattheson. He's a schoolteacher in Mountain Fire."

"I see," Cousins replied. "Andréa Veronique Mattheson. I did know that. But you go by Andréa Veronique?"

"Yes," Andréa Veronique said. "Since I was young."

"Andréa Veronique—very distinguished, very lovely name. By the way, you're still young." Cousins smiled and again extended his hand.

"I have a proposal I'd like to discuss with you," Cousins said. "I represent a pro-choice advocacy group that believes a woman has the right to choose." Cousins paused for a moment and looked at Andréa Veronique with an inquiring expression on his face. "You didn't address the subject in your remarks; I'm not sure where you stand. But I will say that you come across as very evenhanded, very fair-minded in your approach to the issues. From what I can gather, there's nothing extreme about your views."

Cousins tilted his chin down slightly and peered over his spectacles. "I imagine you believe that a woman's reproductive decisions are hers to make with no interference from anyone else," he said as more of a statement than a question. Without waiting for Andréa Veronique to respond, Cousins continued. "We'd like to get behind a candidate who will support our agenda. Money is not an object. Media coverage will put the person we support at the forefront of the race. Our resources will virtually guarantee his or her election. In addition, there's a bonus for the candidate we support. Specifically, for you personally, if you're that person. We can set up a time to discuss the details further if this interests you, but I can assure you the offer will be substantial. In the meantime, your campaigning just got easier." Cousins smiled broadly.

"You realize I'm running as an independent?"

"Of course. In the end, it doesn't matter. We would prefer . . ." Cousins's voice tailed off. "In this race we need a fresh face. Somebody with no issues. Levelheaded, dignified sounding. Someone who we hope can reach across the aisle and appeal to center-left voters. I think you fit the bill."

Andréa Veronique was stunned. In a moment's time, the election was seemingly being handed to her. All of her passion for the convictions she held had translated into a very detailed, comprehensive plan of initiatives that she believed were needed to effectively run the country. Those plans could now be enacted. The platform was there for the taking.

"Who are the members of the group you represent?"

"If you're elected you'll meet your beneficiaries soon enough, I'm sure of that, but today that's immaterial, my dear. What's important is the ideals they represent. We're looking for someone who will fearlessly, dauntlessly represent these views. We think you have what it takes to successfully advance our cause. Here's my card."

Andréa Veronique's mind was racing with a montage of thoughts. She believed in human rights, in the need to reduce suffering, in both parties' efforts toward eliminating inequality. Health care needed to be available to everyone, without exception. Government needed to provide basic needs like food and shelter. As a society, global warming needed to be addressed. But abortion? Her mind flashed to the moment her first daughter was born, how she had held Verity in her arms and embraced the new life that God had given her. How was she to support policies that would encourage the taking of that life in a mother's womb?

"Can I review your offer and let you know?"

"Of course, but we need to know quickly. We have another candidate we'll get behind if you're not the one."

Cousins looked at Andréa Veronique inquisitively. "Look, this is a great opportunity. Lots of benefits ahead, like the bonus I mentioned. Not to mention the congressional salary. A House rep makes $174,000. Not too shabby, and it's yours if you want it. Call me. Let me know."

That evening at dinner, Andréa Veronique shared the conversation she had earlier that day with Arthur Cousins.

"Mom, we can't be killing babies. That's what my friend Rachel's mom said. People that support abortion are killing babies."

Andréa Veronique looked appalled. "Honey, we're not going to be killing babies. Don't even think such a thing."

The children excused themselves from the table and Andréa Veronique looked anxiously at Stuart. "How should I view this? It's an incredible offer. But abortion?"

Stuart nodded thoughtfully. "Neither one of us feel good about abortion. We decided before . . . we would never make that decision ourselves. Nothing has changed with our own personal views. But you're running for Congress. If you're elected, there may be times when you're asked to support pro-choice legislation. We've talked about this. You know that."

"I know . . ." Andréa Veronique sighed, shook her head, and pursed her lips momentarily before continuing. "It just happened so fast, that's all. I feel like I was blindsided. I wasn't expecting to be approached by a representative from the abortion . . . pro-choice movement after my speech, let alone have a monetary offer thrown at me."

Stuart reached across the table and took Andréa Veronique's hand. "Andréa. I hate this as much as you do, but we knew going into the campaign that you would have to deal with this. There's a lot of good you can accomplish if you're elected. Abortion is only one issue." Stuart reached his other hand across the table, holding her hand between his. He had an earnest look about him, but then his face brightened with a newfound eagerness.

"I guess the other thing that's been on my mind lately is what the pastor at the new church said Sunday. God wants to bless us. He wants us to prosper. We've been struggling for so long now. There's not a day that goes by that I don't wish I could provide a better life for you."

"Stuart, stop." Tears welled up in Andréa Veronique's eyes as she said softly, "You do provide for me. Don't say that."

"We're both almost thirty-six, and we haven't bought our first house. If you're elected, our financial problems are over. Maybe this is God's way of blessing us after years of living on a teacher's salary."

Jack Broholm had an impressive home office filled with treasures of various sorts. Sports memorabilia, signed photographs of presidents handed down from his grandfather, and autographed baseballs of Hall of Fame members were all part of a notable memorabilia collection from his childhood in Anaheim, California.

In the mid-'60s his parents moved from Fargo to Phoenix before settling in Anaheim in a residential area about a mile from Angel Stadium and less than a half mile from the airplane park. Over the years, Jack would joke, "I went from the coldest spot in the country to the hottest before ending up in a perfect climate." Jack's family lived on a block perpendicular to the sports field for Katella High School and not far from James Guinn Elementary School where Jack attended third through sixth grade. He was consumed with baseball as a child.

Jack looked at his bookcase and was reminded of the time he had jumped onto the stairwell of the New York Mets team bus and pleaded for Yogi Berra's autograph. It was 1968 and Berra was a coach for the Mets. It was about ten thirty on a weekend night, and the teams had just finished an exhibition game. The players boarded the bus, and the driver was preparing to exit the stadium. Just before the folding door of the bus clamped shut, Jack jumped onto the steps and pleaded, "Please, we just want to get Yogi Berra's autograph." The security guard was about to give Jack the boot, but Yogi must have said it was okay. Jack and his small entourage quickly ascended the steps of the bus and began passing their autograph books and other paraphernalia from one player to the next until the items reached Berra, who was sitting midway on the right-hand side of the bus. Yogi signed everything that was passed to him, and the kids hopped off the bus. It was a thrilling story for a fifth grader, a story Jack told many times over the next year.

His autograph collection was impressive; a display of sports luminaries filled the room.

Jack's office had a tall five-columned English mahogany bookcase taking up much of the wall to the right of his desk. Sitting prominently on the top middle shelves of the bookcase rested an NBA basketball signed by Jerry West and Elgin Baylor, and an NFL football signed by Merlin Olsen and Deacon Jones. A framed picture signed by NHL legend Gordie Howe sat alongside a Christmas card signed by former heavyweight champion of the world Jack Dempsey. The card was given to Jack by his older brother, Ted, also an autograph collector, who in the course of writing to Jack Dempsey's Manhattan restaurant requesting a signed picture of the former champ was surprised when he received a Christmas card that year. Ted used to joke and tell Jack, "You were named after Jack Dempsey."

On the second shelf of the bookcase were autographed baseballs of Willie Mays, Hank Aaron, Frank Robinson, Bob Feller, Maury Wills, and Mickey Mantle, who was Jack's favorite player as a boy, as well as a panoply of other famous names. The year before, he had given a signed Bradford Exchange plate of Joe DiMaggio to his son, and that was the plan for the years ahead: give away all the treasures he had collected since childhood. He hadn't been an active collector for many years and had little interest in baseball at this time in his life.

In Jack's office closet, resting against the back wall, each article wrapped carefully in cream-colored manila paper, were signed photographs, some personalized to Jack's grandfather, of former presidents. The group included Herbert Hoover, Franklin D. Roosevelt, Harry Truman, Dwight D. Eisenhower, and Ronald Reagan— the latter of whom was pictured at a prayer breakfast at the state capitol building during his time as governor of California.

Jack's thoughts turned to business. His consulting business had been slow, and most of his workday was spent buying and selling securities.

His thoughts then turned to his stock portfolio and yesterday's market drop, which had resulted in a 1.45 percent reduction in his holdings. Jack sat down at his desk and looked at the time in the lower right-hand corner of his computer. Seven o'clock—thirty minutes before the opening bell on Wall Street, which rang at 9:30 a.m. eastern time. Jack sat at his desk and logged into his online brokerage account. He quickly gleaned through his stock portfolio and then listed sell orders for two securities. The screen showed twenty-two open stock positions and five open options contracts. Three of the option contracts were in the red, two were positive, but each had originally been opened with a two-to-three-month expiration date, so none were in immediate danger of expiring. The contracts were for in-the-money call options, increasing the odds for a profitable transaction.

Jack stroked his thin gray mustache with his thumb and forefinger and looked thoughtfully at the computer screen. One contract in particular concerned him. He had purchased ten contracts of a fast-growing technology company at a strike price of $85.00—$5.00 under the $90.00 asking price for the security. When he initiated the transaction, he was confident the stock price would go up, favorably impacting the value of the option. Earnings were expected to beat analyst expectations, long-term fundamentals were solid, technical indicators were good, and investors were pouring money into the stock—until yesterday's news report just before the market closed. The company announced it was issuing additional shares to raise capital to buy a small technology firm that was expected to support the existing business model. The company stated they were gaining "enhanced proprietary software." This would be a "strategic move for both companies," the press release announced. But the additional shares were perceived by investors to dilute the share value, and the stock price dropped 10 percent just before market close. Premarket trading showed a further drop in price.

Jack took a deep breath, sighed, and shut down the trading site. Profitable trades were exhilarating, but recent losing trades had been stressful. On most days Jack was distracted, unable to give the energy and focus needed to successfully navigate the changing markets. He wanted to make profitable trades, but he was conflicted. The world of finance had occupied his thoughts for most of his adult life. His career was centered on financial transactions—buying and selling stocks, bonds, ETFs, options, occasional futures contracts, and sometimes lesser-known financial instruments—in their entirety, consuming his day to the point he could think of little else. Some days he was so preoccupied with looking at charts, graphs, candlestick patterns, and other market-related data that he would hardly move from his desk for three or four hours. Surely this isn't what the Lord wants for me at this stage of life, Jack thought.

His day typically started in prayer and Bible reading. Jack had been a New King James man ever since the version was first published in 1982, but he relished other translations as well. He was reading the Bible cover to cover, which he had done most years of his marriage. Jack's daily devotions were focused on the persecuted church: a church in great stress worldwide in places like Somalia, Nigeria, Sudan, and China. One of his devotionals, *Anguished Cries From the Underground Church*, detailed stories of extreme persecution taking place throughout the world. He was also reading from *Foxe's Book of Martyrs*, stories about the suffering of saints from ages past, many of whom had been burned at the stake for holding fast to the Word of God. Jack's mind was wrestling increasingly with not simply the prosperity-minded church he and the other men had debated about but the affluence he walked in, even though the prosperity gospel wasn't a message he embraced.

As a young man managing a portfolio on the Chicago Board of Trade, Jack reveled in the intensity and stimulus that came with buying and selling futures and options contracts. "A young man's job," he told friends. "Not for the faint of heart." Yet he remained an active trader.

After leaving Anaheim, his parents moved the family to Wisconsin where Jack graduated high school and then attended the University of Wisconsin in Madison. Fresh out of college, with an MBA in finance, he landed a job on the Chicago Board of Trade assisting a trader in managing a $1 million portfolio for a small commodities investor from Milwaukee. On a typical day, Jack bought and sold agricultural-related contracts for corn, wheat, soy beans, and cattle. Thirty years ago, at the urging of a family member, he left Chicago for Mountain Fire, bought a small business consulting firm, and soon expanded the client base to five states—New Mexico, Colorado, Texas, Arizona, and Utah. For a time, the business branched into the commercial loan refinancing arena, but Jack was no longer pursuing loan projects and no longer had contractual ties with Equity Resources, at one time his largest client. Jack spent his days developing financial pro formas for business start-ups and expansions, analyzing P&L statements, and directing cost control and marketing strategies for small-to-midsize companies. The enterprise was successful; in the early years the business flourished. But then, after an ill-advised, overleveraged investment failed, the company suffered markedly and Jack declared bankruptcy. It was a hard lesson. Following a desperate period in Jack's life, which saw him withdraw from ministry for a time, the consulting business rebounded. Many of his clients returned, and to supplement his business, Jack began buying and selling securities again. Financially, he had prospered. College tuition for his son and daughter was paid for. He and his wife lived comfortably in a nice section of Mountain Fire, the mortgage long retired. Jack was active in ministry, part of the weekly pastoral prayer group even though he was a layman, and well respected in the community.

What was the Lord saying to him? How could his life be so comfortable with millions of saints worldwide suffering so immensely?

By all appearances, Jack led an abundant life.

Materially speaking, there were no "needs" in his life. But something seemed out of kilter, off-balance, off track. His life was a contradiction, an anomaly. Something didn't seem right.

It was this backdrop of thoughts that Jack found himself increasingly wrestling with. He knew he wasn't deserving, but what should he do?

To the Christian, the word *depression* has a range of meanings. To some, depression in a fellow believer represents a life less than victorious, a life not walking in victory, a life that somehow has allowed the enemy to take hold and thwart the peace and joy intended for all believers in Christ. Others, not discounting the exhortation to walk in victory nor in any way diminishing the spiritual attacks Christians experience, might suggest that, at times, circumstances in life contribute to emotional pains not always recognized by those attending to happier moments of life. To the psychologist or trained medical doctor, depression is a mental health condition, a condition affecting the mind—a physiological state of being sometimes caused by a chemical imbalance—no less an illness than any other physical ailment. To the counselor, depression might be an emotional state caused by life's pain and hardship—the loss of a child, a divorce, losing a job, and any number of life's trials—all contributing to sorrow, all causing strain and preventing the patient from the joys of a happy life.

By any clinical diagnosis, Robert Thompson was in

a deep state of depression. The years had gone by faster than he could have ever imagined. This wasn't how he envisioned retirement. He had always been goal-oriented, but now, after stepping down from the pulpit, his pursuits and daily activities had come to a crashing stop. He tried to stay active. Robert would chronicle events, planning his schedule well in advance, meticulously detailing meeting notes from people he had met or spoken with. He continued attending the weekly pastoral prayer times and managed to conceal much of the pain he felt, but the lack of motivation was wearing on him. Throughout his years as a pastor and missionary he had set out to organize every aspect of his life, but now, being retired, there were no real expectations from anyone and, as a result, no pressure to accomplish much of anything. No goals and no sense of accomplishment that came from fulfilling those goals. And now a loneliness had set in. And with that loneliness and the little incentive he felt most days, a depression had taken hold.

Robert had lived much of his life initiating and completing worthwhile, admirable, and needed endeavors, but he never felt caught up. He was always striving. The lists were never finalized. Something always remained undone. Now with no day-to-day ministry goals, there was limited motivation, no spring in his steps.

His office bookcase was filled with study Bibles, theological dissertations, small cards with Scripture passages and beautifully adorned pictures of three crosses on a hillside, an empty tomb, and the heading "HE IS RISEN!"

Robert's faith had not wavered. He was a regular parishioner of the Presbyterian church in Mountain Fire he had pastored at for a number of years after his missionary work in South America. He corresponded frequently with current and former members of the mission. He greeted and conversed with the new pastor, board members, and parishioners on Sunday before and after each service. But the days in between were taking a toll.

"Please, Lord," Robert whispered, as he sat gazing out the window at a darkened, cloudless gray sky. "Please tell me what You want me to do."

Chapter Six

Andréa Veronique waved frantically at the shuttle driver, who veered suddenly to the left and within moments was parked alongside the curb. She was twenty minutes off schedule, not expecting a delay from the accident and single-lane traffic that followed.

"What time does your plane leave?" the driver asked.

"Six thirty," she replied. "I left at three this morning, which should have given me ample time. I ran into an accident near Grants."

"I'll get you there in time, don't worry," the man said, maneuvering the van carefully between a parked bus and the oncoming traffic lane before accelerating the speed of the vehicle so rapidly that Andréa Veronique lost her balance. "Sorry," the driver said as she grabbed the rail in front of her.

James Radisson greeted her in front of the gate and helped her exit the last step from the shuttle van.

"You look worried," he said as they walked toward the doors to the terminal. "Don't be. We're good. The flight was delayed forty-five minutes."

Andréa Veronique sighed. "There was an accident on the way. I was worried we'd miss our flight."

"No worries," Radisson said. "We'll adjust."

At seven o'clock they were walking down the jetway, and by 7:20 the plane was lifting off the runway.

Minutes earlier, just before takeoff, Andréa Veronique looked up from her window seat at a tall, sandy-haired man standing in the aisle. "I think I'm on the window," he said.

"Yes, I thought maybe we had an empty seat. I was hoping we had an empty seat," Andréa said and smiled. "Nothing personal."

"I understand, believe me," the man replied.

Radisson, looking annoyed, stood up from his seat near the aisle and stepped back. Andréa worked her way to the aisle and waited for the man to sit down and then sat down in the middle seat.

Radisson sat down again in the aisle seat, removed an iPad from his briefcase, connected to Wi-Fi, and began reviewing emails as the flight captain finished his remarks.

Andréa Veronique turned to the man and extended her hand. "Andréa Veronique Mattheson," she said confidently.

"Clifton Rockwell. Sorry to make you get up," he said, taking her hand. "I've never missed a flight, but I'm always on the wire. The less time I spend in airports, the better."

"Where are you from?" Andréa Veronique asked.

"Albuquerque," Clifton replied.

"What part of Albuquerque?"

"NE Heights."

"NE Heights? Wow, nice!"

"We like it. We bought our home during the housing crunch in 2009. Basically, at the bottom of the real estate downturn. Everything equal, not sure we could pull it off today." Clifton laughed.

"My husband and I live in Mountain Fire, but we drive by the Heights if we're taking a trip to Taos or into Colorado for a vacation. It's a beautiful area. What do you do?"

"I'm a district manager for Artisan Building Supplies, headquarters Dallas. We sell lumber and other building materials. I have Albuquerque, Santa Fe, Farmington, Mountain Fire. Some smaller stores as well."

"So you're flying to Dallas for meetings?"

"Yes. It'll be a short trip. Full plate though. Action-packed from the time I arrive until I fly out tomorrow evening."

"Great! Impressive," Andréa Veronique said. "My husband frequents your Mountain Fire store. He seems to have projects going all the time."

"What about the two of you? Rockwell said, motioning toward James Radisson. "You appear to be together. What's your agenda?"

Andréa Veronique looked at Radisson, unsure for a moment who was going to respond. He nodded, as if to say, "Keep going."

"Following an eleven o'clock meeting this morning in Dallas, we drive to Austin where Mr. Radisson's news organization has an affiliate station. They're doing a feature story on me. I'm running for a congressional seat in the upcoming election. Pretty exciting, should be a big boost for my campaign. I give a speech in Austin tonight; we polish up the story tomorrow, fly home on Thursday, so yeah, just like you, busy trip. My husband and I have two daughters. I'm sure Stuart will be glad when I get back."

They shared pleasantries for a few more minutes and then Andréa Veronique asked for the man's support. "I hope you'll vote for me. I won't let you down. My commitment is to my constituency—that means you." Andréa Veronique extended her hand once again.

Rockwell looked at Andréa Veronique inquisitively. "I very well may. I'll certainly be voting in the upcoming election. I'm very active in the political process, but at this point I don't know where you stand on any of the issues."

"Fire away!" she said confidently.

"Are you sure?"

"Go for it! Put me on the front line. If I can't answer a couple of questions on a plane, I'm not the right person for the job."

Radisson looked annoyed that Andréa Veronique's attention was diverted, but he nodded at Rockwell and said, "It's your show. Let it fly. You just became part of the feature story."

"I'll be famous too," Rockwell said and laughed.

"Where do I start?" he asked, pausing thoughtfully before continuing.

"I want to qualify that this isn't about Donald Trump's Republican presidency. The left would say we've lowered our standards. Others would counter and say, no, we're simply tired of seeing unelected bureaucrats, along with the media . . ." He looked at Radisson and said, "Sorry, but it's true. Hear me out."

Radisson closed his eyes and smirked.

"My question is, why is the country so divided?" Rockwell asked and then added, not trying to disguise the arrogance he felt, "In my opinion, there is no uniting the country. Do you know what the main reason is?"

Rockwell looked at James Radisson, who tilted his head back and raised his eyebrows as if to say, "Go ahead. You obviously know it all."

Clifton Rockwell looked at Andréa Veronique, who said quietly, "Tell me."

"What do you think it is?" Rockwell said, glancing back and forth between Andréa Veronique and Radisson. "You're running for office . . ." He paused and looked straight at Andréa Veronique. "And you're a leading media voice out of Washington." He glanced at Radisson. "So before I tell you my thoughts, I'm asking you, what do *you* think the dominant reason is?"

"The economy," Andréa Veronique replied.

"To expand on Andréa Veronique's response, the overall economic divide," Radisson said, clearly impatient with the exercise.

"Voters care about the economy. Agreed," replied Rockwell. "We all remember Clinton's comment years ago. And yes, the wealthiest part of the population bears no resemblance to the working class of America. But that's not new. That's been the situation in times past. In World War II there was an economic divide, maybe not as pronounced as today, but a strong divide without question. Nevertheless, the country united around the war effort in spite of the economic disparity. So, no, I don't think that's the answer. Asked another way, what policy position is the most divisive in America?"

A voice over the intercom interrupted their discourse, and for the next few minutes a flight attendant entertained the passengers with a monologue on par with a late-night comedy show.

When the intercom was silent Radisson wasted no time in handing Andréa Veronique an agenda, and for the next thirty minutes they conversed about programming, format, image, and the Q&A to follow her speech. Radisson shared the direction he was hoping to take the story. Andréa Veronique nodded in agreement.

The pilot announced that the plane would be landing in about ten minutes, and Andréa Veronique turned her attention back to Rockwell. "Sorry we were interrupted. It was really nice talking to you. Stop and see me at one of my rallies. I'm out in front of the public almost daily it seems. A lot of campaign work locally. If you see a poster, stop by. How often do you get to Mountain Fire?"

"I'm there every week or so," Rockwell replied.

"Do you have any contacts outside of work? I've met a lot of people in recent weeks. Anyone in town I might know?"

"I have fifty to sixty employees at the Mountain Fire store at any given time, so obviously I have work relationships with some of them. Outside of the store, I know a few people. I know one of the City Council members, Andrew Walker. There's a business consultant the company has used in the past, a casual friend of mine. His name is Jack Broholm. He's very active in the Christian community."

"I know Andrew Walker. I've met Mr. Broholm."

"Really!"

They were interrupted once again by the pilot's voice over the intercom. "Flight attendants, prepare for landing." Rockwell, Andréa Veronique, and James Radisson all lurched forward slightly as the plane abruptly began its descent.

Clifton looked at Andréa Veronique. "We're running out of time. I still don't know where you stand on what I view as one of the most important issues facing the country. What's your position on abortion? Are you pro-life or pro-choice?"

The question came at Andréa Veronique like a chilling surge of water from an icy sea. The confidence she felt an hour and a half ago was suddenly gone.

"I don't think anyone really *wants* to get an abortion," she said, starting her answer in a rhythmic tone but her voice faltering as she finished the sentence. Her eyes lowered, averting her attention from Rockwell's intense stare. She turned toward the window and looked at the thin stream of light from the slightly jarred window shade settling on the seat in front of her. Neither Andréa Veronique nor Clifton Rockwell said anything for what seemed a much longer period of time than the actual twenty or thirty second lull in the conversation. James Radisson glanced back and forth between the two but was silent.

Rockwell spoke first. "You said earlier that you knew Jack Broholm. The business consultant in Mountain Fire?"

"I don't really know him. My husband and I met Mr. Broholm at Abundant Blessings Word of Faith, a new church in town."

"I thought Jack went to Faith Gospel Tabernacle?" Clifton said, more to himself than to Andréa Veronique.

"I believe you're correct. He told us he was visiting the church to meet the new pastor and invite him to a weekly prayer meeting with some of the local pastors."

"Oh, okay, makes sense." Rockwell nodded. "The reason I bring Jack Broholm up is to give you something else to think about as it relates to your position on abortion, whatever that position may be. Are you familiar with the large prayer assemblies they hold in Mountain Fire?"

"I've never been to one. I did see posters around town and heard radio advertisements promoting the last event."

"Jack attends Faith Gospel Tabernacle. The pastor of that church—his name is Benjamin Sharon, you may have heard of him, he's well-known statewide in church circles—is the organizer of the prayer assemblies. Christians from all over the state come to these meetings. I've been to one myself. I'm not trying to sound . . ." his voice tailed off, "and I don't pretend to speak for everyone at those prayer meetings, but I can just about assure you that these folks won't be voting for a pro-choice candidate." Rockwell paused. "Just an FYI."

"There's a much bigger, much broader base to be concerned about than the so-called Christian far right," Radisson interjected. "Andréa Veronique has a very balanced platform; she'll be all right. But hey, thanks for your input." Radisson lifted his chin, nodded smugly, looked away from Rockwell's scrutinizing gaze, and then slightly rolled his eyes. The plane landed, and the rows were emptying one by one as Radisson thrust his hand toward Rockwell's, grasping it firmly and then raising it forward in more of an arm jolt than a shake. Rockwell held Radisson's hand through the duration of the shake and then squeezed tightly, creating an awkward moment before releasing his grip. The three exited the plane, left the gate, and began walking through the terminal.

Radisson stopped suddenly and answered his phone. Andréa Veronique glanced at Clifton Rockwell. "Good luck," she said.

Rockwell continued walking but then looked back and called out, "Remember!"

Andréa Veronique and Radisson turned toward Rockwell, who was now about thirty feet away. "On some issues there is no middle ground," he said loudly.

Andréa Veronique turned away and looked down, her glance averting to a small child running toward his mother at the adjacent gate.

Radisson shook his head and rolled his eyes. "He doesn't know anything," he muttered to her as they approached the escalator.

She was surprised by the limousine that awaited them as they left the concourse.

"You don't think I've sacrificed enough riding coach with you?" Radisson said with a grin.

Chapter Seven

The parking lot was packed when Jack Broholm maneuvered his vehicle into a space minutes before the service began at Abundant Blessings Word of Faith church. Jack walked briskly toward the entrance as a couple intersected his path.

"We keep running into each other," Andréa Veronique said as she and Stuart raced ahead of Jack, reaching the door first, before turning around to shake hands. Jack raised both arms, taking hold of a hand from both Andréa Veronique and Stuart, and greeted the young couple warmly.

"You know who to vote for, Mr. Broholm," Andréa Veronique said, smiling broadly and then gracefully proceeding down the hall, seemingly as comfortable in high heels and a skirt as she would have been in jogging attire, moments later disappearing into the auditorium.

The lights were dimmed when Jack entered the sanctuary and sat down in a seat about halfway between the back aisle and the stage. The auditorium had three sections of bluish-gray chairs, cushioned on the seats and backs, attached together neatly in straight rows of ten. Jack settled into a seat toward the end of one of the middle rows.

Beacon lights flashed across the stage, capturing glimpses of the worship team ensemble standing quietly on the platform. Moments later the worship team leader said, "Everybody stand! Let's worship the Lord this morning!"

Jack stood to his feet and looked at the stage filled with singers and musicians. The music began with a contemporary song Jack recognized from an Albuquerque Christian radio station. Wow, this is loud, Jack thought to himself. After four songs, Jack was beside himself. The music wasn't just loud, it was blaring. It appeared the musicians were playing over a recorded sound track, creating a thunderous, heavy, bass-driven roar. At times the words to the lyrics were shrill. Jack thought of covering his ears but refrained. The stage was filled with amplifiers, microphones, an enclosed percussions set, and other band equipment. He looked at the lead singers standing to the front of the musicians and accompanying instruments layered across the stage. Attractive faces, colorful outfits, and interesting personalities filled the platform, highlighted by the strobe lights flashing across the stage and throughout the auditorium.

It's a good thing David Janssen isn't here, Jack thought.

Jack tried to pray through the songs, but he felt

agitated, critical. They need to replace the sound man, he thought. Three decibel levels too loud, at least.

The final song ended, piercing through the arena.

The concert atmosphere left Jack so rattled he could barely follow the sermon text. The message was a non-judgmental, no-condemnation homily of encouragement. The preacher closed his message saying, "God understands your needs, and He accepts you where you're at. Walk in His destiny, church."

Before ending the service, Reverend Parker cried out, "How many here today need a financial miracle? Raise your hand if you need abundant blessings in your life!" Hands shot up throughout the room. "Be an extravagant giver if you want to be bountifully enriched!"

The ushers passed velvet, burgundy-colored offering receptacles down the rows of the sanctuary, and Reverend Parker closed the service with a prayer.

It wasn't lost on Jack as to why he had come. As the parishioners worked their way to the aisles, Jack approached the podium and again waited patiently for Reverend Parker. Overhead lights had been turned on in the auditorium following the service, and happy faces with joyful expressions gathered around the minister. Jack finally had an opportunity and extended his hand. Reverend Parker took his hand and smiled warmly at Jack.

"Reverend Parker, Jack Broholm. I wanted to say hi and formally meet you. I was here a couple of weeks ago, but you needed to run before we could talk. As I recall, your wife was waiting for you, which I understand. I'm not a pastor, just to be clear, but I meet with a group of pastors each week for prayer. On behalf of the group, I'd like to invite you to join us next Thursday for our prayer time. We're meeting at the Nazarene church over the noon hour. I'd be happy to pick you up and we can ride over to the church together. We usually spend a few minutes talking, having fellowship, and then we spend forty-five minutes, give or take, in prayer. Usually done by one o'clock and everyone gets back to work. We'd love to have you come."

Reverend Parker had been holding Jack's hand through the entire invitation but now let go and leaned back. "It is very thoughtful of you to think about me, Jack. I appreciate you reaching out. As it is, I'm afraid I'm going to have to pass. Church leadership has given me and the rest of the staff some pretty hefty attendance goals. Most of the time I don't have time to blink." Reverend Parker laughed and said, "But thanks again. Thanks for coming this morning. Hope to see you again."

Parker quickly turned toward another parishioner who tugged at his arm and said, "Lunch is waiting, Reverend. The families are waiting outside."

Reverend Parker grinned broadly at Jack. "Sorry to rush. We've had this potluck planned for new members. Gotta run. Thanks again, Jack."

As Jack was leaving the auditorium, he noticed the sound room off to his left. He approached the room and saw a young man, about eighteen, wearing a T-shirt that said, "Destined for Blessings and Favor." Jack walked up to the young man and smiled. "Good morning. How are you?"

The young man nodded. "Doing great, you?"

"Good, good. Hey, please don't think I'm being critical, and by the way, this is a complicated job. I'm sure you have a great deal of skill when it comes to sound systems, but I wanted to mention to you that the sound was maybe," Jack's voice rose as he continued, "accidentally turned up too loud this morning? The music was really blaring where I was sitting, about halfway down the aisle."

The young man laughed. "No accident, sir. They like it loud. Those are my instructions. Sorry if it bothered you."

"Wow!" Jack exclaimed. "Okay . . . well, thank you for your service."

Jack thanked the young man again and left the building.

Jack felt guilty driving home. He tried to be non-judgmental in the so-called "worship wars" surrounding church music, but this was easier to do in the comfort of his own church home. Jack had long considered himself a connoisseur of Christian preaching. He had frequented numerous churches over the past twenty years, sometimes when traveling, other times when acting as an ambassador for the Mountain Fire prayer assemblies. In the course of those visitations to other congregations, he listened to and participated in a wide variety of worship music styles. But today was unnerving. The songs were what David Janssen decried as anthem-driven, ballad-driven, chorus-repetitive "entertainment music"—songs that had no place in a worship service. Jack understood David's description. He was familiar with each song from the radio or even local churches. They weren't his style either. The songs at Faith Gospel Tabernacle were worshipful. Some were traditional hymns of the faith, some contemporary, some in Spanish, some in Navajo, some in Hebrew, but the selections had a reverence that invoked heartfelt thoughts of awe and gratitude, not the reverberating pulses of some of the contemporary songs that today left him unsettled.

The men were particularly vocal at Thursday's prayer meeting when Jack Broholm updated them on his visit to Abundant Blessings Word of Faith Church.

"Don't give up on him," one of the men said. "He's a good man. He's just trying to build a church. We need to pray for him."

The voices continued:

"Any pastor who lives in a multimillion-dollar home, uses church funds to buy two-hundred-million-dollar jets—I'm not talking about the new pastor, I'm referring to the TV evangelists—is fleecing the flock. You will know them by their fruit."

"I'll grant you that. Some of them may be deceived, but some are outright charlatans. In Paul's last address to the elders of the church in Ephesus, he said, 'I have coveted no one's silver or gold or apparel.' That's not the message we get from a lot of these guys. I agree. They're fleecing the flock."

"But we're talking about this man . . ."

Elijah Rawlins, chaplain of the local hospital, spoke next. "I've been in Mountain Fire for eight years. The last time I looked, there were less than fifty other Blacks in town. I went from being in the majority in Philly to being part of a minority in a small town in New Mexico. I don't agree with the message he's preaching, but I don't think we should shun him either."

"I try not to be judgmental, but we can't abandon the truth. God wants us to be discerning."

"It's the message," David Janssen interjected. "The prosperity gospel is not the gospel!" David paused and looked around the circle at the men. "The message is heretical. We can't support heresy. *I won't* support heresy!"

Janssen's last comment was met with silence. Some of the men nodded; some looked down.

"Other than John, all of the original disciples after Judas were martyred," Jack said softly. "I've been reading from *Foxe's Book of Martyrs* in my morning devotions and studying the persecuted church in general. Paul was shipwrecked, beaten, stoned. Reformers were burned at the stake. I know we live in a different time. I wanted to reach out . . . I can't get my arms around the message either."

Robert Thompson was the last to speak. "Men," he began. "Our opinions and our sentiments toward the new preacher in town are of no value unless they're aligned with the Word of God. Allow me to read two Scripture passages to you." Robert opened the Bible that had rested on his lap since he first arrived at the church, a small building on the outskirts of Mountain Fire that served a congregation of about fifty Nazarene believers, pastored by Thomas Begaye, who was elevated to senior pastor after the passing of Reverend Hall.

"I will be reading from the *New American Standard Bible.* Jesus says in Matthew 6, verse 24, 'No one can serve two masters; for either he will hate the one and love the other, or he will hold to one and despise the other. You cannot serve God and mammon.' Mammon means wealth, gentlemen."

None of the men as much as flinched.

"The second passage I feel led to read is Matthew 6, verses 19–21. Jesus tells us, 'Do not lay up for yourselves treasures upon earth, where moth and rust destroy, and where thieves break in and steal. But lay up for yourselves treasures in heaven, where neither moth nor rust destroys, and where thieves do not break in or steal; for where your treasure is, there will your heart be also.'

"This is the Lord speaking in these passages. These verses apply to us all."

The men nodded; the mood was somber. They had spent almost the full hour discussing the new pastor, prosperity teaching, and well-known television evangelists but had not spent their customary time in prayer. "I know some of you need to get back to your church. Let me close in prayer," Reverend Begaye said.

Jack Broholm awoke early the next morning and sat down in a chair by the window of a second-floor bedroom that he used as a morning prayer room. The chair sat in a corner near a window on the east side of the house. He had risen earlier than normal this morning, shortly before dawn, unable to sleep, his mind racing with a collage of concerns: the prosperity church and how it related to him, the persecuted church throughout the world, and the immense suffering he'd been reading about in his daily devotions. He thought of saints of old from the 1500s who had been imprisoned and then burned at the stake for their rejection of church teachings and their insistence on adhering to the Word of God. Then his mind shifted to business objectives and the day's trading strategies. He tried to avoid thinking about investments and securities trading during his morning time of reflection and prayer, but invariably his mind wandered, however briefly, to work plans involving business clients, marketing efforts geared toward attracting new customers, his current port-folio holdings, and the stock and bond markets.

The sun began its rise to a new day, shining brightly through the slats of the window panes, forming glit-tering lines of light on the wall to his left. Jack prayed about a myriad of concerns: for family members, for the worldwide Christian church, for the local community. He then spent time reading Scripture from *The One Year Chronological Bible* published by Tyndale in the New King James Version. On most days, Jack tried to read one segment from the Old Testament and one segment from the New Testament. After finishing his Scripture reading, Jack opened a devotional he had been reading from for the past week, *Daybreak News Reach*, which published stories about the underground church. Jack read about a young Sudanese boy whose dream was to acquire a used bicycle, a bicycle he could use to bring sorghum and wheat and other foodstuffs back to his home. Jack put the article down and stared solemnly at the picture of the smiling Sudanese family standing together in front of a thatched hut in the small village. *A bicycle? A used bicycle? The boy's dream was to acquire a used bicycle?* A wave of guilt engulfed him. How was he to process this? How could he even begin to understand the austere daily existence of this family? How could he reconcile the disparity he felt?

Jack dropped to his knees and bowed his head. "Help me to understand, Lord," he prayed quietly.

In his mind's eye Jack pictured the living room of his four-bedroom home, noticing first the brick fireplace, then the golden-colored chandelier hanging from the raised ceiling. His eyes settled for a moment on the antique P.A. Starck pipe organ handed down from his wife's grandmother, and he thought about the offer he had just received from a local dealer. The built-in oak bookcase on the far wall was filled with hardcover books—one shelf containing several clothbound Bibles. The article referenced the Sudanese boy's father. The boy's father's dream was to have a pocket-size New Testament like the one the pastor had at the clandestine church service the family attended. After one of the secret meetings, the pastor had torn a page from one of the Gospels and given it to the man. Jack began to weep quietly. "Lord, what are You telling me in all this?" he prayed.

Chapter Eight

Clifton Rockwell left the Ruidoso store, got in his company truck—a 2016 black Chevy Silverado—checked his cell phone, and read the text from his wife, Nicole. "I'm praying for you!" the message said, accompanied by three red hearts. "Drive safely. See you tonight."

Clifton considered himself a Christian. He was raised in a Christian home by Henry and Faye Rockwell, devout Christians by all accounts. He rebelled at a young age: smoking, drinking, and otherwise indulging in unsavory activities, but then, at his father's urging, in his senior year of college, he attended Billy Graham's final Albuquerque crusade in 1998, held at The Pit. At the end of the service, he responded to the altar call, went forward, and accepted Christ as his Savior.

But Rockwell was a dichotomy of sorts. In his twenties, he was as flawed as he was passionate, entertaining vices that most members of the small American Baptist church he attended would refer to as backsliding. As noble as his pro-life stance was, as firmly as he was committed to an array of conservative political causes, when it came to matters of faith, he was often worldly-minded and, to one degree or another, depending on the setting, he entertained sinful vices that he knew were inconsistent with his profession of faith. He wanted to be saved, but a full surrender?

The commitment to his causes, his intense personality and driving ambition, and his tunnel vision for climbing the corporate ladder, in practice far exceeded any notion of what God might have him do. There was a self-righteousness that accompanied his mindset. He was smarter, better educated, more disciplined, and more committed than the next person. Clifton Rockwell's carnality was not completely lost on him. He distantly perceived the irony. His faults would be dealt with eventually. In the meantime, he felt a call to action, to be a voice for conservative America.

Rockwell was a workaholic. In the early years of family life when both boys were still at home, he routinely worked sixty-hour weeks, at times seventy-hour weeks, and on occasion an eighty-hour week.

"I'll hear someone say they work eighty-hour weeks," he lectured his managers, "but when I ask them what their hours are, they'll give me numbers that don't add up. Do you know how you get to an eighty-hour week? Let me tell you: You work Monday through Friday from seven in the morning to eight o'clock at night, Saturday from eight in the morning to six in the evening, and Sunday afternoon from one to six. Most people exaggerate their hours."

But as prideful as he was in working longer and harder than anyone else, or so he thought, Rockwell was not unaware of the price he had paid. As the years passed and his self-awareness increased, he felt almost haunted at times by the neglect he had imposed on his family. He remembered a conversation with his dad, who said, "I'm gonna burst your ego, son. History is filled with administrators, entrepreneurs, and business managers. Skilled men and women, to be sure. But are they exceptional in the scheme of history? Only a very few. No, it's the great men of God who are the exceptions." He then went on to say, "You can devote all of your time and energy to work and neglect your family, but you'll have regrets later. When you're my age, you'll wish you had spent more time playing catch with Danny and Sam instead of working late every evening."

By his early forties, he hadn't smoked or drank for ten years, but his less than stellar example of what a Christian man should be, combined with working long hours absent from his family, had taken a toll. His sons grew up in church but, like many teenagers, strayed into areas unguarded, and Clifton was not there to run interference. He lived with the regrets of having children not completely sold out to God, and he blamed himself.

"Dad, when can we go fishing?"

"How about this weekend?" he would reply. Most of the time "this weekend" never came.

There was a trade-off that Rockwell readily accepted. Work was never neglected nor was his political focus. He was a tried-and-true Republican. Clifton considered himself in the upper 1 percentile of the population when it came to knowledge of national politics. He memorized the Gettysburg Address when he was in sixth grade. "Of the people, by the people, for the people" was his political mantra. He echoed the patriotic phrases from political leaders on both sides of the aisle: "The United States is the greatest nation on earth," "The United States is the greatest country in the world," and "The United States is the greatest country in the history of the world."

Rockwell would say, "I'm a patriot, not a nationalist, but first and foremost a Christian." But Rockwell was indeed a nationalist, and most of his close associates would say he *was not* "first and foremost a Christian."

There were Christian friends in Rockwell's life, some of whom questioned his zeal, suggesting that his energy would be better served focusing on the unsaved.

"Granted, politics is not the main thing," Rockwell acknowledged. "But I'd rather know what's going on then be kept in the dark." He rarely shared his faith.

Rockwell knew the political climate and made sure that everyone around him knew that he knew. He considered himself an authority on current events and would debate anyone giving him the first inkling of a challenge. He thrived on the stimulus of winning, of being right.

As much as his intense ambition lent itself well to a management career, he at times entertained a political career, though he despised career politicians and un-elected bureaucrats who governed within the status quo, preferring candidates and elected officials who were bold enough to provoke the ruling class, who had the moxie to "burn bridges" or "go down with the ship" if it meant standing up for the republic.

His mind routinely played out the agenda his platform would stand on if he were running for governor of New Mexico: He would be uncompromisingly pro-life. He believed *Roe v. Wade* was the worst judicial decision in the history of the Supreme Court. He would stand for life in New Mexico and, in the meantime, would never vote for a candidate who *was not* pro-life.

Secondly, he would complete the electrical grid state-wide and ensure that water was available on every square inch of the Navajo Reservation. In Rockwell's mind, the failure to complete the state's utilities infrastructure was criminal. How could politicians disregard such basic services, year after year, term after term? If need be, a statewide tax would be imposed to pay for the projects, but Rockwell's primary vision involved hiring the best fundraiser in the country and tapping into the billions of dollars sitting dormant in charitable foundation accounts. Rockwell was a capitalist but a cynical capitalist. He disparaged the lack of organization and what he viewed as weak, poorly coordinated efforts in distributing funds to so many obvious and worthy projects. His leading example: the International Growth and Development Foundation. On average, an inflow of one billion dollars a year; on average, a fund balance of one billion dollars. Why maintain such an extreme cushion? "As the money comes in, let it flow out," Rockwell repeatedly said. "Use the capital in a timely manner. It's needed now!"

Third on his agenda would be economic development. He would work diligently to bring light manufacturing and software development companies to New Mexico. Every resident that wanted a job would have a job.

Finally, Rockwell would be indefatigable in fighting crime. Drugs and other criminal activities would decline rapidly under his watch. "There's not an ounce of my being that won't be tough on crime," Rockwell would tell friends.

His thoughts turned to Andréa Veronique Mattheson. He hoped she wasn't in over her head. She seemed bright but too nice for Washington. James Radisson and NRI Broadcasting Affiliates' coverage might help her get elected, but even if she does get in, she's on the wrong side of history. Wrong party, wrong ideals, questionable direction, absolutely the wrong media affiliation, he thought. Certainly not what he would do.

It was dusk as Clifton reached the outskirts of Albuquerque, but the foothills of the Sandia Mountains to the east of I-25 stood tall above the valley as he drove north toward Tramway Boulevard. Rockwell and his wife, Nicole, lived in a beautiful home in the NE Heights foothills, an area spotted with jagged rocks, desert flowers, and other southwest foliage gracefully overlooking the valley and night lights of Albuquerque.

Rockwell pulled into the driveway, hardly noticing the beauty of the evening, his mind racing with Artisan Building Supplies quarterly EBITDAR results, upcoming personnel moves within his stores, and the management conference call he had scheduled for Friday.

Chapter Nine

For Robert Thompson, the days brought little relief. The victories, once prominently brought to mind, were seldom thought about. He seemed to only remember the failures. No more enthusiastic plans, no more stimulus from achievements, just waiting. But waiting for what, he didn't know.

Robert had shaved almost every day of his adult life, forty-plus years of discipline and structure would not have permitted even the thought of an unshaven face, but today Thompson sat deep in thought, a two-day old silver stubble detracting from the sadness in his troubled eyes.

Robert loved great literature. As he sat in his office, lost in his thoughts, Robert reflected on his high school and Bible college years, his time in seminary, and the ensuing years of ministry. Even now, Robert didn't neglect reading—he was disciplined in daily Bible reading, devotions, and other spiritual books of the faith—but spending time reading historical classics he had once enjoyed in his youth would take away from doing, from getting things done. He had never learned how to relax. There was always work to accomplish. "Do you want to get things done? Then get organized," Robert used to tell his students.

He was intentional in virtually every one of his activities. His daily work structure combined diligence with an exacting focus and was carried out with an almost clinical precision, but the skills he always believed were divinely inspired now seemed as distant as the youthful prowess of an aged athlete. He didn't understand why he felt so listless. His life had been filled with what he deemed as worthy responsibilities and objectives, but now there were no more deadlines, just gray days.

Throughout his years of ministry, Robert had been a prolific writer. Whether memorandums to church staff, articles for various ministry-related journals, or books devoted largely to theological studies, writing filled his work hours and often carried over to whatever leisure time he allowed himself.

He had planned a trilogy. After the success of *Once a Fortnight*, he would follow with *A Decade Gone By*, and then, finally, the great American novel, *The Barren Soil*.

"Very poignant," the agent had written following one of Robert's submissions. "The story has great verisimilitude," he said.

Robert rarely followed a conventional path. He remembered the agent who had said, "None of the major publishers use Times New Roman." Perhaps true, but it was a typeset that Robert liked, so he didn't change.

He was dismayed by the literary debate involving pronouns for God. He had long known that Hebrew writing did not differentiate between upper- and lowercase letters, but psychologically the hurdle was too great. There was no way he could not capitalize a reference to God—regardless of Greek and Hebrew writing norms two to four thousand years ago. Style considerations had changed. He was in the camp that believed capitalizing pronouns was a display of respect, and in fact, whether anyone else felt that way or not, Robert did.

Miriam had majored in English and minored in history. Robert's literary studies were impressive but paled in contrast to Miriam's credentials. To Robert, she was the consummate copy editor and proofreader with an impeccable eye for grammatical error, polished syntax, and eloquent prose. Miriam edited virtually all of Robert's writings, graciously answering every question Robert posed, generally presiding triumphantly over any disagreements the two might have. But there was no competition; they were a team.

During their years of ministry in South America, Miriam taught English to students of all ages. In addition to his pastoral duties, Robert taught a systematic theology course to men in the church. Miriam was patient. Robert, although thorough, was always steps ahead of his students, oftentimes leaving them wondering what he meant. Sometimes they went to Miriam for clarification.

His fastidious approach to virtually every area of his life, whether counseling, teaching, preaching, or writing, had made the work of editing or making revisions a joyous process, but work that he previously enjoyed had become tedious and laborious. He was working on a book of short stories: uplifting, edifying stories of victorious Christian living, of God's deliverance for His children in the midst of life's troubles. And then he stopped writing. It wasn't writer's block. It wasn't that his faculties were diminished. Robert Thompson simply felt too depressed and too weary to go on with what he believed to be a worthy endeavor, a Christ-honoring use of his talents and his time, but a work that seemed another life away from the discouragement he felt.

His best years of ministry were in settings when there was no media interference—periods when he was unencumbered by email or the colorful, sensory daily news briefs on internet news sites, no newspapers, no television, albeit a radio, but generally sans electronic devices. Sometimes he would go weeks at a time with only occasional communiqués from the field mission office.

Robert Thompson stared vacantly at the list of activities he had planned for the week. Three days into the list of goals and nothing was accomplished. Robert felt despondent. The depression he was feeling seemed heavier with each passing day.

Annie Fuller, having been the receptionist at Faith Gospel Tabernacle prior to Benjamin Sharon's arrival in Mountain Fire and having now spent greater than thirty-five years answering the church's incoming calls, had developed an extraordinary, almost uncanny ability to associate names with voices, sometimes fielding calls requesting information on church activities or service times, but not uncommonly someone calling specifically for Benjamin, and before Benjamin, Reverend Peterson, now long since retired. She instantly recognized the voices of any number of local pastors, a number of whom were part of the weekly pastoral prayer group, and many who joined together for the community body of Christ prayer assemblies. She also immediately recognized many of the church's parishioners, though it was only a small percentage of the five hundred plus members who called with any regularity. Her voice-to-name association encompassed not merely identifying regional Navajo, Hispanic, Caucasian, African American, Middle Eastern, and Asian accents on the other end of the line, but a mastery of associating those accents with names, regardless of whether or not the name and ethnicity seemed related.

But today, the female voice on the other end of the phone was unrecognizable, other than a very slight northeastern accent at times discernible when Benjamin spoke.

"Good morning, this is Annie Fuller at Faith Gospel Tabernacle. How may I help you?"

"Yes, I'm calling for Pastor Sharon," the woman said softly.

"I'm sorry, but he's not in. May I take a message for him?" Annie asked politely.

"I'd rather not leave a message. I'm an old friend and would like the call to be a surprise. Can you tell me when

I might be able to reach him?"

"Well, I'm afraid he won't be available for several months. He's out of the country on a sabbatical."

"Oh my!" The caller's voice amplified but then faltered for a moment. "I wasn't expecting that. Is there any way I can get ahold of him? I have an old cell phone number, but the number must have changed."

Before Annie could respond, the woman continued. "When you say he's out of the country on a sabbatical . . . does this involve ministry work for the church?"

"Well, ministry work for the kingdom but not specific to Faith Gospel Tabernacle. Are you a Christian yourself?"

The caller seemed to hesitate but then said softly, "I am a Christian, yes, I am."

The woman paused, not sure what to say next. "I shouldn't be surprised by Benjamin's, I mean Pastor Sharon's absence. Where are his travels taking him, if I could ask?" she said, before quickly adding, "Forgive me. I'm putting you in an awkward position."

"No, not at all," Annie said kindly. "Let's see, today is Monday. Benjamin has been in Israel for the past week or so, let me see . . . one moment, please, I'm grabbing his itinerary." Annie reached for a file on her desk and continued talking. "Benjamin flies from Tel Aviv to Barcelona on Friday. He's been in Jerusalem for the past five days, I guess, or thereabouts. It's kind of a zigzag schedule based on his speaking engagements. Over the coming weeks he'll be in Luxembourg, Wittenberg, back in Israel to Tiberias near the Sea of Galilee, not necessarily in that order. Would you like a more detailed itinerary?"

"You're willing to give me his itinerary?" the woman exclaimed.

"Well, you said you were an old friend and you also said you were a Christian, so, with those important facts in mind, I don't have a problem telling you. Let me also say that his itinerary is readily available to a number of local church members already. Benjamin has a number of speaking engagements in the weeks ahead. He's asked the Elder Board here at the church, as well as his circle of pastoral friends in the area, to lift him up in prayer. He's asked them to pray over each of the engagements. I imagine some of the pastors have shared this information with members of their own congregations. So I'm not speaking out of turn in any way. There's a close community of Christian believers here."

"Oh, thank you so much. Mrs. Fuller, correct?"

"Yes, it is Mrs. Fuller. Everyone calls me Annie."

"I'm so grateful. You've been so helpful, Annie. More than you know. I don't need the entire itinerary, but again, thank you so much. But you're sure? Benjamin, Pastor Sharon, I mean, leaves for Barcelona on Friday?"

"Yes, Benjamin flies from Tel Aviv to Barcelona on Friday. I should be sure. I booked the flight." Annie laughed. "Would you like his number as well?"

"You would give me his cell number too?"

"Yes. It's not often anyone asks, but Benjamin has told me that if someone is persistent, it must be important.

He wants to be available if someone needs him."

Annie gave the woman Benjamin's cell number and then asked, "You don't want to give me your name, sweetie?"

"My name is . . . oh, please, Annie. This needs to be a surprise. We've only spoken for a few minutes, but I feel like I know you, like we're friends. You would understand if I told you."

"Certainly, I would. It was so nice chatting with you."

The call ended, and Annie smiled to herself as she reflected on the conversation. Although there was no one else in the room, she said aloud, "I think I know who that was. What a wonderful blessing."

Chapter Ten

J ack and his wife, Natalie, were faithful givers, believing that the Bible was clear on storehouse tithing, that the tithe was the minimum God required.

He had tithed faithfully since he was a teenager working his first job delivering newspapers in Anaheim. His parents instructed him early in his youth, and his own studies later confirmed—the Bible was clear about the Christian's mandate to tithe. The principles were clear; the instructions laid out in the Word were clear. The Lord spoke to Israel through the prophet Malachi and said:

> " 'Bring all the tithes into the storehouse,
> That there may be food in My house,
> And try Me now in this,'
> Says the LORD of hosts,
> If I will not open for you the windows of heaven
> And pour out for you such blessing
> That there will not be room enough to receive it.' "
> (Malachi 3:10 NKJV)

Jack agreed with the largely accepted teaching in modern evangelical churches that the storehouse was referring to the local church and the tithe was understood to represent 10 percent of one's income. He was sometimes amused by the gross income versus net income debate. This is simple, he thought. If I earn $10.00, I need to tithe 10 percent, which means I'll give the church one dollar. "There may be other deductions as well, but that's the reality of earning a paycheck," he would tell others when discussing the subject. "The government withholds their share in taxes, even though I don't agree with much of their spending," he would add. "A certain part goes to pay for insurance, and in some cases future retirement funds are withheld—all from the gross pay amount. After all the deductions, I'm left with a net income to disperse for other expenses. Every other deduction comes off the top. Why would I shortchange my giving to God?"

Jack loved the English Standard Version Scripture passage from Proverbs that clearly described generous giving:

> "One gives freely, yet grows all the richer;
> another withholds what he should give, and
> only suffers want."
> (Proverbs 11:24 ESV)

He committed to memory the following verse:

"The generous man [is a source of blessing and] shall be prosperous *and* enriched, And he who waters will himself be watered [reaping the generosity he has sown]."
(Proverbs 11:25 AMP)

Jack was well-known within the local body of Christ, having worked closely with Benjamin Sharon in organizing the prayer assemblies. Although not a pastor, he would occasionally be asked to fill the pulpit in one of the affiliated churches, though he never accepted a stipend, saying, "I'm giving back a fraction of what God has given me."

His closet held the same blue jean jacket, Levi jeans, sweaters, and shirts that he'd had for the past twenty years. He could afford new clothes, but the question was, why? These were perfectly good garments; they weren't worn out, a bit tighter than years before, but most of the clothes still fit. And they fit his personality—no need to change. Jack supported a number of ministries with monthly donations above and beyond the tithe.

Jack thought of the material blessings that had been showered on him over the course of his life: an upbringing centered around family, church, and most importantly God. A happy childhood filled with sports and other school activities, a quality education in good schools with dedicated teachers, a career that paid well, a comfortable home, the enjoyment of traveling to new places, and, after the Lord Himself, at the top of the list of blessings that

God had provided, a faithful wife who loved Jesus and great kids who were walking with the Lord. The list goes on and on, Jack thought. "How have I escaped so much of the pain that so many others in the world have had to endure?" he said quietly to himself.

Jack stared blankly at the words and read the page a second time. The devotion from *Anguished Cries From the Underground Church* shared a story of a group of Nigerian Christians who were attacked and brutalized by the Boko Haram. It happened in the first century and it's still happening today! Jack cried out in his spirit.

Jack finished his morning Scripture and devotional readings and had just started work when a phone call came in. An hour later, his thoughts turned to the trading platform that was still open on his desktop computer. He quickly changed the view from the Positions page to the Charts tab. Candlesticks for both SPY and QQQ had spiked since the market opened. Jack sighed. He had taken what turned out to be a lengthy call from a client and missed out on the rally.

During periods of strong market rallies his tech stocks would often increase 3–4 percent daily; his overall portfolio would jump 2 percent. Peak bull market rallies at their heights were supported by a buying frenzy that often drove underperforming equities to unsustainable support levels. Jack avoided risky securities; most companies he invested in were profitable.

But in a normal market, the level of profitability would never justify the price spikes and enormous returns many investors were experiencing. At one juncture in a twelve-month period following the 2008–2009 Great Recession, the Fed's easy money policies contributed to an increase of 75 percent in his holdings.

During the recession his holdings suffered a 30 percent drop—less than many investors, however, who had taken on aggressive, high-growth financial instruments that lost much of their value during the mortgage crash.

Jack was not involved in short selling and had never purchased credit default swaps or other risky credit derivatives and complex financial products that even many hedge fund managers didn't understand, let alone the unwary customer purchasing those products. The market had been rife with subprime mortgages—loans with interest rates higher than the prime lending rate that were being marketed to borrowers with low credit scores. A loan package doomed to fail, a financial paradox: a borrower who had not been creditworthy in the past was now being given a higher interest rate loan, decreasing the repayment ability.

Jack had never forgotten the reports of suicides during the 2000 dot-com crash. High technology start-up companies that had exploded in value even though they had never earned a profit and in many cases had not yet brought a product to market, suddenly crashed, losing 90 percent of their value and creating despair among investors whose buying frenzies had driven stock prices to exorbitant, unsupportable levels. At some point the bubble had to burst, and it did so perilously for many speculators.

Bankruptcies and foreclosures in the more recent Great Recession left a new set of investors reeling. The housing meltdown led to turbulent days in the market, oftentimes leaving the retail investor holding the bag.

Jack had shared many times that he never held positions in any of the risky credit-swap derivatives, and thankfully he had little market exposure during the dotcom crash. During the housing crisis he was building his consulting business and avoided the worst of the downturn.

His consulting business was good during those periods, and fortunately he limited his stock portfolio holdings to a mix of companies providing needed services to the economy, companies that would rebound following a market correction, and most of his holdings recovered.

"Okay, everyone's dialed in," Rockwell said, as he began the conference call.

"I have several concerns that I want to review today, and then after I've gone through my list, I have some great news to share with you.

"Overall, as a district, we're having a good month. We should finish the quarter well.

"Margins are good, but sales need to come up. As a district, we're missing our EBITDAR target by half a point. Sales in the second half of the month will be stronger than the first, so we'll gain some ground before month end. We can make this up, but we need to buckle down now. Make sure your sales collateral is up. I don't want to show up at your store and find boxes of promotional materials sitting in the back room. If you're missing anything, get with corporate ASAP!

"The not-so-good news, guys and gals. Help me understand how we can be down in sales and fail to keep our stores stocked. Out-of-stock items are killing us! We need to keep our shelves full. I walk into stores and see empty pegs, empty spaces on merchandise shelving, racks that are missing product, and then I walk into the warehouse and see product sitting in boxes. We have the inventory. Back orders from nearly every one of our suppliers have been minimal. We need to do a better job of getting the merchandise on the floor as soon as it arrives. Watch your labor, but don't cut corners on stocking. On Wednesday, you have orders coming in. Make sure you're staffed. We can't sell items that aren't on the shelf. The public needs to be able to see the item and touch the item. If it's not there, they may or may not ask if we have it.

"On a positive note, Annika, outstanding job managing your inventory! I was hard pressed last week to find missing product. Your store is a showcase not just for the district but for the entire region. I'm very proud of your performance."

"Thank you, Clifton," Annika said.

"Compliment well deserved. Sierra, excellent job as well.

"Moving on, folks. Watch your expenses like a hawk. Make sure you're not spending more than you have. Payroll, supplies, maintenance, and other controllable costs—make sure you stay within your budgeted percentages! No surprises at the end of the month. Get with me after this call if there's any target area you don't think you're going to meet. We'll talk about an action plan.

"Let's talk about appearance. I was in one of our competitor's stores last weekend looking around. Lots of housekeeping issues. Ceiling lights out, papers strewn across the parking lot, trash cans spilling over. Employees with no name tags, lots of problems.

"Our stores need to be immaculate, inside and out. Don't get sidetracked putting out fires. If you allow it, personnel problems will eat you alive.

"As I've told you guys a million times, we won't hesitate to prosecute theft. Be ruthless with your controls. If you catch a shoplifter, call the police immediately. If an employee is stealing, get a confession and have him arrested. You need to make an example or the theft will continue.

"Don't be naïve. Most of our theft is internal. I have more employee theft stories than any DM in the company," he added, with more than a tinge of pride.

"Winding down . . ." Rockwell's tone softened ever so slightly as he neared the end of his remarks. "Folks, I made the out of stocks sound worse than they are. Having said that, what's our goal? Merchandise front-faced, attractively displayed, one hundred percent fully stocked, nothing less. I know you're pushing every day. Collectively, all of you are working very hard. You know the drill. Be relentless; don't let up! Let's make sure we're working smart. Stay focused on the things that are going to yield the biggest results.

"Last thing, and you guys are going to be happy to hear this. As I mentioned to you a few weeks ago, last month's regional visit went very well. Reynolds was so impressed that he authorized a $500 bonus for each of you, payable on the last check of the quarter."

Audible "all right," "yes," and other positive exclamations interrupted whatever Rockwell was going to say next. When the voices subsided, he continued. "Congratulations. This is coming from funds outside the normal bonus pool, so it's above and beyond anything else you'll be getting. Great job!"

Rockwell opened the call to his GMs, and one by one they reported on previously arranged topics affecting the management team as a group. True McElravy, the Mountain Fire general manager, talked about hiring, employee retention, and employee turnover initiatives; Annika Johnson and Sierra Scott, managers of the two Santa Fe stores, reported, respectively, on merchandising and inventory control policies; Bobby Jones, John Romero, and Palin Edwards, who each ran one of the three Albuquerque stores, teamed up and gave a presentation on appearance and organizational standards; Eliana Fredricks, who ran a small store in Ruidoso, and Raymond Nez, the manager of the Roswell store, talked about local marketing strategies.

"Wrapping up, team. One more thing and we'll get on with our day. All of you know the answer, but I'll ask the question anyway. What's the top line on your profit and loss statement?"

"Sales, revenue," the voices on the call responded.

"Focus on driving sales! Make it happen, people! I'll see each of you over the next couple of weeks," Rockwell said at the end of the two-hour scheduled call.

Two days later, Clifton and a new store manager, Anthony Rizzuto, walked through the building of his Farmington store, preparing to leave for the night.

"Six o'clock," Anthony said as he and Clifton exited the store and headed toward their vehicles. "Late night for you again," he added.

"Par for the course," Clifton replied.

"What time will you get home?" Anthony asked.

"Nine, give or take."

"I'll bet your wife gets tired of that."

"She's used to it. It's been the program for a long time."

As they walked through the parking lot, a well-dressed, dignified-looking man who had just left the store glanced at the men. "Are you guys managers here?" he asked.

"Yes," answered Clifton, extending his hand. "Clifton Rockwell. I'm the district manager. This is Anthony Rizzuto, my store general manager."

"Gentlemen," the man began, "I'm sixty-eight years old, and I just had the worst service I've ever had in my life."

"What happened?" Anthony Rizzuto exclaimed.

"What happened, sir?" Rockwell asked with a pained expression on his face.

"Before I tell you, let me say clearly, I don't blame the young lady behind the counter. I don't blame her for not greeting me. I don't blame her for not asking me if I found everything okay, for not thanking me after I paid for my items, for not making eye contact with me even once during the transaction." The man paused and looked intently at the men. "Do you know who I blame?"

The men looked down. "You blame us, sir," Rizzuto said.

"And rightfully so, I'm afraid. I apologize, sir," Clifton quickly added.

"Do you know who else I blame?" the man continued. "I blame your CEO, who needs to get out in his stores more often. And I don't mean the once-every-ten-years television show publicity stunt. And I'm not talking about the infrequent site visits with one of your regionals. I'm talking about getting out in the stores unannounced, where no one knows him, and just observing the service his workers give. You know, I just read where the average corporate CEO makes two hundred times what the frontline worker in his or her organization makes, and the number gets higher by the month. And this is what the consumer gets. Half the time, he's making this kind of money running a company that's losing millions of dollars a year. It's contemptible! The salaries are obscene! Not just your guy. Corporate CEO compensation is disgraceful!"

Rockwell looked distraught. Rizzuto looked worried. "My profuse apologies, sir," Clifton said in a troubled tone.

"Can I give you my business card good for 10 percent off your next purchase?" Rizzuto asked as he reached into his jacket pocket.

"Absolutely not," the man said, calming down a bit. "I'm not looking for anything free. Listen, I hate to pick on you guys. Your service is no worse than the service I get from your competitors. No different. Most of the time I don't say anything. I just happened to run into you guys. Bottom line is I have no expectations, so most of the time this type of thing doesn't faze me. I've taken enough of your time. Thanks for listening." The man turned and began to walk away but then looked back and said, "You can do one thing for me."

"Yes, sir," Rockwell replied.

"Tell your CEO to get out in his stores. Or her stores, whatever the case may be. And tell him to take a huge pay cut. He doesn't deserve what he's making. None of 'em do."

The man got in a red late model Porsche and drove off.

"Ouch! Unbelievable," Rockwell said, shaking his head.

"I'll deal with it." Rizzuto spoke hurriedly. "I'll fix it."

"Counsel her. Don't fire her," Rockwell responded. "You're already short five associates."

"Got it. I'll take care of it."

Rockwell turned to leave. "Needless to say, unacceptable, Anthony. Time to kick things up a notch. Get your training into overdrive," he said as he reached for the door handle of his truck.

"I'm all over it, sir. We take great pride in our customer service offering. I don't know what happened. I'm on it."

Clifton exited the parking lot, drove several blocks through the old industrial section of Farmington, and within minutes was on U.S. Route 64 heading east toward Bloomfield. He reflected on the customer's comments, relieved he was at the store and given the opportunity to field the complaint. At least he talked to us instead of sending a complaint through the pipeline, he thought. Rockwell hated to be micromanaged. The last thing he wanted was additional oversight in his district. For the most part, they left him alone. If the complaint had gone through the customer experience call line, it would have gone directly to the CEO and from there back down to the regional manager, Mack Reynolds, who Rockwell reported to. Way too many unneeded voices. I've got this covered, he thought.

Rockwell glanced at the text from Nicole: "Praying for your protection today. Wish you didn't have to drive on that highway. Be careful."

Rockwell's thoughts turned back to the encounter he had with the customer. No excuse for the lack of responsiveness by one of his employees. Hopefully the story was exaggerated. Who is this guy, Rockwell thought. He obviously made his money somewhere. He's driving a Porsche. He's clearly not living on the streets.

Rockwell had met the CEO, Don Williams, on a number of occasions, and although Artisan Building Supplies was a privately held company and executive salaries were not publicly disclosed, he was 99 percent certain that Williams didn't make even close to two hundred times more than the frontline employees.

Ownership of the company was confined to Artisan family members with only token shares going to top management. Williams was well compensated but nothing extreme. In fact, the number wasn't too far from where Rockwell wanted to be in the not-too-distant future.

At Bloomfield, Clifton turned onto U.S. 550 and continued on in a southeastwardly direction toward Albuquerque. He reflected on the conversation he had with Nicole the night before.

"I've been praying earnestly for you," she said. "I want my husband to be more than just a nominal Christian. I'm not looking down on you. I just want something better for both of us."

Rockwell sighed. What did she expect from him? Wasn't he giving enough? he thought. Hopefully, she'd be in a good mood when he got home.

His thoughts turned back to work—upcoming meetings, budget reports, sales targets, expense control initiatives, and finally, future management promotions he aspired to raced through his mind. His mind was still racing when he pulled into the driveway that night. It was close to ten. The lights were out. Rockwell was relieved. No questions to answer tonight, he thought.

Chapter Eleven

I'm surprised this is such a dilemma," Cousins said moments after they sat down. "Is your quandary due to religious reasons?"

"I suppose, to some extent," Andréa Veronique replied.

"What's your church background?" Cousins asked.

"I had an orthodox upbringing. Well, my family did anyhow. My parents attended St. Elijah Antiochian Orthodox Christian Church in Oklahoma City, but we moved to Wilmette, Illinois, when I was seven years old. Church attendance was sporadic after that."

"And you graduated with a political science degree from Northwestern. With honors, I might add. Very distinguished. Remarkable, indeed."

"How did you know?" Andréa Veronique looked surprised.

"Public record. Notwithstanding the fact that we take great care to research our candidates."

"You mentioned a bonus. Is that ethical?" Andréa Veronique asked.

"Oh, my dear!" Cousins laughed. "Look, we'll cover our bases. We'll schedule several speeches, appearances. You'll earn the money. Everything's on the up. Nothing to be concerned about."

Cousins looked intently at Andréa Veronique. "I'm a person of faith myself. We both are. But who are we to impose our beliefs on everyone else? We live in a diverse country; we need to be sensitive to a broad spectrum of thoughts. That's the coalition we're in. That's what the caucus expects. You won't agree with your constituents on everything."

"I'm conflicted on the abortion agenda," Andréa Veronique said. "I feel like I'm compromising . . ."

"Andréa, my dear." Cousins lifted her left hand from the table and held it between his. "There will be many other compromises. This may or may not be the first. It won't be the last."

Andréa Veronique looked down and pulled her hand back. "I've been wrestling with a couple of things that I need to figure out. If I'm in, I'm in. All the way. Just give me a few more days to work through this. I'll let you know soon."

"Fair enough," Cousins said and sighed. "I've waited this long. I suppose I can wait a little longer. But frankly, I'm running out of time. I need to know by the end of the month. At the latest."

With that, Cousins flagged down the server, paid the check, and abruptly left the diner, leaving Andréa Veronique alone at the table, immersed in a range of emotions.

That night, well into the wee hours and with Stuart fast asleep, Andréa Veronique lay awake, her mind churning over two distinct choices she faced—one position or the other that she needed to take in her candidacy—and for some reason, which she did not fully understand, haunted by memories from her childhood of lying in bed listening to her parents fight, praying, "Please, God, don't let my parents get divorced." She would cover her ears, drowning out the arguments, but the fighting continued until she fell asleep, her face pressed against a pillow and wet from her crying.

Her mind flashed to childhood memories of visiting her grandparents in Oklahoma in the ensuing summers after moving to Wilmette. Her grandpa and grandma lived in a suburb of Oklahoma City, in a development comprised of four parallel streets, each about a mile long and spotted with brick ranch-style homes on two-acre parcels.

Her grandparents' property had eleven sycamores and three maple trees—an autumn blaze, October glory, and silver maple—lush, vibrant shades of green in the spring and summer, a red hues, gold and orange splashed color spectacle in the fall. In the corner of the yard, a gnarled, crooked pine tree twisted its way upward in a jagged pattern, dropping cones and pine needles on the grass. She loved playing under the rugged, gnarly tree, collecting the pine cones in a basket she displayed near the fence. Andréa Veronique always imagined the tree to be a hunched over old man, walking unsteadily through a nearby woods, at times faltering and stumbling off the path before steadying himself with a knobby cane and continuing his journey. He was carrying a knapsack, and a small bird sat perched on his shoulder. She never understood why she looked at the pine tree in this way, but the startling image of the old man made her cry.

She viewed the pine cones as a buttress, a line of defense.

Seven tall evergreens bordered the adjacent property to the north. A line of oak trees bordered the front yards of three homes on one of the cross streets; the neighborhood was filled with elms, loblolly pines, Oklahoma red buds, and crape myrtles. Trees, blue skies, and sunny days filled her memories along with the occasional view of a fox and an assortment of colorful birds—scissor-tailed flycatchers darting from fence post to tree limb, hummingbirds zipping around the feeder hanging from the soffit on the back porch, an occasional cardinal, and once in a while, to her delight, a bluebird. Sometimes, when she and her grandpa were out walking, a Mississippi kite would swoop down just above her grandpa's hat—she was much shorter, so she was spared the unnerving dive and disconcerting warning inches above his head. He took it in stride, saying, "There must be a nest nearby. She's just protecting her young."

But her favorite bird was the ever-present mockingbird, singing incessant melodies throughout the day, much to Andréa Veronique's delight.

The summer she turned ten, her grandpa enrolled her in a weeklong vacation Bible school class at a Baptist church in town. It was an enjoyable time of learning Bible stories and verses, making crafts, and playing with other kids her age. Each day of vacation Bible school, at the end of the day, the teacher would ask the kids if they would like to accept Jesus into their hearts as Savior. On the third day of class, she raised her hand and followed along with the teacher in a prayer. In the years that followed, if asked, she would say that she was saved when she was ten.

One of her earliest childhood memories was before her parents moved to Wilmette. She was about five. Her mom put her in the back seat, buckled her seatbelt, started the engine, but then turned the key and stopped the engine after remembering something she had forgotten in the house. Andréa Veronique remembered the car rolling toward the street when a man suddenly jumped into the front seat and put the car in gear. The man was gone when her mother came back. In the years following her prayer at vacation Bible school that summer, she wondered if the man had been an angel.

After she turned twelve or thirteen, her dad would let her ride her bike to Lake Michigan. She only crashed the bike on the sidewalk once, but before a middle-aged couple could reach her to help, she had sprung to her feet and sped off, turning and waving to them as she pedaled off toward the lake.

She'd lock her bike in the bike stand and then walk along the sandy beach watching the waves lap along the shore, picking up a small seashell and tossing it into the lake or, if it was especially shiny or the color particularly intriguing, washing it off in the water and then placing it in her pocket. Sometimes, on a weekend, she and her dad would catch the train at the Howard Station Depot in Evanston and ride downtown. She loved looking at Wrigley Field and the other old buildings and was always struck by the austerity of the tenement housing they passed. Her father was an engineer, and the family lived in a white three-bedroom home with two second-floor gables and a screened-in porch facing the backyard.

The fighting continued until Andréa Veronique left for college, but her parents stayed together.

She held memories of peaceful, happy times for the most part, although there were other incidents. Arguments on the playground, fractured relationships in junior high and high school, balancing college and part-time job responsibilities—all the typical challenges many young people face. But for as long as she could remember, Dad would say, "Andréa Veronique is a survivor. She always lands on her feet. She's tough. She'll be all right."

To the wonderment of many of her friends, about halfway through her freshman year in college she stopped telling people she was saved.

Early on, she too had marriage problems, usually relating to money. They were always scraping to get by, raising kids, trying to figure out how and when each of their respective dreams should be acted on.

Where would they be without help from her dad and Stuart's parents? They were unable to make their last move on their own. Part of the move went on credit cards; part of it came from family.

And then her life trajectory changed. Two years after moving to Mountain Fire, New Mexico, for Stuart's teaching job, Andréa Veronique ran for an open county commissioner seat and was elected by an overwhelming majority. She had a degree in political science, but it was her personality that endeared her to the voters. She was attractive, well-dressed, smart, a good speaker, and passionate about improving the community. Less than a year into her term she was running for a United States House of Representatives seat. The past year had been a whirlwind.

Her thoughts turned to her last conversation with Cousins and the turmoil she felt.

Andréa Veronique glanced at the calendar of events that were scheduled for the remainder of the month: three speeches, a fundraising call, a follow-up interview with James Radisson, and a meeting with Cousins. She had always thrived on pressure, but the stress of the last few days was weighing on her. For an instant, a fleeting moment, she felt like giving up. *How did my life become so complicated?* she wondered.

Andréa Veronique stood up, took a deep breath, picked up a folder containing notes for her meeting with Radisson, and began reviewing the talking points she would need for the interview. *If I'm going to get through this, I need to be strong,* she said to herself.

Chapter Twelve

⁂

Greetings to each of you. It's a great honor and blessing and privilege to be here in Madrid to share with you from God's Word. Before I begin, I would like to introduce three guests of mine that have joined us today. Sitting to my left is a very dear friend from New York, Miss Sarai Levy. Sarai, don't be shy, please stand up." Sarai stood, turned toward the audience, smiled sheepishly, lifted her arm in a somewhat timid manner, and waved unassertively before sitting back down.

"Thank you, Sarai. I'm also pleased to have two new friends, Mr. Gideon Mendelson and his daughter, Rivka. I won't ask my new friends to stand, but I do want them to know how much I appreciate them being here. Thank you, Gideon. Thank you, Rivka.

"I've been asked to read from Scripture, and I'm honored to do so. Please open your Bibles with me to Isaiah chapter 53."

Benjamin held his Bible in his hands and began reading:

" 'Who hath believed our report? and to whom is the arm of the LORD revealed? For he shall grow up before him as a tender plant, and as a root out of a dry ground: he hath no form nor comeliness; and when we shall see him, there is no beauty that we should desire him. He is despised and rejected of men; a man of sorrows, and acquainted with grief: and we hid as it were our faces from him; he was despised, and we esteemed him not.

" 'Surely he hath borne our griefs, and carried our sorrows: yet we did esteem him stricken, smitten of God, and afflicted. But he was wounded for our transgressions, he was bruised for our iniquities: the chastisement of our peace was upon him; and with his stripes we are healed. All we like sheep have gone astray; we have turned every one to his own way; and the LORD hath laid on him the iniquity of us all.

" 'He was oppressed, and he was afflicted, yet he opened not his mouth: he is brought as a lamb to the slaughter, and as a sheep before her shearers is dumb, so he openeth not his mouth. He was taken from prison and from judgment: and who shall declare his generation? for he was cut off out of the land of the living: for the transgression of my people was he stricken. And he made his grave with the wicked, and with the rich in his death; because he had done no violence, neither was any deceit in his mouth.

" 'Yet it pleased the LORD to bruise him; he hath put him to grief: when thou shalt make his soul an offering for sin, he shall see his seed, he shall prolong his days, and the pleasure of the LORD shall prosper in his hand. He shall see of the travail of his soul, and shall be satisfied: by his knowledge shall my righteous servant justify many; for he shall bear their iniquities. Therefore will I divide him a portion with the great, and he shall divide the spoil with the strong; because he hath poured out his soul unto death: and he was numbered with the transgressors: and he bare the sin of many, and made intercession for the transgressors.'
(Isaiah 53:1–12)

"Chavurah, my dear Jewish friends, and perhaps some of you in this assembly who have been grafted into Yeshua. The prophet Isaiah is talking about Yeshua Hamashiach, Jesus the Messiah, God the Father's Suffering Servant. He is the one who Micah prophesied would be born in Bethlehem Ephratah, the One 'whose goings forth have been from of old, from everlasting.'

"Yeshua is the one our fathers have been waiting for. There is salvation under heaven in no one but Yeshua."

Benjamin began singing, first in English, then in Hebrew, his tenor voice beautifully sounding the Scripture passage from Numbers chapter 6,

" 'The LORD bless thee, and keep thee:
the LORD make his face shine upon thee,
and be gracious unto thee:
the LORD lift up his countenance upon thee,
and give thee peace.' "

By most standards, Sarai Levy was a wealthy woman. After her conversion just weeks before her conversation with Annie Fuller, she studiously read through the New Testament, astounded by the words she was reading, awestruck, like so many Jewish believers before her, that the New Testament authors were predominately Jewish, writing about a Jewish Messiah—a Messiah learned in the Prophets and Jewish law and tradition. As she read, she was overwhelmed by the thought that she had been a sinner on her way to hell when suddenly she was snatched from a fire into Yeshua's arms. The skepticism she had felt when she first walked into the church was replaced with utter astonishment. The minister, a Jewish man, was talking about a new birth in Yeshua. It was as if a wave of truth had covered her like a tidal wave, engulfed her entire body, and saturated every pore of her being. Her entire life had gone by without knowing the truth about Jesus, Yeshua, the Son of God who sacrificed Himself for her sins, and now she wept as she listened to the words, consciously inviting the Spirit of the Living God to take hold of her, to lift her to another place, to never let her go.

Benjamin had tried to tell her, many years before. The conversation was as vivid as the night they had spoken.

"I was hoping you'd call to say good night," she said, happy to hear his voice.

"I called, but not to say good night. We need to meet right away. I have something very important to share with you."

"Benjamin, what's wrong? It's almost ten o'clock." Sarai sounded alarmed.

"Please, Sarai, it's important." Benjamin had an urgency in his voice. "I'm at Katz's. When can you be here?"

"I was getting ready for bed. We meet with Rabbi Danielson at nine tomorrow morning . . ."

"Sarai, it can't wait."

"I'm in my nightgown. I'll get dressed. I'll catch a cab. I'll try to be there within a half hour, maybe twenty minutes."

Sarai set the phone down, dressed, grabbed a light tan-colored jacket, moved quickly to the elevator, and a minute later was standing on the sidewalk near the street. She waved toward a cab that was slowly working its way toward her apartment building and handed the driver an address, to which he said, "I know where Katz's Deli is. I've been driving a cab in Manhattan for thirty years."

Benjamin was seated when Sarai arrived. He jumped up, took her hand, and approached the counter. "Would you like anything, Sarai? Dessert? I haven't eaten since this afternoon." He glanced at the attendant behind the counter. "Two espressos, please, and a pastrami sandwich. Sliced. Sarai?"

"No, thank you. Nothing for me. I'll never get to sleep if I have coffee at this hour. Benjamin, why are we here? Tell me what's going on."

"Sarai, I was at a church service tonight. A Christian gathering. My mind is going a million miles an hour right now. I hardly know where to begin. I'll try to figure it all out later. I was at a small church on Thirty-First Street. The minister introduced a Jewish man, a Christian Jewish man, who shared a story from the Bible about Yeshua, Jesus the Christ. The One we've been waiting for. We've been waiting for Messiah, and He's already come! Jesus, Yeshua, is Messiah! I have far more questions than answers, but I responded to an invitation tonight to surrender my life to Yeshua. I know in my heart that God was speaking to me. Sarai, I've become a Christian! I'm telling you tonight that Yeshua is the true Messiah!"

Sarai looked at Benjamin in disbelief, her mind whirling in a state of shock. "Benjamin, do you hear yourself? What are you saying?" she cried out. "What's happened to you? We're getting married in less than a month. In the largest Jewish synagogue in Brooklyn. What will your father say? We know what he'll say. He'll disown you! Both of our families . . ."

Sarai buried her face in her hands and began to sob. "No, no, no, no, you can't do this, Benjamin!"

Benjamin's testimony the next morning was met with incredulity and bewilderment. Benjamin shared his story with Rabbi Danielson, who said, "Please, go right now and talk to your father."

An hour later, Benjamin and Sarai met with his father and mother. His words were met with disbelief, then anger. The wedding was postponed and soon after canceled. Benjamin and Sarai continued to meet, though clandestinely, for each of their families were now embittered toward Benjamin. Sarai remained committed to the marriage but did not embrace Yeshua as Messiah. Three months after the anxiously awaited wedding date, their relationship ended and Benjamin left for seminary school.

The years went by with little contact between the two, although they had met in San Francisco years before where Sarai had accompanied Benjamin to a Jews For Jesus presentation. How had she not understood? How had she not believed? How had she been so blind?

Non-Jewish Christian friends occasionally shared their testimonies with her, but the message had never taken hold in her heart. Now the gospel message had come alive. She was amazed as she read the Epistles. Paul, a Jewish Christian convert who had persecuted believers, was writing about the one true God, Yeshua! Something she had failed to see her entire life! Peter, James, Jude, the writer of Hebrews, and John, all Jewish followers of Jesus, were teaching salvation through Yeshua alone!

Barely leaving her apartment, she read Matthew, Mark, Luke, and John in their entirety no less than three times the first week she was saved. And now the question of wealth overwhelmed her. What was she to do with her estate—real estate holdings, money market accounts, stocks and treasury bonds, financial assets—by most people's standards, a small fortune? She had always traveled freely, bought anything she desired, dined at the finest restaurants, and never gave cost a second thought. It wasn't that she was particularly covetous or even desirous of worldly gain; she simply always had the affluence that came with being the only daughter of a wealthy entrepreneur. Extravagance had been showered on her since she was a child. Following her father's death she was the sole recipient, the only heir, to a substantial inheritance; the designated overseer to his charitable foundation—a fund active with endowments to causes, some of which she quickly recognized as conflicting with her new faith.

It's not that she was so attracted to a lifetime of opulence that anything less would be unsatisfying or in some way insufferable; it was simply that she had never known anything else. Her travels on behalf of her father's endowments took her to many parts of the country, places with interesting scenery, diverse cultures, responsive people, and, in many settings, a slower, more relaxed pace of life than the coterie of financial advisors and legal counselors she worked with enjoyed. She was always glad to get home. Not because she missed the luxuriousness of her lifestyle but more so because she missed her daily routine. She was happy to be the administrator and trustee of her father's estate, she enjoyed consulting with attorneys about general funding decisions for the foundation she was responsible for, and she enjoyed signing documents, talking on the phone, and otherwise immersing herself in a world of philanthropy and benevolence she felt was virtuous, honorable, and meaningful. In the afternoon she would go out for lunch or tea at a local Manhattan café, take a stroll in Central Park, and sometimes in the evening take in a play. She had a small group of female friends, most of them Jewish, but some Christian.

Sarai was raised in a strict Jewish household by a rigid Orthodox Jewish businessman, Zev Levy. Mr. Levy's father, Dov Levy, amassed a fortune buying, refurbishing, and selling commercial real estate properties in Brooklyn, Queens, and Long Island. Zev expanded the business into Manhattan. Zev was a celebrated Zionist lending support to the Likud – National Liberal Movement, a party founded by Ariel Sharon and Menachem Begin and represented later by Benjamin Netanyahu as prime minister of Israel.

Zev Levy was a distinguished member and large financial supporter of the synagogue where Rabbi Isaac Sharon served. Mr. Levy and Rabbi Sharon maintained far more than a congregationalist-rabbi relationship, but were like brothers, attending the same schools in Long Island, having grown up themselves in the same synagogue since grade school, celebrated bar mitzvah in the same month, Shevat, almost to the same day, January 27, went to the same high school, and only separated in a notable way when Isaac Sharon left for rabbinical seminary training.

Following his ordination, Isaac Sharon served as rabbi, first in a small temple in Long Island, but later, covering a span of forty years, at synagogues in all five boroughs of New York City, the final destination a synagogue in Manhattan where he served the last ten years of his life. It was during this time that Rabbi Sharon's son, Benjamin, asked Zev Levy for his daughter's hand in marriage. Like their fathers, Benjamin and Sarai had known each other since childhood. After Rabbi Sharon returned from rabbinical training, and with Zev Levy's real estate development career well underway, the two were often united in the same synagogue service as Rabbi Sharon moved from borough to borough, and frequently the families were together at festive gatherings. But it was not until college—Sarai was a sophomore, Benjamin a senior—that they became an inseparable couple. Their wedding ceremony would follow Benjamin's return from Israel. His absence with only occasional returns to the States would be the longest five years of Sarai's life.

How could he have accepted that position and postponed the most enduring, poetic fairy tale she could ever imagine? What an enraptured life together they would have enjoyed. Why would Benjamin accept a separation from the only woman he was ever meant to be with? Why would her father encourage and help orchestrate such a move?

In the early years of her childhood, the family observed Shabbat and other Jewish holidays. As the years passed and Zev Levy became consumed with his empire, as he proudly described his business, the orthodoxy prevalent in Sarai's upbringing lessened. By the time Sarai was in college neither she nor Benjamin had abandoned Judaism, but likewise neither described themselves as religious Jews, much to the chagrin of Rabbi Sharon,

Benjamin's uncles, and other family members, all who had expected Benjamin to become yet another rabbi in a long line of rabbis.

Their marriage, nonetheless, would be held at Congregation Beth Abraham, a synagogue in Brooklyn, and would be attended by select members of no less than eight synagogues Rabbi Sharon had served at and by a coterie of influential businessmen and pro-Israeli Zionists, some coming from Israel. The guest list was planned with meticulous detail. The synagogue would be filled to capacity.

As the years went by, Sarai busied herself with planning and executing charitable work and found some level of happiness, but there was a loneliness in her eyes, and at certain moments she felt an emptiness that she believed was a result of her departure from the Jewish orthodoxy she was raised in.

Now, close to thirty-five years later she was flying to Barcelona to see Benjamin Sharon, the man who was supposed to be her husband, who abandoned Judaism, embraced Christianity, was forsaken by family . . .

Sarai had a King James Bible a Christian friend had given her years before. Resting in a nightstand, the Bible had scarcely been opened, never to the B'rit Chadashah, the Hebrew term for the new covenant, what Christians called the New Testament. After immersing herself in the text, her mind kept coming back to the words of Jesus she read in Matthew 19, first from the King James Version, then from a contemporary English translation recommended to her by the friend who invited her to the service, and then over and over from *The Complete Jewish Study Bible* given to her at Times Square Church the night she heard the Jewish man's testimony of a new birth in Yeshua, the night she herself said yes to Yeshua.

She read,

"Yeshua said to him, 'If you are serious about reaching the goal, go and sell your possessions, give to the poor, and you will have riches in heaven. Then come, follow me!' But when the young man heard this, he went away sad, because he was wealthy.

"Then Yeshua said to his *talmidim*, 'Yes. I tell you that it will be very hard for a rich man to enter the Kingdom of Heaven. Furthermore, I tell you that it is easier for a camel to pass through a needle's eye than for a rich man to enter the Kingdom of God.'" (Matthew 19: 21–24 CJB)

What an astonishing statement! she cried out in her spirit. How should I interpret this? What does this mean for me? Sarai needed counsel. Benjamin would know, she thought.

Chapter Thirteen

The flight from New York's LaGuardia arrived in Barcelona thirty minutes late. Sarai looked anxiously at the terminal clock as she maneuvered through the crowd. What would he think? Why had she not told him she was coming? How presumptuous to show up unannounced. What if there was someone else in his life?

Suddenly she spotted him! Oh my, she thought. Seeing him in the distance, she walked briskly toward the gate. She noticed Benjamin turn slightly to his left and look back. He saw me. He looked right at me, she thought. They were now separated by about fifty feet. Sarai thought her heart would burst. Where was he going? Why didn't he come back after seeing her? Annie said he was flying from Tel Aviv to Barcelona. There was no mention of a connecting flight upon arrival.

"Benjamin," she cried out, but an announcement about an unaccompanied child blared through the intercom, drowning out her cry. She ran toward the gate, catching a final glimpse of his arm, and then suddenly the gate closed with a heavy thud. In an instant he was gone.

Sarai raised her arms in a state of panic but then gathered her senses. What time is it in New Mexico? she wondered. Annie will know if Benjamin's itinerary changed.

Moments before, Benjamin disembarked from his flight, went to the restroom, ordered a soft drink from a specialty beverage stand, and then heard his name called out above the din of the crowd and blare of the loudspeaker. He turned abruptly to see a woman racing toward a nearby gate, lift her arms in dismay, and then stop as she reached for her cell phone. Her hair was shoulder length, black with silver streaks, a woman about five foot five, slender, with a lovely, familiar voice, even if his name had been shouted in an amalgam of sound. He knew the woman. Benjamin walked steadily toward her when she suddenly turned and looked up.

"Sarai?" He sounded surprised, puzzled, but ecstatic.

"Benjamin!" she exclaimed. "I saw you get on the plane! What happened?"

"No, you are mistaken. It wasn't me that you saw boarding a plane. I'm right here. What are you doing here?"

"Benjamin! I gave my heart to Yeshua! I wanted to tell you in person. I called the church and was told you had left for Israel and Europe and wouldn't be back for three months. It couldn't wait. I booked a flight from New York to Barcelona.

"Oh, Benjamin." Sarai looked at Benjamin and suddenly burst into tears.

"Please, please don't cry." Benjamin gently placed his hands on her shoulders and then took her hand, leading her through a sudden influx of passengers who had just disembarked from a plane at the gate they were standing near. The two worked their way through the terminal and found an empty table at the Caffé di Fiore.

"Please, let's sit down. Tell me everything."

For the next hour and a half, Sarai breathtakingly shared her conversion, her testimony interrupted by references to shared incidents from their lives going back to childhood, high school, and college; Benjamin's time in Israel; work involving her father's estate; frequent questions for Benjamin about the Christian faith, his pastoral work, his sabbatical, but not pausing long enough for him to reply to any of the queries, a narrative impeded by occasional crying but a crying of joy at the place she found herself in.

"Scarcely a day has gone by for the past thirty-five years that I haven't asked Yeshua to save your soul. I'm at a loss for words to describe the happiness I feel. To say that I'm overjoyed is a considerable understatement."

The mood turned light and Benjamin smiled. "You are as beautiful today as you were at twenty-five."

"I appreciate your kind words, although we both know that they're not true. I don't even try to get the gray lines out anymore."

The two shared a lighthearted laugh, and then

Benjamin commented, "We didn't discuss the obvious. What are your plans?"

"I know this will sound . . . perhaps it won't make sense, but I have an engagement tomorrow afternoon in New York, a meeting with a Realtor, buyers, lawyers that I need to be back for. I booked a round-trip flight. I fly back into LaGuardia tonight. The flight leaves in two hours. I had no idea how our conversation would go. I wasn't even sure I'd find you. I just knew I had to try and that I needed to meet with you in person, not on the phone. Yeshua answered my prayer."

"Our prayers. My specific prayer didn't anticipate this, but Yeshua Himself planned this encounter. To Him be the glory!" Benjamin said.

Benjamin looked down, his mind pondering a scenario that he suddenly suggested. "After I leave the airport, I'm traveling by train to Madrid. On Monday afternoon I'll be speaking to a Messianic congregation at a small church. A good friend, a Jewish believer, invited me to speak.

"It would be so nice if you could be there with me."

"Benjamin, I would love to be there. I will finish my business on Saturday, pack a suitcase, and be on a plane to Madrid."

"Let me walk you to your gate. I'll stay with you until your flight is in the air."

Benjamin and Sarai made their way through the terminal, excitedly discussing arrangements for their next meeting in Madrid.

No sooner than Sarai parted, Benjamin was approached by a uniformed man who identified himself as the head of airport security.

"Mr. Sharon, Jorge Fredrick. I'm the chief security officer for the Barcelona Airport-El Prat."

The man flashed a badge displaying his name and title.

"What can I do for you?" Benjamin replied.

"Mr. Sharon, please come with me. We have some questions we'd like to ask you."

"What kind of questions? Come with you where?"

The man pointed to an open room just off from the security check-in to their right.

"Please cooperate, Mr. Sharon. We have some questions to ask you."

Reluctantly, and with considerable reservation, Benjamin walked with the man toward the room.

"Sit down, please. Were you in Barcelona on Wednesday, Mr. Sharon?"

"No, I was in Jerusalem on Wednesday. I flew here today."

"Allow me to show you a video recording from two days ago, Mr. Sharon."

Fredrick turned on a recording and played footage of a man standing in front of a jewelry store in downtown Barcelona. The man appeared to have exited the store, flagged a cab, and then left the scene moments before police cars converged on the street in front of the business. Mr. Fredrick replayed the scene of the man exiting the entryway near the door of the store. He then rewound the video, enlarged the image, and in slow motion played the footage as the man proceeded to the street corner and got into a cab.

"Is not the man in the recording you, Mr. Sharon?"

Benjamin was incredulous. "Of course it's not me," he exclaimed. "I wasn't in Barcelona on Wednesday. I was in Israel."

"Let me play the shot one more time, Mr. Sharon."

Once again, he rewound the tape and played the scene. The man in the footage looked remarkably like Benjamin.

"This is unbelievable. I can't believe we're having this conversation."

"No, what's unbelievable is your response, Mr. Sharon. I ask you again, were you in Barcelona on Wednesday?"

"I explained to you. I flew here from Tel Aviv, Israel, to speak at a church in Madrid. My flight was delayed. Check the flight itinerary. You'll see my name."

"I'm sorry, Mr. Sharon, but we'll need to detain you."

"I need to contact the American Embassy."

In a rapid-fire cluster of events that ended with the arrival of a police captain from the Barcelona police station, a succession of recurrent apologies from the captain, security officer, and airport executive that emerged on the scene, and a conciliatory offer for a flight upgrade, Benjamin, stunned by the questioning, left the airport and caught a shuttle for the train station.

Late that afternoon, he boarded the Renfe AVE high-speed train at the Barcelona Sants station and settled in for the two-and-a-half-hour trip to Madrid. Benjamin had a window seat in a two-seat row with an open aisle seat and the facing row empty. Benjamin leaned back in the seat and closed his eyes. He had the section to himself. He could relax and try to make sense of what happened. The events of the last few hours had been surreal—as shocking and stunning and dreamlike as anything he had experienced since the phone call with Khalid so many years before. The story would have invoked disbelief from himself had he been listening to the account from a friend. His thoughts turned to Sarai Levy. After all these years! And yet, he had prayed for Sarai for how long? Why was he surprised that Yeshua had dramatically revealed Himself to her and saved her soul? All glory to my Lord and King, Yeshua! Benjamin prayed silently. His mind turned back to Sarai and the exhilaration and rapture he felt listening to her share her testimony of Yeshua's grace in her life. What an incredible day, he thought, with a sense of wonderment overcoming him in such a way that he felt like standing in the aisle and shouting to the entire group of passengers and crew the goodness of God. The God that he, Benjamin, served. The Creator, the One who made the heavens and the earth, the God Most High who sent his Son, Yeshua, the giver of life, to atone for man's sins, and the God of salvation who had just imparted eternal life to a woman he had fervently lifted up in prayer for thirty-five years. And Yeshua answered his prayer!

Benjamin was jolted from his thoughts when an

elderly man wearing a kippah sat down next to the window in the seat directly across from him. The man greeted Benjamin in Spanish and then opened the table in front of him, preparing for the dinner that would soon be served. In the meantime, he set a book down, folded his hands, and smiled at Benjamin. After exchanging greetings and brief introductions, Benjamin politely offered, "I do speak some Spanish, but my English is much better."

"I speak English, yes, I do. I've been to America many times," the man said in a deep, husky voice. There was a kindness and glitter in his eyes as he spoke.

"Do you live in Barcelona or Madrid?" Benjamin asked.

"Madrid," the man replied, his thick Spanish accent prominently on display with every word spoken.

Benjamin prayed silently asking the Lord to prepare the man's heart for whatever might be said between the two.

"I'm glad it wasn't you," the man said.

Benjamin looked at the man inquisitively. "I don't understand," he said.

"The man arrested for the jewelry heist. There is a striking resemblance. But here you are on the train. The man I saw on the monitor was taken off in handcuffs."

The man paused and laughed a deep, hearty laugh. "Here you are on the train. It couldn't have been you," he said before adding, "He was involved in a string of larcenies, the reporter said. It caused quite a little intrigue, if you can imagine."

"I understand now," Benjamin said. "I won't bother you with all of the details, but yes, there was some confusion at the airport earlier this afternoon. You're not the only one who thought there was a similarity in our appearance."

A waiter arrived, pushing a dinner cart, and set a tray in front of each of the men.

"May I recite a blessing?" the man asked.

"Please do," Benjamin replied.

The men bowed their heads as the man prayed.

"I see your kippah and the Tanakh you placed on the table. I'm reminded of my father. He was a rabbi in New York City."

"A rabbi! In New York! How interesting! Was he part of an Orthodox synagogue?"

"Yes, Orthodox. I come from a long line of rabbis in my family."

Benjamin looked at the man and smiled warmly. "I'm a Messianic Jew. I believe that Yeshua is the Messiah. I understand that you may not believe in Yeshua. I'm not trying to make you uncomfortable."

The man looked surprised when Benjamin said the name Yeshua, but then, to Benjamin's own surprise, the man said, "I have known many Christians in my lifetime. Not a great many Jewish Christians but some."

The men sat silently for a time eating their dinner, a neatly arranged meal of chicken, vegetables, a small salad and roll, and a pastry with a swirl of strawberry glaze.

"What were you doing in Israel, if I may ask?" the man said.

"Some of the time visiting old friends," Benjamin replied. "There are several speaking engagements I'm preparing for. Part of the time on this recent trip was spent visiting historical biblical sites, places where Yeshua ministered. I'm on a sabbatical from the church I pastor in the United States. I was hoping for some vacation time, but it seems most of my time is spent studying and preparing sermons." Benjamin laughed. "Have you been to Israel?" he asked the man.

"My, yes. Many times. I studied Hebrew in Jerusalem when I was a young man. Too many years ago," the man said, his eyes glistening with the memory. My favorite mizmôr, psalm I should say, from the Tehillim says, 'Let them be ashamed and turned backward, All they that hate Zion' (Psalm 129:5 Tanakh 1917). In the Tanakh, the prophet Isaiah says the ransomed of the Lord will return and come to Zion with singing. Some of your translations say Jerusalem. What a blessed day that will be." He then said, "I look forward to that day."

"We share a love for the prophets. I should tell you that I'm a Christian Zionist," Benjamin said. "In the coming days I'll be speaking on Zionism in Jerusalem. I've shared the message a number of times over the years, but it will be an honor for me to address an audience in Zion."

"Fascinating, fascinating." The man unfolded the table belonging to the adjacent seat and moved his tray over. He folded the table in front of him, put his hands in his lap, and for a moment looked intently at Benjamin. "I'm not antagonistic. I said I've known many Christians in my lifetime. In fact, I have Christian friends."

The man gazed out the window and, without looking up at Benjamin, said, "I'm waiting for Messiah."

A short time later the man said, "We have another hour before we reach Madrid. I can close my eyes and rest, which I would normally do if I were alone. Or I can take advantage of being in the company of a man who I sense has lived a life worth sharing. What is your preference?"

"I'm happy to spend time with you. What would you like to ask me?"

"I've heard other confirmations, declarations, if you agree with that description, but I'm interested to hear your statement of belief. Tell me. How did you come to be a supporter of Yeshua? How did you determine that Yeshua was Messiah? I truly want to know. Tell me your story. Don't hold back."

Thank you, Yeshua, Lord Jesus, Benjamin prayed silently. Pour out Your Spirit upon me, please. Anoint me with Your words.

For the next hour Benjamin shared his dramatic conversion, his loss of family, his pastoral ministry, his work in calling the body of Christ together in prayer, and lastly, his surprise visit from Sarai at an airport halfway around the world—"I'm exaggerating, not quite halfway" he added—and her recent commitment to Yeshua.

"Sarai? This was your Jewish bride in New York? Did I understand this right?"

"Yes, all of these years later. I never stopped praying for her," Benjamin replied.

A short time later, the train arrived in Madrid. After exiting the train, they took an escalator from the terminal platform to level 1, and then began working their way through the station.

"I've navigated this train station many times. If you allow me, I'll get you to the street sooner than you might on your own," the man told Benjamin.

As they approached a set of automatic doors, the man stumbled. Benjamin rested his hand under the man's arm, steadying him, and the two walked slowly toward the door. Just before reaching the exit, the man said, "I need to sit down for a little while. I'm meeting my daughter. She'll find me." Benjamin helped the man to a bench and gently held his arm and left hand. It was a soft hand, bruised from the brunt of minor bumps and scrapes, wrinkled and worn from age. The man looked at Benjamin. "Thank you for your company tonight," he said.

"It was my pleasure. Shalom, my friend."

As Benjamin turned in the direction of the car rental counters, the man said, "Pastor Sharon. I didn't say this to you on the train. I'm not especially well. I don't think I'm long in this world. Will you remember me in your prayers?"

"Certainly, absolutely I will pray for you. I will remember you in my prayers. Would you mind . . . would you allow me to pray for you right now, before we part?"

The man glanced to his left and then turned slowly

to his right. "I don't see my daughter. I suppose we have time. I asked you to pray for me and you said yes. How can I say no?"

Benjamin gently placed his hands on each side of the man's head and began to pray. "*Adonai*, God of Abraham, Isaac, and Jacob. God of Moses and the Israelites. God of the Hebrew Scriptures. You are the one true God, the only true God. You alone deserve all the praise and all the honor and all the glory.

"Lord God Almighty, I lift up my new friend, Gideon Mendelson, before You. Gideon is in need of healing. I ask You, in the mighty name of Yeshua, to heal my friend and to touch his soul with Your presence. In the mighty name of Yeshua, amen."

Benjamin looked up to see a woman standing at Mr. Mendelson's side, her face looking panic-stricken, as though she had just witnessed a horrific act at a crime scene. "Father, what are you doing?" she exclaimed in Spanish while tugging at Mr. Mendelson's arm. "Get up, we must be going."

"Please let me help," Benjamin said as he gently put his hand under Gideon's other arm. "Your father had a difficult time walking from the train. Let me help you take him to your car."

Without looking at Benjamin, the woman nodded, reluctantly accepting his help. The three walked slowly to a train station exit door and left the building. They crossed the street running in front of the terminal, proceeded to a parking lot, and came to a small compact car, a blue Dacia

Sandero. Benjamin opened the passenger-side door and helped Gideon into the car. Mr. Mendelson's daughter opened the driver's-side door and sat down. Benjamin looked at the woman and said, "I failed to introduce myself. My name is Benjamin Sharon." The woman nodded without looking up at Benjamin.

"Shalom, my friend," Benjamin said to Gideon.

"Thank you for praying for me," Mr. Mendelson said, reaching and grasping Benjamin's hand. "Shalom, shalom."

Just as Benjamin began to close the car door, he suddenly stopped, looked intently back and forth between Mr. Mendelson and his daughter, and said, "On Monday, at one in the afternoon, I will be speaking to a group of Messianic Jewish believers at a small venue called Él Está Vivo. Here is the address."

Benjamin handed Gideon a business card. "Two cards were sent to me. Now I know why." Benjamin smiled warmly at the two. "I would be so honored if you would be my guests."

Mr. Mendelson's daughter looked frightened, but Gideon replied, "Thank you, thank you . . . I don't know . . . but thank you."

Benjamin closed the car door and prayed silently as they drove away. *Please, Lord, bring them to the reading of Your Word.*

That Monday afternoon after reading Isaiah 53 and singing from Numbers chapter 6, Benjamin looked at the assembled congregation, mostly elderly Messianic Jewish believers, but an audience that today included Sarai Levy, Gideon Mendelson, and Rivka Mendelson.

"You are Jews by birth, but each of you had to respond at one time or another to Yeshua's calling. Please bow your heads and pray with me. If you are here today and need Yeshua, and will make Him Lord of your life, please come to this altar and let me pray for you."

Benjamin finished his prayer with the words, "Yeshua, You alone are King!" and then looked up to see Gideon and Rivka Mendelson standing at the front of the small gathering hall. Sarai stood behind them resting her hands on their shoulders.

"Papa, Yeshua has been calling me for the longest time now. I've been hearing so many testimonies, but I didn't know what you would say. I was afraid."

"It's okay, my child." Gideon Mendelson clutched Benjamin's hand. "Here is my full-grown daughter, standing at the altar of Yeshua, alongside an old man with few years left in this life.

"We both believe. He's been speaking to both of us longer than I care to admit. We will need support," Gideon said.

"Friends, gather around this new brother and his daughter. Lay your hands on them and pray with me," Benjamin said.

Members of the small church congregation gathered around Gideon and Rivka Mendelson, praying aloud, thanking Yeshua for the salvation that He alone offers. There were many tears and much crying before the assembly of men and women slowly separated and the service ended.

Chapter Fourteen

The wind and rain had Jack Broholm tossing and turning through much of the night. The weather alerts had accurately forecast the 60 mph wind gusts and flash flooding he had read about before bed. He arose at 5:30, descended the steps from the upstairs master bedroom, walked past an oak dining room table, its lustrous shine dancing in the predawn light, grabbed a cold coffee bottle from the refrigerator, and headed back upstairs to his prayer corner. The discord he felt the week before had persisted in the days that followed and was still present on this dark, rainy morning. Jack prayed through a list of concerns, spent time as he always did reading the Word, and then leafed through a devotional book he had just received in the mail the day before. The book was a compilation of testimonies published by Firelight Media Group, an organization devoted to stories about the persecuted church. Jack opened the book to the first testimony:

"Benji fell between two bodies and lay motionless, his mind swirling in fear. An hour before, a man had entered the village just after dawn, claiming to be a pastor, saying he had a message to share with the Christians, and requesting a prayer meeting with the believers. Many of the village inhabitants arrived at the small building serving as a church. As the people waited, the man suddenly left the church, and then, moments later a group of masked attackers converged on the group of fifty men, women, and children. Benji listened in horror as screams of 'Kill the infidels' blared through the one-room hut, and for an instant he looked in shock as raised machetes swung through the room and piercing cries from anguished faces broke out among the people. Within minutes the wailing was over and dead bodies lay strewn across the dirt floor. Benji felt wetness across his left arm as if he had walked into a light rain, and he knew it was blood from his mother who lay motionless at his side. To his right, his brother was silent. Where was his father? One of the marauders yelled, in Arabic, not Somali, Benji's native tongue, 'They're all dead. Run, let's go.' Benji, twelve years old, and one other man who also was left for dead, survived the brutal attack by lying motionless in the mass of dead bodies."

The man ended his testimony with the words, "Pray for the Christians in Somalia. They know the danger of serving God. All the villagers who died had chosen to follow Jesus. Their love for God was great."

Jack read the testimony and cried out to the Lord in his spirit. How can man be so evil? How can this be happening in the twenty-first century? Where are the defenders of the weak and innocent?

Jack flipped the page and stopped at a headline:

Jen Wang

Under the caption was a picture of a middle-aged Chinese woman followed by her testimony.

"I came from mainland with promise of good job," she wrote in English. "My husband left me. I had nothing more in China. I come to Los Angeles. They told me in China I would see the ocean. I was put in large room with six or seven other women and given a sewing machine. I made textiles all day. We were awakened at 4:00 a.m. every morning. We worked until ten at night. I was allowed to shower three times a week, and I was let out into a yard for fifteen minutes at a time each day. There was a radio in the room. One day I listened to a man tell about Jesus. I said, 'Jesus if you exist, please save me from this terrible place.' I felt He told me, 'First I need to save your soul.' I yielded myself to

Him. I relinquished my life to Him. Not many days later inspectors came to visit the facility. One of the women screamed that she was being held prisoner against her will. The next thing I know, authorities had freed us and arrested the shop owner. I'm so grateful to God for saving me. Saving my soul and saving me from the cruel labor each day. I didn't know God when I was brought here, but now I know Him."

"Lord, please help Jen Wang," Jack prayed aloud. "How can this happen in the United States of America?"

The crown of thorns is a symbol of majesty and grandeur that no earthly king's crown of gold or other precious stones could ever rival. To the Christian, the crown of thorns displays the beauty, the wonder, the immense love, and the splendor of the One who sacrificially paid the ultimate price—Himself, to atone for sins no other sacrifice could satisfy. To the believer in Christ Jesus, the crown of thorns represents the exceeding humility of the Creator of the universe enduring shame and scorn and physical death from an unimaginable evil on behalf of His redeemed children, those redeemed by the blood of the Lamb, those trusting in Jesus, the Savior who paid the supreme price for their salvation.

Some believers display replicas of the crown on a living or dining room wall, beautifully intertwined with vines or roses or other colorful flowers. Other decorative pieces show an attractive earth tone wreath, a garland of sorts, pleasing to behold.

In its starkest array, the crown of thorns was a mangled arrangement of thorn vines, twisted and compressed to fit on the brow of Jesus, the Son of God who knew no sin. The gospel writers tell of the mockery He endured. The crown was placed on His head, and mocking soldiers derided Him and hit Him with their hands.

"And the soldiers twisted a crown of thorns and put it on His head, and they put on Him a purple robe. Then they said, 'Hail, King of the Jews!' And they struck Him with their hands."
(John 19:2–3 NKJV)

To the Christian, thorns are also associated with "thorny ground"—the unproductive life distracted by worldly pursuits that Jesus spoke of in His parable of the sower.

After a restless night of sleep, Jack arose early, well before the sun shone its first rays of the new day, and now, in the moments following his Bible reading, devotions, and morning prayer, he was overcome with a discomforting, unsettling sense that his life had been far too easy—for all practical purposes void of any sacrifice of note—and, in its richness of material gain, all about his own comfort.

Though the pathway from the crown of thorns leads to resurrection, joy, and eternal life for all who believe, the crown of thorns reminds the Christian of the immense suffering our Lord endured and the suffering also of those who will follow Him.

"Indeed, all who desire to live a godly life in Christ Jesus will be persecuted."
(2 Timothy 3:12 ESV)

Jack read the passage thoughtfully, pondering its meaning. Lord, how does this relate to my life? he prayed silently. I haven't suffered persecution. My life has been as comfortable as anyone could ever imagine.

The verse from 2 Timothy was included in a group of Scripture passages that he had placed prominently in a montage of sorts, the first passage on the list containing the words of Jesus:

"Remember the word that I said to you, 'A servant is not greater than his master.' If they persecuted Me, they will also persecute you. If they kept My word, they will keep yours also."
(John 15:20 NKJV)

In Philippians, Paul wrote to the congregation in Philippi:

"For you have been granted [the privilege] for Christ's sake, not only to believe *and* confidently trust in Him, but also to suffer for His sake."
(Philippians 1:29 AMP)

And to those in Rome, he wrote,

"And if [we are His] children, [then we are His] heirs also: heirs of God and fellow heirs with Christ [sharing His spiritual blessing and inheritance], if indeed we share in His suffering so that we may also share in His glory."
(Romans 8:17 AMP)

Jack had read these passages many times before, and today he read them once again. How could anyone not recognize the suffering that saints would endure in this life? he thought.

"Now Saul was consenting to his death.
"At that time a great persecution arose against the church which was at Jerusalem; and they were all scattered throughout the regions of Judea and Samaria, except the apostles. And devout men carried Stephen *to his burial,* and made great lamentation over him.
"As for Saul, he made havoc of the church, entering every house, and dragging off men and women, committing *them* to prison."
(Acts 8:1–3 NKJV)

"I've had no sacrifice, no hardship, no persecution, Lord," Jack spoke softly, though to an empty room.
It was a crown of twisted thorns but a crown of purity,

stature, magnitude, and supreme authority for the preeminent Lord and King!

A crown of thorns, a lineage to the royal diadem.

Chapter Fifteen

ood morning, everyone! What a blessing it is to
be here to celebrate the kingship and lordship
of Yeshua Hamashiach, Jesus the Messiah! Thank you,
Rabbi Abramson, for the esteemed privilege and honor
you have given me today, to come and share a message
with you that Yeshua has laid on my heart. I am overjoyed
beyond words to be here this morning, and I would like
to thank each of you for being here as well.

"The Scripture text for my message this morning is
chapter 90 from the Book of Psalms. As we begin, please
bow with me in prayer.

"Lord Jesus, Yeshua. We know that Your Word is
a sharp two-edged sword, piercing asunder to the very
innermost parts of our hearts and minds, our souls, our
very consciousness. Speak to us from Your Word, please.
Let each of us better understand the gravity of our lives,
the moment in time you've granted to each of us. In the
precious name of Jesus, we pray. Amen.

"The Book of Psalms, referred to as 'the Old

Testament Hymnal,' is comprised of 150 sacred writings, divinely inspired narratives, that include songs, prayers, poems, confessions of sin, cries for deliverance, pleas for God's mercy, petitions for justice, and certainly acknowledgment of His eternal power. Many of the psalms are attributed to David, some to Moses, some to Asaph, and others to writers unknown. A number of biblical scholars ascribe authorship of Psalm 90 to Moses. In years past, the King James Bible was published with titles listed at the beginning of some of the psalms. My King James Bible, which was published by the American Bible Society in 1972, has the title

'God's Eternity and Man's
Transitoriness
A Prayer of Moses the man of God'

written as a heading before Psalm 90. *The Reece Chronological Bible* places Psalm 90 at 1,461 BC, early into the exodus of the Israelites from Egypt. We read about this period of history in the Old Testament in Deuteronomy chapter 1 and in the book of Numbers in chapters 14 and 15.

"In Psalm chapter 90 we read the prayer of Moses, recorded in the Holy Scriptures as a testament of God's eternal nature, man's brief time—but a moment—on earth, and the proclamation of man's need for the blessings of God in this life.

"Under the anointing of the Holy Spirit, Moses prays:

" 'LORD, thou hast been our dwelling place in all generations. Before the mountains were brought forth, or ever thou hadst formed the earth and the world, even from everlasting to everlasting, thou art God.

" 'Thou turnest man to destruction; and sayest, Return, ye children of men. For a thousand years in thy sight are but as yesterday when it is past, and as a watch in the night.

" 'Thou carriest them away as with a flood; they are as a sleep: in the morning they are like grass which growth up. In the morning it flourisheth, and growth up; in the evening it is cut down, and withereth.

" 'For we are consumed by thine anger, and by thy wrath are we troubled. Thou hast set our iniquities before thee, our secret sins in the light of thy countenance.

" 'For all our days are passed away in thy wrath: we spend our years as a tale that is told. The days of our years are threescore years and ten; and if by reason of strength they be fourscore years, yet is their strength labor and sorrow; for it is soon cut off, and we fly away.

" 'Who knoweth the power of thine anger? Even according to thy fear, so is thy wrath. So teach us to number our days, that we may apply our hearts unto wisdom.

" 'Return, O LORD, how long? And let it repent

thee concerning thy servants. O satisfy us early with thy mercy; that we may rejoice and be glad all our days. Make us glad according to the days wherein thou hast afflicted us, and the years wherein we have seen evil. Let thy work appear unto thy servants, and thy glory unto their children. And let the beauty of the LORD our God be upon us: and establish thou the work of our hands upon us; yea, the work of our hands establish thou it' (KJV).

"The psalmist begins by saying, 'Lord, thou hast been our dwelling place in all generations.' Acts 17:28 says, 'For in Him we live, and move, and have our being.' Jesus said, 'Abide in me, and I in you.' Psalm 91 states, 'He is my refuge and my fortress,' and refers to the Most High as 'thy habitation.'

"When we come to know Jesus as our Lord and Savior, after recognizing our sinfulness, repenting of our sins, and asking Him to come into our hearts, we become born again of the Spirit of God. It's a miraculous transformation. Jesus lives in us, and we, in turn, become part of the body of Christ.

"And that's just the beginning of our walk with Him. We're to dwell in His presence, and sense His presence. We're to walk with Him and throughout our lives become more like Him.

"Verse 2 of Psalm 90 is the second Scripture passage listed in the *Reece Chronological Bible*, which is a wonderful volume of work laying out God's Word in chronological order—in the order in which the events occurred.

"The work, which is a complete edition of the King James Bible, starts with John 1 verses 1 and 2. 'In the beginning was the Word, and the Word was with God, and the Word was God. The same was in the beginning with God.'

"The next Scripture passage is Psalm 90 verse 2: 'Before the mountains were brought forth, or ever thou hadst formed the earth and the world, even from everlasting to everlasting, thou art God.'

"The third passage is from Genesis 1:1: 'In the beginning God created the heaven and the earth.'

"But before God created the universe, He existed throughout all of eternity. There's a theological word that describes God's existence: The word is *aseity*. It means that God's existence is in and of Himself. It's an incomprehensible truth, a God without beginning or end, yet a truth that we accept by faith in Jesus.

"In verse 4 the psalmist tells us that 'a thousand years in thy sight are but as yesterday when it is past, and as a watch in the night.'

"In the backdrop of God's eternal nature in which a thousand years to the Lord are but as yesterday, or in one translation, but an hour, the Bible contrasts our brief time in this life. 'Thou carriest them away as with a flood; they are as a sleep.'

"The Living Bible so eloquently expresses this passage by saying, 'We glide along the tides of time as swiftly as a racing river and vanish as quickly as a dream.'

"The psalmist goes on and compares us to grass which is green in the morning but is cut down and withers in the evening.

"In James we read that life is like a vapor, a mist. Here today and then gone.

"Yet even as we live out this brief moment of time that we call life, we're reminded that we serve a holy God who cannot look upon sin. Our awareness of God's anger and wrath against sin and evil, and the sensitivity that we feel about our own sins and impurities, is expressed in verses 7 and 8 where the psalmist laments, 'For we are consumed by thine anger, and by thy wrath are we troubled. Thou hast set our iniquities before thee, our secret sins in the light of thy countenance.'

"Verse 9 begins, 'For all our days are passed away in thy wrath,' and verse 11 says, 'Who knoweth the power of thine anger? Even according to thy fear, so is thy wrath.'

"At times, our shortfalls, our failures, our iniquities, our sins trouble us.

"But God has shown us a different way! The Bible says that 'if we confess our sins, he is faithful and just to forgive us our sins, and to cleanse us from all unrighteous-ness' (1 John 1:9). Even as we're occasionally reminded of our sins, we cling to the promises of God. We know that we're redeemed by the blood of the Lamb, we're washed clean by the precious blood of Jesus, Yeshua, we know that His mercies are 'new every morning . . . great is His faithfulness.' We cling to the biblical promise that our sins have been thrown out as far as the east is from the west, we know that 'by grace are ye saved through faith; and that not of yourselves: it is the gift of God: Not of works, lest any man should boast' (Ephesians 2:8–9).

"The Bible says,

> 'For if you confess with your mouth
>   that *Yeshua* is Lord,
> and believe in your heart
>   that God raised Him from the dead,
>   you will be saved.'
> (Romans 10:9 TLV)

"The Word tells us, 'For God so loved the world . . .' Think about these words, 'For God so loved . . .' It's an incomprehensible love. The Scripture passage goes on to say, 'For God sent not his Son into the world to condemn the world; but that the world through him might be saved' (John 3:17).

"The Bible tells us, 'For the wages of sin is death; but the gift of God is eternal life through Jesus Christ our Lord' (Romans 6:23).

"What a glorious plan of salvation, and we rest in that peace, we rest in that comfort, knowing that we believe on the Lord Jesus unto eternal life.

"In verse 10 the psalmist says, 'The days of our years are threescore years and ten; and if by reason of strength they be fourscore years, yet is their strength labor and sorrow; for it is soon cut off, and we fly away.'

"The Word of God tells us that we're given seventy years in this world and if we're a hardy soul, we may even live to be eighty.

"Before the flood, men lived to be hundreds of years old. The Bible tells us that Noah lived to be nine hundred and fifty years old. His father, Lamech, died at the age of seven hundred and seventy-seven. What a blessed number that is! His father, Methuselah, lived to be nine hundred and sixty-nine.

"After the flood, as the generations passed, man's years in this world became less and less. King David lived to be about seventy; Solomon, I've seen a range of fifty-three to fifty-eight years old. The life expectancy rate for men in the United States in 1919, the first year after World War I, was fifty-three and a half, fifty-six years for women. That rose to sixty years old for men in 1921 but dropped into the upper 50s for men during much of the 1920s. When Social Security was enacted in 1935, the life expectancy for men was fifty-nine point nine; for women sixty-three point nine.

"Today we live in a society that puts a great deal of emphasis on good health, exercise, vitamins, nutritious meals, and, aside from the Lord's divine healing touch that we as believers sometimes experience in this life by God's grace, we're blessed to have the best medical care in the history of the world. Many men and women live to be eighty or ninety years old, and there are a number of centenarians today—people who live to be one hundred years old.

"But even though medical and technological break-throughs and healthy lifestyle choices have contributed to our increased longevity, we understand as we look back on the generations since the flood that man is given seventy years in this world, and maybe, if they are a strong soul, they live to be eighty.

"Under the anointing of the Holy Spirit, Moses reminds us, 'So teach us to number our days, that we may apply our hearts unto wisdom.'

"How much more then should we redeem the time, number our days, and occupy until the Lord returns?

"We're to 'redeem the time,' buy back the wasted years, take hold of the lost opportunities, recognize how short our lives are, and be diligent, faithful followers of Jesus, occupying . . . what does it mean to occupy? It means to influence our surroundings. Living faithful lives until the Lord returns.

"And what is our life? *What is our life?* But to know Him, and the power of His resurrection, and the fellowship of His sufferings, and to learn to love Him more, and to learn to trust Him more, as we look to Him, Jesus, Yeshua, the Author and Finisher of our faith. The One who leads us through this life along that spiritual highway as it were, taking us from grace to grace, faith to faith, glory to glory, strength to strength, victory to victory, leading us, indwelling us, anointing us by the power of the Holy Spirit, helping us to stay the course, and press toward the mark, and to grow in the grace and knowledge of Jesus.

"In verses 13–15, Moses pleads for the Lord's mercy and petitions Him to turn away His anger from the people and to reveal His love and kindness and joy from their earliest youth to the end of their lives. Moses asks the Lord to give the people gladness in proportion to their former misery and to replace the evil years with good.

"It's not too late for the Lord to change the direction of our lives; to lift our sight from the trials and the valleys to the victories and the mountaintops; to replace the trying years and fill us with His love and His joy.

"The Scripture tells us in verse 16, 'Let thy work appear unto thy servants, and thy glory unto their children.'

"We desire that God blesses our lives. That He gives us His favor and grants us success. In our families, in our jobs, in our ministries.

"In Matthew chapter 25, Jesus tells us the story about the three men who received talents, and we know that God expects us to use our talents, our skills, our abilities, and the knowledge that He's given us to further His kingdom and advance the work of the gospel of Jesus Christ.

"The church is the body of Christ, comprised of people from many walks of life. People with diverse talents. Talents that are to be used to advance His kingdom.

"In Ephesians we read, 'And whatsoever ye do in word or deed, do all in the name of the Lord Jesus, giving thanks to God and the Father by Him' (Colossians 3:17).

"We're to be thankful for our careers, our occupations, the income He's entrusted to us, our families, our success, our favor. And recognize that we're to be representatives of Him—in whatever position in life we may serve.

" 'Let thy work appear unto thy servants, and thy glory unto their children.' And we desire God's divine glory in the lives of our children as well. It's not enough that our kids say a sinner's prayer when they're five years old. We desire that our children grow up and become devout Christians, as hopefully each of us would say that we are. And I don't mean devout in a self-righteous or pious or holier-than-thou way, but I mean we're serious believers. We study to show ourselves approved; our faith goes to work with us; it's with us when we're in the world; it's with us when no one is watching. And we desire that our children, too, have a deep, personal relationship with Jesus; that they're committed, sold-out believers for Him.

"The beginning of verse 17, the last passage in this wonderful psalm, says, 'And let the beauty of the LORD our God be upon us.'

"In Revelation chapter 1, we read of the power, the majesty, the splendor, and the *beauty* of our Lord in the Revelation of Jesus Christ which the apostle John, under the anointing of the Holy Spirit, penned on the isle of Patmos. John wrote, 'His head and his hairs were white like wool, as white as snow; and his eyes were as a flame of fire; and his feet like unto fine brass, as if they burned in a furnace; and his voice as the sound of many waters. And he had in his right hand seven stars: and out of his mouth went a sharp two-edged sword: and his countenance was as the sun shineth in his strength.'

"In the last chapter of the Bible, Revelation chapter 22, we read, 'And there shall be no night there; and they need no candle, neither light of the sun; for the Lord God giveth them light.'

"Truly, what a beautiful name, what a beautiful Savior we serve. Amen?

"The Scripture passage ends by saying, 'And establish thou the work of our hands upon us; yea, the work of our hands establish thou it.'

"In closing this message on Psalm 90, and as we come near to the end of the service, I'd like to share a few thoughts with you on Psalm 91 and God's deliverance in my life.

"The book *Hand on the Helm*, written by Katherine Pollard Carter, is a wonderful compilation of stories of God's divine intervention in the affairs of men. In this book, the story is told of a British regiment in World War I that each day, every enlisted soldier and officer would either recite or read Psalm 91. Over a span of four years, there was not a single casualty in the brigade, although casualties did occur in the regiments on either side of this group of soldiers. The author notes that after the war was over, religious publications on both sides of the Atlantic wrote about this miraculous testimony.

"At some point, after reading that story many years ago, perhaps when I was in my early thirties . . . I'm sixty-two now, so thirty years ago, give or take, I memorized Psalm 91. Many, if not most, days over the past thirty years I've recited this psalm by memory.

"God has blessed me with a wonderful church family, friends in the local body of Christ, and the privilege of serving Him in many interesting and captivating places. Throughout the years, my life has seen trials, ups and downs, successes, failures, times of difficulty, and times of great blessing—just like all of you. But during the difficult periods, God's hand of deliverance has always been at work in my life.

"I remember asking a good friend, a brother in Christ who was experiencing sickness and health problems, a dear saint who has since gone on to be with the Lord, I asked him, in regard to both of our lives really, 'How many times has God delivered us?' Even in the midst of his trials, the very real pain he was suffering, he replied, 'Every time.'

"Yeshua is a kind and loving and merciful Savior who loves each of us so much more than we can ever imagine and so much more than we could ever deserve. And in that vast arena of His steadfast love, He uses people to help us during some of the most difficult times in life.

"In Psalm chapter 91 the psalmist writes,

" 'He that dwelleth in the secret place of the Most High shall abide under the shadow of the Almighty.

I will say of the LORD, He is my refuge and my fortress: my God; in him will I trust. Surely he shall deliver thee from the snare of the fowler, and from the noisome pestilence. He shall cover thee with his feathers, and under his wings shalt thou trust: his truth shall be thy shield and buckler. Thou shalt not be afraid for the terror by night; nor for the arrow that flieth by day; nor for the pestilence that walketh in darkness; nor for the destruction that wasteth at noonday.

" 'A thousand shall fall at thy side, and ten thousand at thy right hand; but it shall not come nigh thee. Only with thine eyes shalt thou behold and see the reward of the wicked.

" 'Because thou hast made the LORD, which is my refuge, even the Most High, thy habitation; there shall no evil befall thee, neither shall any plague come nigh thy dwelling.

" 'For he shall give his angels charge over thee, to keep thee in all thy ways. They shall bear thee up in their hands, lest thou dash thy foot against a stone. Thou shalt tread upon the lion and adder: the young lion and the dragon shalt thou trample under feet.

" 'Because he hath set his love upon me, therefore will I deliver him: I will set him on high, because he hath known my name. He shall call upon me, and I will answer him: I will be with him in trouble; I will deliver him, and honor him. With long life will I satisfy him, and show him my salvation' (KJV).

"As this part of our service comes to a close, 'May the grace of our Lord Jesus Christ be with you all. May God's love and the Holy Spirit's friendship be yours' (2 Corinthians 13:14 TLB).

" 'Now unto the King eternal, immortal, invisible, the only wise God, be honor and glory for ever and ever. Amen' (1 Timothy 1:17)."

Benjamin looked at the assembly, a congregation of young and old, affluent and well-dressed in appearance and those with plain attire, Orthodox men with kippahs on their heads and modestly dressed women with long-sleeved blouses and below-the-knee dresses or skirts.

"I am so honored to be here this morning. Luxembourg City should be proud to have so many wonderful believers in Yeshua."

Benjamin left the bimah as Rabbi Mordecai Abramson made his way to the front of the Messianic Jewish synagogue. "You have blessed me immensely," Rabbi Abramson said.

"I am honored Yeshua has used me. I so hope I can visit your congregation again someday."

After the service ended, Benjamin, Sarai, and Rabbi Abramson visited for several minutes, interrupted frequently by members of the synagogue who stopped briefly to shake hands, ask about Benjamin's pastoral work in the States, and, in some instances, reference Rabbi Sharon, Benjamin's late father. The introductions were warm and cordial with respectful deference to Sarai, who many supposed to be Mrs. Sharon. As the socializing began to wind down, Rabbi Abramson announced that lunch was ready, and abruptly the congregants began making their way to the social hall.

That evening at a small café near their hotel, Benjamin and Sarai reflected on the prior twenty-four hours.

"I cannot fathom . . . I cannot even begin to imagine how much I've missed out on all these years," Sarai said, expressing both sadness and bewilderment as she shook her head. "I am so happy I found Yeshua . . . no, Yeshua found me!" She looked intently at Benjamin and spoke eagerly. "When I said yes to Yeshua, just a few weeks ago, but it seems much longer now that I'm with you, my mind has been racing with what seems like countless questions. I have so many things to ask you. You don't know how grateful I am to have you in my life again. I know that you will help me through . . ." Sarai stopped suddenly. "I'm sorry, Benjamin. I didn't mean . . . I assumed something . . ." Sarai looked down and began to cry.

Benjamin reached for her hands and held them together before gently lifting her chin. "Sarai, look at me. You did not assume wrong. Yeshua has brought us together. We were always meant to be together. I never stopped thinking about you. I never stopped loving you. I never stopped praying for you. Deep in my spirit I thought this day would come. I have learned to be patient and wait on Yeshua.

"I should add, by the way—unlike me, you don't appear to have aged at all in the last twenty years." Benjamin smiled warmly.

Sarai Levy was an attractive woman with a bright, youthful-looking demeanor, svelte figure, and deep brown eyes.

"Sarai, I want you to be my wife. I want you to join me in my work in New Mexico." Benjamin placed his hands gently on the sides of her face. "You said yes years ago. Will you say yes today? Will you be my wife?"

Sarai's eyes glistened with excitement, and her face looked as though it would burst in joy.

"Yes, yes, yes, yes, Benjamin! Yes, of course I will! I accept, I accept!"

"I would like you to join me for the rest of my sabbatical."

"Benjamin, I already booked the flights," she said sheepishly. "I called Annie and got your itinerary. She booked rooms for me at the hotels you're staying at."

"Annie booked your rooms?"

"Yes, I told you about our earlier call. I've spoken to her twice now. She was so helpful when I first called the church. On our last call Annie referred to me as 'young lady.' "

"Thank you for reminding me that I just proposed to a younger woman."

"Two and a half years hardly makes me a younger woman!"

Chapter Sixteen

Average build, slightly overweight—noticeable primarily in the midsection—Robert Thompson's white hair was combed back but not parted. He had a full head of hair, though it had thinned with age and otherwise served to amplify his indubitable grandfatherly appearance. This morning he sat in the dining room, holding a cup of coffee, staring at the champagne-colored carpet now forming symmetrical lines and patterns in his mind.

"Please get some help, Robert," Miriam said softly.

"Talk to someone at the church. One of your pastor friends. Talk to Benjamin. He's always been supportive."

Robert looked up at his wife. His blue eyes, in happier times sparkling with enthusiasm for the day's work, held a sadness not displayed in years past. "I'll be all right. I'm just trying to figure some things out."

"We've always been so happy." Miriam shook her head. "What happened, Robert? In South America, we never had much. Even when the kids were little and things were always tight, God provided. You felt it was your life's calling to mentor the men at the mission. You were enthralled, that was the word you used, remember? Enthralled to be able to teach and preach God's Word to the families that came each Sunday. I couldn't have been happier teaching English to the children. For ten years we never had any money. But they were wonderful years. And then God led us to Mountain Fire. You had a wonderful congregation that loved and respected you. Our time here has been fruitful and productive with wonderful ministry opportunities in the church and community. The Lord has given you a legacy you can feel good about and be thankful for. It's all because of Him. He's provided for us in so many ways. We went from no savings to a pension and a nice place to live in retirement. I don't understand what you're going through." Tears welled up in Miriam's eyes. "I pray for you each day."

"Don't worry, we'll get through this," Robert said, trying to sound reassuring, but the sadness in his voice was inescapable. "I'll be all right," he repeated.

Robert had a mahogany woodgrain plaque that hung on his office wall that had gone from house to house, state to state, country to country, ministry calling to ministry calling. The plaque read:

NEVER GIVE UP
ALWAYS ENDURE TO THE END
ALWAYS WALK TO THE EDGE OF THE RED SEA

And yet he had given up. His to-do list, once appreciated and enjoyed for the satisfaction that came with achievement—the realization, attainment, and fulfillment of goals and assignments—was not met with mere procrastination but rather with a lack of desire. The types of projects he had begun and completed just three years before, work requiring energy and focus, worthy endeavors, were now met with delay. He found one reason after the other to postpone or even abandon the work completely. Robert felt listless, drained. It wasn't that long ago when he never seemed to reach the end of a project. There was always more he could have done. Imagine the work in South America and the benefits that would have been realized if the funds had been available. He never felt that he had "arrived," and today he was as close to despair as he had ever felt. "Please help me through this, Lord," Robert prayed quietly.

Clifton Rockwell was ecstatic when he arrived home that evening. "I got a raise!" he announced as he walked into the living room. "Mack Reynolds told me there's a regional manager position waiting for me in Dallas."

Nicole Rockwell pursed her lips and looked at Clifton. "What if I don't want to move to Dallas? What if I don't want to be in a marriage where my husband is gone even more than he is now? Then what?"

"Seriously? This is your response to a nice jump in salary and a huge promotion?"

"Clifton, sit down. Please."

Rockwell slumped into the recliner and swiveled it to face his wife, but then straightened up, clearly agitated. "I truly thought you would be happy," he said in an exasperated tone. "We've talked about Dallas in the past. Sam graduates in less than a year. The move won't happen tomorrow. Maybe by the end of the year. This is a great opportunity for us."

"For you, not for *us*," Nicole said sarcastically, looking intently at her husband. "Clifton, listen to me. I've been doing a lot of thinking lately. I'm very unhappy. We have a beautiful home, you have a good salary, we drive nice cars, all of that. But there's more to life than this."

"What haven't I given you?" he said impatiently. "What's wrong with our lives the way they are?"

"Other than being nominal Christians, you mean?"

"Nominal Christians, that's what we are?" he said with an irritable tone in his voice.

"We go to church most Sundays and we pray over our meals, but yes, we are nominal Christians. Hear me out, Clifton. God has been dealing with me. I started going to a weekly women's fellowship and prayer meeting. I yearn to have a closer walk with Him. Let me remind you of something. You remember the Sunday school class years ago when we read *In His Steps*? What was the question posed in the book? 'What would Jesus do?' How do we spend our evenings? Watching political talk shows. But even worse than that is when you turn on a movie. When do we watch anything that's not filled with awful violence and terrible language? Would Jesus watch those movies? Of course not!

"Clifton, you think you're a strong Christian. You're what the Bible would call lukewarm. I've been lukewarm, too, but I don't want to stay there!"

"I don't think we're lukewarm," Clifton answered curtly.

Rockwell wanted that promotion so badly he couldn't imagine what he would do if he didn't get the offer. Why couldn't she understand? Did she take for granted their home, their cars, their vacations, everything his salary allowed? And now there was the opportunity for even more. Rockwell was beside himself thinking about losing a promotion he'd envisioned for longer than he cared to remember.

"Do I need to remind you where we were in September? The October before that? Where we went three years ago?" he said in an exasperated tone.

"Of course not," Nicole replied. "That's not the point of this conversation."

Undeterred, Rockwell continued. "Grand Cayman last September. The Virgin Islands the year before, a Mediterranean cruise the year before that. Don't those things mean anything to you? How do you think we were able to afford those trips?"

"Clifton, I appreciate your hard work. I always have. I always will. I'm grateful for a husband who works hard and earns a good salary. Sam will go off to college soon. It will be just us. There's more to life than you climbing another rung on the corporate ladder. If you take that position in Dallas . . ." Her voice tailed off. "We'll never see each other."

"Think about the salary and the bonus I just told you about," he said impatiently. "How can we pass up this opportunity?" Clifton sprang from the recliner and began pacing through the room.

"Look at you," she said softly. "You're a nervous wreck. Clifton, here's the bottom line—to use a term you can relate to—I'm unhappy. There's more to life than what your next job promotion has to offer. I know God has more for us. We need to find out what He wants us to do. When is the last time we prayed together, other than a quick prayer at dinner? It's been so long I can't remember.

"I have a favor I want to ask you," she continued. "I'd like you to take me to the revival service at Faith Gospel Tabernacle in Mountain Fire. I read about it in the *Albuquerque Journal*. The service is a week from Friday night. It'll be good for us."

"I know about it. It's not a revival service, per se. Jack Broholm, an associate of the company, invited me. He also invited Andréa Mattheson, the congressional candidate I sat next to on the plane."

"Broholm, the Christian businessman in Mountain Fire? What does he do again?"

"He's a consultant, a business analyst. We've used him a couple of times. The last time was when we expand-ed the Farmington store. He did the projections."

"When did you see him?"

"He was picking up something at the Mountain Fire store when I was in town last week. We run into each other from time to time."

"I remember him." She nodded. "He invited you to one of the prayer meetings at Faith Gospel Tabernacle some years back. That seems like a lifetime ago. We met with him that night. Clifton, why don't you spend more time with Jack? You need a strong Christian friend in your life. Invite him and his wife to dinner. We can take them to El Pinto or Sadie's, maybe Los Cuates . . . or downtown for prime rib . . . someplace nice the next time they're in town. I'd love to get to know Mrs. Broholm."

Nicole looked inquisitively at Clifton. "The newspaper said it was a special service. If it's not a revival service, what is it?"

"Broholm said there was a guest speaker. He didn't know much about him, but he said the pastor of Faith Gospel Tabernacle, who's out of town, encouraged the church to promote the service."

"Will you take me? Please?"

Jack Broholm was elated. He had made $500 trading on Monday, a $1,000 profit on Tuesday, another $500 on Wednesday. By market close on Thursday his demeanor had changed.

"How was your day?" Natalie asked

"I lost $2,500 today," he said sullenly.

"Why? What happened? Last night you said the week was starting out well."

"I gauged the direction of the market wrong. The trade went against me. Instead of quickly getting out, I stayed in, thinking it would reverse."

"How many times have I told you it was rigged?"

"It's not rigged," Jack said, followed by a sigh.

"What are you going to do? You've been saying you felt conflicted. We've both felt the Lord moving you in a different direction."

"I do feel pulled," he said quietly, but then, in somewhat of a defensive tone, he continued. "I'm trying to earn a living. This is what I've done since we were married. Usually, with some success."

"Jack, we don't need the money. Your consulting business is sufficient to meet our financial needs."

"I know . . . you're right. I have frequent misgivings about the market," Jack confessed.

"I'm meeting a young lady at the church in a little while. The young mother I told you about. I know God has put it on my heart to minister to her. Pray for me. I'll see you a little later."

Natalie gave him a hug and left the house. Just before closing the door, she said, "Don't worry. The Lord will work this out."

Jack sat at his desk pondering not simply the day's loss but the tug-of-war he felt in his spirit trying to balance work, ministry, and the pressing notion of his own prosperity while so many saints worldwide suffered.

His entire career had been centered around business. The Chicago Board of Trade, his consulting business, stock transactions, spreadsheets tracking a myriad of financial metrics. He wasn't opposed to commerce—buying and selling were part of the fabric of day-to-day life. There were merchants and traders in biblical times.

But the market had changed. He didn't believe it was rigged in the conventional sense of the word, but it was certainly stacked against the average retail investor. By the time news had reached the average retail trader, it had already circulated through Wall Street. And if that disadvantage wasn't enough, today's average investor wasn't competing merely against institutional banks and hedge-fund managers but was now facing off against computers with complex algorithms generating high-frequency trades—programs built on artificial intelligence.

When Jack started his career, investors would buy blue-chip stocks with the thought of holding the shares for five, ten, even fifteen years with the expectation of a higher return than a standard money market fund. Those days are over, Jack thought.

"If you're in for the long term, no problem. Don't worry about the market swings. Buy it and hold it forever," an analyst would say. Right. Buy, hold, and forget about it. Until it falls out of favor with Wall Street, that is. Wake up and find out that's it's lost 25 percent of its value, Jack thought. Too often a company's technology became outdated and replaced by a newer technology, plummeting the stock's price from its once lofty status to a share value that would never again reach its glory days. Now the market was filled with retail traders and hedge funds alike that were constantly looking for the next disruptive technology company—start-ups or early-stage companies promising new, innovative technologies that would change society. Companies that speculators hoped would explode in value. It was no longer investing but rather trading—for both institutional and retail traders. Buying and selling short-term financial instruments instead of buying and holding equities and other securities long-term was now the norm for many young investors. The number of retail traders, in many cases day traders trying to profit on short-term market fluctuations or volatile price swings based on Fed comments or other market news, had skyrocketed in recent years.

He had grown up with the adage "buy low, sell high," easier said than done in periods when securities pricing was dominated by short-term trend investing as markets tried to determine direction. His email inbox was filled with investment research firm recommendations promoting gains of up to one thousand percent for cutting-edge high-tech growth stocks. Yes, Jack thought, those stories exist, but what a facade—most retail traders lose money.

Jack sighed. It's so hard to know how to plan, he thought. Analyst ratings change on a dime. Wall Street analysts, many still in their twenties, who had known only the recent bull market seemed to think prices would always rise. The Fed's quantitative easing and low interest rates were once again providing easy money for companies that could incur debt, grow sales, and continue to sustain losses—as long as they could service debt with nominal interest payments and the companies' market cap continued to climb. At some point the bubble had to burst, Jack thought.

The market had changed and so had Jack. There is an old adage in commerce, "Let the buyer beware," but increasingly, even on profitable trades, Jack was burdened with guilt and a sense of personal obligation: What responsibility do I have for the person on the other end of the trade? he questioned himself.

Trading didn't take up his entire day. There were a number of noteworthy activities he attended to, but there were also bad days of trading—days in which four or five hours of his time were given and for what, $100?

What a waste of time, he thought. Jack did not need to trade options. His consulting business was good. But his preoccupation with trading had become an obsession, his mind absorbed in a sea of candlestick charts, his thoughts consumed with minute-to-minute price swings and market fluctuations.

In a society with an infrastructure of long work weeks, managers and employees who get Saturday and Sunday off anxiously look forward to weekends. Not so with many traders who look forward to Monday morning and the opening bell on Wall Street. Forex traders bring trading to a new level with Forex markets operating twenty-four hours a day from 5:00 p.m. eastern time on Sunday to 4:00 p.m. eastern time on Friday. All the trader needs is a brokerage account and a device to access the platform to buy, sell, take profits, or endure losses—all the while engaging in transactions every bit as addictive as substance abuse, but rather than a drug-induced high, the thrill of a winning trade.

Jack was losing his desire for the markets and recognized that God was taking him to a different place.

Chapter Seventeen

Andréa Veronique handed the microphone to the event organizer and walked toward the crowd, shaking hands and giving high fives to supporters, signing a program bulletin for one of the stage men, stopping several times for selfies, putting her arm around the shoulder of one woman holding an "Andréa Veronique for Congress" placard, smiling cheerfully for the picture—the woman with the placard delighted by the attention—and mingling with an appreciative crowd fully behind their candidate.

Between the makeshift podium and the parking lot about fifty yards from the company of folks still congregating by the stage, raised voices, some shouting, could be heard from a group of men and women lined up on two sides of the walkway leading to the parking area. Most of the group held signs. Andréa Veronique picked up her pace, hoping to avoid the controversy unfolding, but it was too late.

"Where do you stand on abortion rights, Mrs.

Mattheson?" a man with a local television crew said as she approached the central part of the gathering.

"Why haven't you publicly stated your position?" a woman about six feet away shouted angrily.

Another woman holding a sign that said "My Body My Choice" yelled, "Are you with us or against us?"

Andréa Veronique glanced to her right. On the opposite side of the sidewalk, a young Hispanic woman held a sign showing a picture of a fetus with the words "Babies Have Rights." Another woman displayed a sign saying "All Life Has Value."

Andréa Veronique stopped and looked at the cameraman. Just as she started to speak, a college-aged woman screamed, "What about my rights, you fascist!" She moved toward the Hispanic woman but then stopped at the sidewalk separating the two groups. A police officer stepped toward the women. "Back, ladies," he said to the crowd. "This a peaceful protest."

The college-aged woman seemed to back up, but as she did, she spit in the direction of a woman handing out pro-life pamphlets who was talking quietly with a noticeably pregnant teenage girl. One of the colleagues of the college-aged woman quickly pulled her back from the sidewalk and pushed her between a man and woman who shot their signs up, concealing her presence from the officer.

Andréa Veronique turned from the television crew and moved quickly toward the parking lot. A supporter held her arm, shielding her from a woman who shouted, "State your position, Mattheson!"

As Andréa Veronique walked briskly toward the awaiting car, a young woman who looked to be about eighteen hurled a barrage of expletives at the men and women on the pro-life side of the sidewalk. "Get your hands off my body!" she screamed.

Within a minute's time the event had gone from what Andréa Veronique thought was a very encouraging rally to a scene that felt like a bomb had gone off. As she reached the end of the lane, she heard prayers coming from a small group on the edge of the grass. "Dear God," one of the voices said. "Help this country to stand for life."

Whatever composure Andréa Veronique had at the beginning of the event was gone. "What just happened?" she said to the supporters who had accompanied her to the rally. "Get me out of here," she said to the man and woman, her face distraught. "Don't worry, I'll be okay," she added.

Nothing more was said as they rode to the motel where she had left her car. They pulled up near the lobby, and Andréa Veronique practically jumped from the vehicle but then held the door open and leaned in toward the driver. "Thank you so much for your support today. I really appreciate it. I wasn't expecting a storm following the rally. I'm sorry I wasn't better company on the drive back."

The man looked at her thoughtfully and nodded. "We're fine," he said and then added, "It's a hot topic. You're going to have to make your position known."

Andréa Veronique looked at the man, expressionless. "I have a long drive home. Thank you again," she said and then closed the car door.

It would be late when she got home. Her confidence was not entirely shattered, but a crack in the armor, a fragility, had been exposed, rendering emotions not felt since her freshman year in college. She had resolved to put those feelings behind her, to press on in spite of any obstacles. And now, married with two children approaching teenage years, she was ready to tackle the world. A congressional career with financial security, influence, and prestige awaited her. Influence not for the sake of power. Influence, rather, to perform needed services for people in her jurisdiction.

But now she was faced with a choice: support an agenda she did not believe in and see her dreams realized, or go with her convictions and watch large donors buy the election for her opponent.

In a surreal moment she found herself standing at the intersection of two open roads—separate, unconnected— each leading to different places; divergent paths, each with its own distinct scenery and contrasting colors, but incompatible destinations. Both beckoned with open arms.

Why had life become so arduous, so complex? she wondered. Why was she struggling with an issue that was readily accepted by millions of Americans? At least that's what the polls said. Why was she being torn about something that was legal and acceptable to many of her peers? With all of the suffering in the world, why would an individual or group put abortion at the forefront of their agenda? she thought. What was the motive? The movement claimed empathy for women . . .

It was late when she arrived home, still shaken by the threats and hostility she experienced at the rally.

That Sunday morning, Andréa Veronique looked up from her notes. "I'm sorry. I thought I mentioned it to you. I have a fundraising call at ten this morning. You attend, honey. Fill me in when you get home."

Stuart and the girls left for the service. After the call ended, she turned on a live stream of the morning sermon just in time to hear Reverend Parker say, "Giving now is like planting your seed. These are times of preparation that will come back in an abundant harvest."

The phone rang, and she turned off the stream. She could watch the full message later. Or Stuart would fill her in.

She was a moment too late. The call went to voice mail. "Good morning, Andréa Veronique. Arthur Cousins here. I hate to bother you on a Sunday morning, but I have people I need to answer to. It's clear that you're reluctant. I really want you to be our voice, but I need a decision as soon as possible. Mindful of that, I'm going to buy you a little more time. My plans have changed unexpectedly. I'll be out of pocket all week, so we won't be able to get together when I had hoped . . . but then we *have* to sit down and wrap things up. After that, I can't put this off any longer. I'll let you know when I have a firm date. We'll meet at Robyn's Grill. Lunch is on me."

The message stopped. Andréa Veronique reached across the counter to press the voicemail button on the telephone console when she heard Cousins' voice again. "I don't have to tell you this, but if you get to a place of closure, reach out and call me. You have my number."

Cousins ended the message by saying, "This is a great opportunity for you, Andréa Veronique. If I don't hear from you, I'll be in touch."

Be strong, she said to herself. You'll get through this. The last thought she had before Stuart and the girls pulled into the driveway was Verity's voice the night before at bedtime: "Mom, I'm glad you didn't have an abortion before I was born."

In the quiet of the early morning Robert Thompson sat on a dining room chair near a front window in the corner of the room and lifted his eyes toward the darkened street, seeing the only visible light on the block, which glowed dimly from an old-fashioned street lamp in the distance.

The night before, Robert had sat in his study reflecting on his years of ministry. He remembered a time in his life when things seemed especially unsettled. The kids were young, the family was always on the move. Church to church, place to place, new church boards with varying levels of oversight. In the early years of Robert's ministry, he pastored no less than six churches in five states over a span of eight years before finally settling into a long-ten-ured position in Florida. Most of the churches were small, offering salaries unable to support the family's needs, but Miriam worked as a substitute teacher at local schools, which provided a small check and helped supplement the modest ministerial pay. Robert never equated the work to monetary gain. He was grateful for each calling; nevertheless, he questioned the frequency of the moves. "Why is the Lord moving us again, so soon?" he would ask Miriam.

The two would pray about each upcoming move, oftentimes gathering the two boys and two girls into a circle and praying together. There was always a peace following these times of prayer.

Robert had a Leopold Company oak desk in his office that he purchased from an office supply store when he was in his twenties during his first pastoral assignment at a small country church in northeast Missouri. The desk went from Missouri to Kansas to Pennsylvania to South Carolina and then to Florida. It was kept at a relative's home during their years in South America. At one time the desk sat in a schoolteacher's classroom in a now abandoned elementary school in southeast Iowa. The desk was fifty years old when Robert bought it, and he had owned it for close to forty years. Robert cherished the old desk. It had a center drawer with a lock that secured the first two drawers on the right-hand side as well as the center drawer itself, which was used primarily for pens, rings, and small souvenirs gathered from place to place over the years. On each side of the desk, just below the surface of the desktop overhang, slatted openings held solid-oak, 18-inch-long writing boards that pulled out from the underside of the desk just above the top drawers and extended over a foot in length, providing shelving to organize papers and files or allow for additional writing space. The desk was solid and sturdy, the drawers constructed with dovetail joints, the desktop well over an inch thick, elegant and stately with streams of horizontal lines and wavy patches of blended oak colors—dancing patterns of golden-brown hues that were spread from top to bottom—a nostalgic mosaic of craftmanship. The drawers had the original brass handles, tarnished from age but displaying an antique-looking luster that Robert felt becoming of a ninety-year-old desk, so he never polished the brass. The side drawers, always heavy from the weight of the oak, were now weighed down with thick manila files accumulated during his years of ministry.

He opened a file with notes from sermons he had preached over the course of his ministry years in the small churches he pastored in the States, during his time in South America, and then at the Presbyterian church in Mountain Fire. For a moment he was struck by the theme that jumped out at him sermon outline after sermon outline. The teachings were largely about the grace of God; the lessons were about His mercy, His love, and His protection.

He remembered the time during an especially difficult season between pastoral assignments when he felt God saying, "I will put a covering over you." He had never let Robert down.

Robert bowed his head and began to pray softly, affirming the Lord's faithfulness. "Father in heaven, with the psalmist I proclaim that You are a gracious and merciful and righteous God. Thank You for Your loving kindness. Thank You for Your faithfulness." Robert spent the first part of his prayer time in worship, reflecting on the many times God had brought him through trials, and thanking the Lord for His ongoing blessings and mercy. And then in the quietness of the early morning Robert began petitioning God for wisdom and blessing for his family. In his prayer, Robert referenced his wife, his two sons and two daughters, their spouses, his grandchildren, extended family members, and finally, he prayed for himself. In the stillness of the darkened room, Robert silently prayed, Please Lord Jesus, pour out knowledge and understanding, wisdom and discernment, guidance and direction, and Your truth on each of us. Shelter us, protect us, keep us from the enemy's plans to harm us, please, dear God. I ask You to bless each of us with Your presence. Please, Lord. In Jesus' name, amen.

If Robert had been asked to explain what he was feeling at that moment, he would have been taken aback. It was as if a burden had been lifted. There were no sermons to deliver, though preparing and delivering messages from God's Word were among the joys of his life, but the pressure of preparation was gone. There was no travel schedule, no itineraries, no worrying about paying bills, no book-related deadlines, no concerns about being organized, about being productive. Someone, or plural, people, had been praying for him, he thought. Robert then remembered one of his favorite verses:

"Hence, also, He is able to save forever those who draw near to God through Him, since He always lives to make intercession for them. (Hebrews 7:25 NASB)

Lord Jesus, thank you for interceding for me, Robert prayed silently.

Robert began reading the Bible, and soon the morning sun shone brightly through the window, resting its glorious rays on the pages of Scripture held open in his lap. Robert had been reading from the Old Testament book of Malachi and his eyes settled on the passage from Malachi 4:2:

"But for you who fear My name the sun of righteousness will rise with healing in its wings; and you will go forth and skip about like calves from the stall."
(NASB)

"Dear God," Robert said aloud. "Thank You for the morning light. You are the Sun of Righteousness!"

Robert arose in the still early hours of the morning with a sense of peace he hadn't felt for a long time. Robert's trials were not yet over, but a breakthrough was coming, a breakthrough as bright as the morning light.

Chapter Eighteen

J ack Broholm was troubled. He found himself increasingly wrestling with direction, solemnly reflecting on the plight of so many Christians whose lives were filled with adversity, extreme hardship, and seemingly unbearable afflictions at every turn. I have been given so much, Jack thought.

He thought about the saints who were burned at the stake in 1500s England—1555 was a particularly notable year of suffering, persecution, and martyrdom—saints branded as heretics, tried, condemned, and then placed in barrels piled with forest wood for kindling and stubble and straw to fan the flames, fastened to a stake with chains, in some instances given a last chance to recant their teachings that only Jesus, not the Mass, could save a man's soul, and that the Word of God divinely inspired by the Holy Spirit, not the Pope, not the state, was the authority for the believer in Christ.

After failing to recant Protestant truths of the Reformation, the fire was lit, flames leaping through the wood and hay, consuming the dying saint as villagers looked on, some praying, some crying, some supporting the punishment with cheering. Sometimes due to a poorly lit fire, the suffering was prolonged, extending the agony of the dear saint.

England was the predominate power in Europe and, by extension, the entire world. A country at the vanguard of Western civilization with schools of higher learning, renowned universities, esteemed scholars of history and the Christian faith, yet a leading voice of oppression, cruelty, and immense barbarity under the Church of England and the Roman Catholic Church of its day.

How many times did Paul use the word *suffering* and *persecution* in letters to the New Testament church? Jack wondered. Two thousand years removed from the persecution of the early church, hundreds of years following reformers being burned at the stake, and now in the twenty-first century unthinkable atrocities were still being committed by governments throughout the world!

Jack's Christian walk had been steady, unwavering, but for the most part unchallenged. What if he were faced with a tortuous death, or even worse if his family were faced with death, and he was told, "Deny your faith or your wife and children will be put to death"? Jack knew from his studies that even today in Third World countries these ultimatums were being given.

But Jack's dilemma was much closer to home. Broholm was concerned about his own prosperity, his own ongoing questions about affluence, his own comfortable lifestyle, devoid, really, of any of the extreme difficulties and persecutions he read about in his daily devotions. Jesus said, "For everyone to whom much is given, from him much will be required" (Luke 12:48 NKJV). I have been given so much, Jack said to himself. He didn't feel self-righteous in respect to his own standing within the contemporary church, but he felt hypocritical. He was honest enough with himself to know that his own flesh recoiled at the thought of suffering. Jack was a sincere, studied, and serious-minded Christian, but so much of his life was centered around pleasing his own wants and desires.

Jack thought of the millions of displaced people throughout the world, families removed from villages, towns, cities, and countries, their homes taken from them and all of their possessions, whether small tracts of land, livestock, or modes of transportation, and now they were in refugee camps with a small knapsack of goods and the clothes they were wearing when they left home. The village was burned, the homes destroyed, the fields ravaged, and relatives killed. There was nothing to return to. In war-torn regions there was little hope of returning to their homes and the former livelihoods that gave day-to-day meaning to life, however seemingly stark in contrast to the Western mind.

"We interrupt our programming of *Saints Across the Globe* to bring you this special broadcast from the underground church . . ." Jack suddenly remembered the interview with the Nigerian man who had haltingly sought words to describe his image of America. The translator patiently and thoughtfully tried to express the young man's thoughts as he eagerly described a place he had read about in school. "A land of peace and prosperity," the man said, his eyes displaying the excitement he felt talking about "a place where dreams come true."

Jack reflected on the many sermons he had heard about eternal rewards for believers in Christ, sermons involving an expectation of heavenly rewards, about believers ruling over the nations. How could he be so presumptuous to think that he would be given a place of authority over the millions of suffering saints through the ages? I'll be lucky just to be a street cleaner, Jack thought.

But Jack, too, had a dream. It involved an endeavor that, if shared, no one would have doubted its worthiness. Indeed, Jack had shared the details with only Natalie and one other close friend. It involved an open door of ministry with no financial recompense but rather a selfless ministry of sacrifice and service. Walking through the door of this outreach ministry required complete obedience, and his career had gotten in the way. Jack had been blessed bountifully. Now he felt the Lord asking him, "What's more important, additional income or undivided service to Me?" He was cautious in saying, "God told me," always sensitive to "Jesus said" or "the Bible says," and he knew the Scripture passage, "For as many as are led by the Spirit of God, these are sons of God" (Romans 8:14 NKJV). Deep in his spirit he sensed the Holy Spirit telling him that he needed to be willing to give up everything if he were to walk through the open ministry door.

Jack was certain he would not lose everything today. But he knew that he needed *to be willing* to lose everything today. If he were taken away to prison for the sake of the gospel—leaving behind all the luxurious trappings of wealth, leaving behind his home and virtually all of his possessions, leaving behind even family and friends—would he still trust God?

James Montgomery, author of the classic Christmas hymn "Angels, From the Realms of Glory," was left with Moravian caretakers at the young age of six, his parents feeling led by God to go to Barbados as missionaries. They and their six-year-old child were never reunited; the missionaries perished ministering the gospel. In twenty-first-century America, even the best-intentioned missionaries would be repelled by the thought of leaving a small child at a boarding school to attend to missions work in a foreign land. They and many that supported them would deem it irresponsible to leave behind a child. The couple would be thought of as uncaring, to have misplaced any "normal," accepted compassion for the lost for the support of their own child. What type of parent would neglect the care, nurturing, and upbringing of his or her own child? Why would they do that? Jack thought. And then he remembered the verse he had read earlier in the week: Jesus told His disciples, "And everyone who has left houses or brothers or sisters or father or mother or children or farms for My name's sake will receive many times as much, and will inherit eternal life" (Matthew 19:29 AMP).

Jack realized that the concept of eternal life, of being joined together with believing family members for all of eternity, had been accepted beyond question by Montgomery's parents; whatever doubts they may have had were put aside with eternity in mind. They left America for the sake of the gospel, knowing they would see their son again.

Another story came to Jack's mind, a story he first heard when he was a teenager from a man who often shared the gospel in a part of town known for homelessness, addictions, and crime. It was a story involving evangelism that Jack had not thought of for many years but a story that came to his remembrance today. It was a story about eternity. In the story, an eagle flew across the ocean and picked up one grain of sand and then flew back across the ocean and set the granule down on the other side. The eagle then repeated the trek. Once again it flew across the ocean, picked up one grain of sand and then returned, again setting the grain of sand down on the other side. Jack remembered the end of the story: if the eagle's journey were repeated until every last grain of sand had been removed from the ocean shore, the time elapsed would be but one second of eternity. Jack understood; the lesson was crystal clear. He needed to be at the place in this life where there was nothing left to cling to. "This world is not my home," Jack said aloud.

Benjamin Sharon's itinerary included a stop in Wittenberg, Germany, to the church where Martin Luther nailed his ninety-five theses to the door of the Castle Church. The theses contained the five central tenets of the Protestant Reformation, which were listed prominently in the bulletins being handed out at the entrance when Benjamin and Sarai entered the building.

"Sola Gratia 'Grace Alone' "
"Sola Fide 'Faith Alone' "
"Solus Christus 'Christ Alone' "
"Sola Scriptura 'Scripture Alone' "
"Soli Deo Gloria 'To the Glory of God Alone' "

Benjamin and Sarai walked slowly down the checkered aisle of the recently renovated castle and sat down in a pew toward the front of the cathedral.

"We have a special treat, Sarai. I planned my trip, our trip at this point, I should say . . ." Benjamin smiled at his bride-to-be. "The trip to Castle Church was planned to correspond with a stop in Wittenberg by the Alpine Village Men's Glee Club, an ensemble from Zurich."

"How exciting," Sarai whispered. "How many choir members are in the group?"

"I read they would be taking sixty-five on the tour. I believe the membership approaches one hundred when they're performing in Switzerland."

Sarai glanced at the ensemble at the front of the cathedral, young men standing erect in unison with colored uniforms of earth tone browns and pastoral greens giving the appearance of students in a mountain village.

The service began with the doxology. A magnificent blend of alto, tenor, and bass voices resounded from the chancel, resonating to the heights of the vaulted cathedral ceiling.

"Praise God, from whom all blessings flow;
Praise Him, all creatures here below;
Praise Him above, ye heav'nly host;
Praise Father, Son, and Holy Ghost.
Amen."

The men's glee club conductor turned and motioned to the packed parishioners; the assembly rose to their feet as the lyrics to "A Mighty Fortress Is Our God" rang through the hall in German Deutsch and was followed by "Christ the Lord Is Risen Today" in English.

Sarai Levy sat mesmerized, listening to the enraptured praises reaching forth to her new King, Yeshua. The world's finest orchestras had gathered at Carnegie Hall and Radio City Music Hall, some performing secular concerts, some Jewish musical presentations, some joyous Christmas specials. She had attended many of these events within the fashionable and privileged circles she lived in for so many years, but nothing compared to the magnificent sounds emanating from the orchestra and visiting choir. She could not imagine a more grandiose, lofty, sublime, and heavenly sound than the voices and instruments seemingly captivating every part of her heart and soul.

> "All hail the power of Jesus' name!
> Let angels prostrate fall.
> Bring forth the royal diadem,
> and crown him Lord of all."

Benjamin reached for Sarai's hand and lifted it upward as the lyrics to the first stanza resounded through the cathedral.

> "Bring forth the royal diadem,
> and crown him Lord of all!"

The service closed with the hymn "Praise to the Lord, the Almighty."

> "Praise to the Lord, the Almighty, the King of creation!
> O my soul, praise him, for he is your health and salvation!"

As the assembly slowly ushered out of the church, Benjamin and Sarai sat quietly in their pew.

"Do we need to leave?" she whispered.

"We have lots of time. I am so happy you are here with me tonight. Yeshua deserves all of the glory!"

At the airport the next morning, Benjamin sent a text message to David Janssen.

"Shalom, my friend. Boarding a flight shortly. Leaving Leipzig for Tel Aviv. Visited Castle Church in Wittenberg last night. You would have loved the service. Give my best to Elisha, and greet the men for me at the next prayer meeting. I have a wonderful announcement to make when I return.
Benjamin"

"Have you thought about the adjustments you'll be making? Have you considered our living arrangements?" Benjamin asked.

Sarai raised her eyebrows and feigned a surprised look. "I don't need to think about that," she said matter-of-factly. "We've been to Madrid. If you tell me we're moving to Madrid, I'm fine with that. We've been to Luxembourg. Luxembourg is fine. We've now been to Wittenberg. If we can attend Castle Church every day, Wittenberg is fine. We'll be in Jerusalem and Tiberias. Even better."

"Are you forgetting that I pastor a church in New Mexico?"

"New Mexico . . . hmm . . . is that part of the continental United States?" she asked playfully.

"Yes, now I remember . . . you pastor a church in western New Mexico. Mountain Fire, New Mexico, to be precise," she said, continuing the banter. "A town very similar to Manhattan, if I'm not mistaken."

"Yes, very much alike. How did I not remember the similarities? But I need to be transparent. There is no

Central Park view from my living room window."

The two shared an extended laugh and then Benjamin spoke again. "I will be so proud to introduce the former Sarai Levy as Mrs. Benjamin Sharon. Mountain Fire is not New York City, but it has a very special charm. It's a place I've called home for many years now. Friendships have been formed that will last my lifetime, our lifetime."

Benjamin paused and looked intently at his soon-to-be wife. "I have a great love for my congregation. If in times ahead the Lord should lead us on, it will be difficult to leave. We will follow the Lord's leading and pray for future guidance. We will go wherever He may prompt us to go, if and when that day comes."

"I am so excited, Benjamin," Sarai said, her eyes glistening with delight. "Now it's my turn to be transparent, as you say. After our wedding, I'm afraid you will have to suffer a distant view of Central Park before your sabbatical ends."

Chapter Nineteen

At this time, I'd like to take a moment to introduce our speaker, Reverend Daniel Phillips, from the Crownpoint area, who will be bringing us a special message tonight. As all of you who regularly attend services here at Faith Gospel Tabernacle know, Pastor Sharon is on an overseas sabbatical. He's been preaching the gospel in Europe as well as in Israel, and he has asked Pastor Joshua, several of the elders, and several guest speakers to share the pulpit in his absence. Let's remember to keep Benjamin in our prayers during the time he's away. I know that the Lord will honor these prayers and bless the work He's put before Benjamin. So, without further ado, I'm honored and pleased to ask our guest, Reverend Phillips, to please step forward and share with us what God has laid on your heart. Reverend Phillips, welcome."

The congregation gave a polite round of applause, and Reverend Phillips stepped into the pulpit and placed his notes on the lectern.

"Thank you, Griff, for your warm greeting. Good

evening, church! You may have noticed in the bulletin you received when you came in tonight that the title of my sermon address is 'Where Are the Watchmen?' The message is a four-part series on some of the challenges I believe the church in our nation is facing today. I would like to put your minds to rest by saying that each of these segments is rather short." Reverend Phillips paused and smiled at the congregation.

Jack Broholm had taken a separate car and arrived at the church shortly after Natalie, who had saved a seat toward the front of the sanctuary. Jack sat down several minutes before Reverend Phillips began speaking.

"Who is he?" a man whispered to his wife as the speaker began his opening remarks.

"I'm not sure. I don't believe he's spoken here before," she said.

Jack leaned across Natalie's lap and whispered to the couple. "He pastors a small church north of Crownpoint."

Six or seven seats to his right sat Juan Gutierrez and his wife, Florencia. Jack smiled and waved to the couple and then looked behind him and glanced up at the balcony. The sanctuary was full.

Jack glanced at the sermon outline in the bulletin he was given by one of the ushers as he walked through the lobby doors into the sanctuary:

Where Are the Watchmen?

I.   The Slumbering Church of America
     (Part 1 of a 4-Part Series)

II. Where Are the Watchmen?
     (Part 2 of a 4-Part Series)

III. When God Lifts His Hand of Protection
     (Part 3 of a 4-Part Series)

IV. A Call to Prayer
     (Part 4 of a 4-Part Series)

After a very brief introduction, Reverend Phillips went straight to his text. "If you're listening to this message today, please pause for a moment and ask the Lord to quicken your heart and mind to receive whatever truth He desires to reveal to you. The message I'm going to share is perhaps not mainstream or status quo, though it does, I believe, meet the muster of providing biblical admonishment and sound doctrine to a world in which, increasingly, God's people are left to fend for themselves, surrounded by cultural voices crying out an acceptance message for life choices, lifestyles, that for two thousand years have been antithetical to orthodox Christianity and which today remain diametrically opposed to the Word of God.

"The church of America is asleep, anesthetized by a

world of entertainment and luxury. We live in a fantasy world of sorts. A land of make believe, perpetuated by an entertainment world of television, movies, music, athletic achievement, and wealth, has blinded us to biblical truths. Our lifestyles have put us far from the exhortation in 1 Peter chapter 4, where Peter under the inspiration of the Holy Spirit writes: 'But the end of all things is at hand: be ye therefore sober, and watch unto prayer' (1 Peter 4:7).

"We've become a self-indulgent society of pleasure and sensuality, no longer blushing at even the most flagrant display of indiscretion. When has a society ever so epitomized the biblical depiction of 'lust of the flesh, lust of the eyes, and the pride of life,' and remained at the vanguard of world leadership? Not the Babylonians, not the Persians, not the Greeks, not the Romans, and, certainly the future will foretell, not the United States of America. Sadly, in an effort to be nonjudgmental and embrace the culture, the church has at times become not simply friends to the sinner, but associates and partners, complicit in an anti-biblical ideology, winking at sin, working hard not to offend, blending inconspicuously into a world of moral compromise.

"We've become a nation where evil masquerades as 'art' and 'freedom of expression.' The movie, television, and music industries unpretentiously masquerading under a harmless definition of *entertainment*, sometimes using the word *family*, nonetheless have become industries filled with hordes of devils shaping and molding the world we live in.

"In Isaiah chapter 5 we read, 'Woe unto them that call evil good, and good evil; that put darkness for light, and light for darkness; that put bitter for sweet, and sweet for bitter!' (Isaiah 5:20).

"We live in a culture that's an antithesis to the gospel of Jesus Christ. Much of the music and movie industries stand in direct opposition to the Word of God and our Christian faith. It's easy to become anesthetized to a culture that promotes sin as something glamorous and carefree. It becomes convenient to speak of certain sins by saying, 'Well, that's legal,' or 'That's accepted,' or 'Everyone does that.' But we're to be a 'peculiar people,' declaring the praises of Him who 'called us out of darkness into His marvelous light.'

"And as a seeker-friendly church attempts to embrace the culture, our downward spiral as a nation accelerates. We, the church, were never called to become part of the culture, but rather, Christians were to impact and change the culture through the proclamation of the gospel. Never were we to embrace the culture, let alone *become like* the culture, but rather we were to work diligently to change the culture.

"There was a chasm between the debauchery of Rome and the Orthodox Jews and new Jewish Christian converts. The Gospels and Epistles are filled with admonishments and exhortations: dos and don'ts on how to live, if you will.

"We hear much about God's love and His desire to bless us, but remember, Jesus said, 'Take up your cross,' and 'If you save your life, you will lose it.' We don't always hear about repentance and a full surrender to Jesus.

"In the twentieth century, nationalism is perhaps best embodied by Germany of the 1930s and early to mid-1940s. German citizens who were not nationalists—many of course were Christians—went underground, harboring families like those of Anne Frank and providing a means of escape for the so-called undesirables of Nationalist Germany, which of course was the Nazi regime. These Germans who had gone underground to help those in need were not nationalists, but rather their true country, their true home, was in the care and protection of those that a nationalistic state would seek to destroy. Likewise, after over sixty million abortions and countless international wars imposing our governing will on other nations, wars that did not initiate free peoples nor democratic societies but rather enriched multinational corporations, it would be impossible for a Christian in America to be a 'nationalist' in their loyalty to country.

"Our only true hope is in Jesus, crying out to God in prayer, repenting of our sins before Almighty God, petitioning Him in obedience for the solution to social ills, crying out to Him for mercy on a society on the verge of destruction. Perhaps He would send a reprieve of judgment, His justice, for a nation that was once enlightened but is now descending to a place of no return."

The speaker paused and took a drink from a clear water glass that had been placed on the inside shelf of the lectern and then continued.

"So what happened? How did the sincere beliefs of the early settlers—believers in Christ who had left their homeland, England, for a new country where they could worship God freely, where a newly established government protected the rights of these believers, not ostracized them for their beliefs, and in whose ranks included many professing Christians, men and women of faith who acknowledged the sovereignty of Almighty God and understood that His divine hand had clearly been involved in establishing this new nation in which men and women could worship their Creator in truth and righteousness—disintegrate into a nation of apostasy and unbelief?

"The American dream is not the gospel, yet material blessing and prosperity is often placed at the forefront of the Christian life. The cross, and any reference of suffering, has been replaced by an Americanized view of pursuing the dreams and visions we have for our lives— our destinies—not a sacrificial giving of our lives for the sake of the gospel. The United States has 50 percent of the world's wealth but only 6 percent of the world's population, yet too often we never seem to have enough. We want more.

"In Revelation chapter 3, Jesus speaks of the Laodicean church, an end-times church that is 'neither cold nor hot,' but rather lukewarm, a church repulsive in nature, one that Jesus said He would spew out of His mouth. Could this end-times church be represented largely by the United States of America?—a country so prosperous and so mighty that American Christians believe that luxury and prosperity are God-given rights that we should pursue, expect, and cling to, and if this prosperity is not evident in our lives, well, we must be doing something wrong. God must be punishing us.

"Jesus said, 'The servant is not greater than his Lord. If they have persecuted me, they will also persecute you,' and 'In this world ye will have tribulation.'

"Philippians 2:12 says, 'Work out your own salvation with fear and trembling.' The New Living Translation says, 'Work hard to show the results of your salvation, obeying God with deep reverence and fear.' *The Message* says, 'Be energetic in your life of salvation, reverent and sensitive before God.'

"Remember, iniquities are not always the egregious sins we think of . . . lying, stealing, adultery. In Mark chapter 4, Jesus told His disciples that 'the thorny ground represents the hearts of people who listen to the Good News and receive it, but all too quickly the attractions of this world and the delights of wealth, and the search for success and lure of nice things come in and crowd out God's message from their hearts, so that no crop is produced' (Mark 4:18–19 TLB). Dearest friends . . . what an indictment!

"The world presses in with its ease and comfort and luxurious attractions, but we're to stay close to the Lord and 'guard our hearts and minds in Christ Jesus.' There is a place of safety in the Lord that we as believers dare not depart from.

"The ultimate goal is not to 'Make America Great Again.' The United States, as well as all of Western civilization throughout history, is only as great as the collective righteousness of Christians, lived out in society as salt and light. America's only hope is a revived church, interceding for righteousness and beseeching God to turn back evil and create opportunities for the gospel to go forth in truth and power.

"The Bible says, 'Blessed is the nation whose God is the LORD, The people whom He has chosen for His own inheritance' (Psalm 33:12 NASB), and that 'Righteousness exalts a nation, But sin is a reproach to any people' (Proverbs 14:34 NKJV).

"Supreme Court decisions involving abortion would have been unthinkable in generations past.

"Where are the watchmen, church?

"Sound the alarm! is a common term used in our society to alert people to great danger that might lie ahead. In the book of Revelation, a voice from heaven calls out, 'Come out of her, my people, that ye be not partakers of her sins, and that ye receive not of her plagues' (Revelation 18:4).

"All of us who proclaim the name of Jesus need to stand in the gap for our nation. We need to intercede on behalf of our families and friends and those who are lost and perishing outside the cross.

"Sound the trumpet! Blow the shofar! Hearken the danger that lies ahead! Time is short! Hearken the soon coming King!

"Ladies and gentlemen, these are precarious days. Don't be content to wait until things return to normal, standing by waiting for things to return to the way they were. Things are not going to return to normal. Be proactive in seeking the Lord. Turn to Him now with all your heart."

The speaker paused and took another drink. The congregation was still. The sanctuary was silent.

Chapter Twenty

T he speaker continued. "Throughout the Old Testament we read of God's punishments on a backsliding people, the Jewish nation of Israel, a people referred to in the book of Zechariah as the 'apple of God's eye,' a people throughout the Old Testament referred to as God's chosen people. And yet, in times of disobedience and idol worship, God's hand of judgment was raised. Remember that, due to unbelief, many of the Israelites died in the wilderness and were not allowed to enter the promised land.

"Does God still move in the affairs of men? I think most, if not all, Evangelical Christians would say, 'Of course He does.' Those who have studied American history would agree that our nation has seen countless times of God's intervention in times of trouble. Yet we sometimes recoil at the word *judgment*. Do contemporary Christians believe that God is merely a benevolent father, always encouraging, always blessing, winking at sin, never angry with injustice, never angry when His people profess His name but live ungodly lives? The Roaring Twenties, also known as the Decade of Decadence, was followed by the Great Depression, an era in our country's history that brought great hardship and suffering for the masses. Even in modern-day America, a case can strongly be made for God's hand of judgment on a nation filled with immorality.

"Where is the weeping and agony over the ever-increasing sins of a nation that once recognized the perilous danger of defying the God of the Bible, the maker of heaven and earth, the Creator of the universe? Where is the deep-felt emotion over the sins of a country that many believe is, even now, in the throes of judgment? If only our heart's cry matched the intensity of a college sports team's 'faithful' in victory or the disheartened faces of the losing team's fans. Where is the fervor, the zeal, and the joy in the body of Christ over great spiritual victories? The travailing in prayer over the persecuted church, over Christians held captive—at times being beaten and tortured for their faith in Christ. Where is the disappointment and deep anguish over the grip of sin that has captured this nation?

"How long will God be patient in holding back judgment against a nation guilty of sixty million abortions? How has this infanticide been possible in a country with so many professing Christians?

"In the book of Habakkuk, we read of the Old Testament prophet, in a vision from God, crying out to the Lord for help and justice. In chapter 1, Habakkuk writes, 'Wherever I look I see oppression and bribery and men who love to argue and to fight. The law is not enforced, and there is no justice given in the courts, for the wicked far outnumber the righteous, and bribes and trickery prevail' (Habakkuk 1:3–4 TLB). The Lord replies that he is doing something in Habakkuk's lifetime that he, Habakkuk, will need to see to believe. The Lord said He would raise up a cruel and violent people, the Chaldeans, who would invade God's chosen people, but then He would defeat this aggressor by His mighty hand and divinely save His people, Israel. For his part, Habakkuk had come to a place of trust in the Lord, regardless of the advancing enemy. In verses 17 and 18 of Habakkuk chapter 3, the prophet says, 'Even though the fig trees are all destroyed, and there is neither blossom left nor fruit; though the olive crops all fail, and the fields lie barren; even if the flocks die in the fields and the cattle barns are empty, yet I will rejoice in the Lord; I will be happy in the God of my salvation' (TLB).

"In other words, even if I lose everything, I will trust the Lord. In the twenty-first-century church of America, how so far away many of us are from the faith of Habakkuk. I'm preaching to myself, church.

"Ask yourself: What if I lost everything? What if I was mocked and ridiculed for my faith? What if I was imprisoned, beaten, made to endure extreme heat or extreme cold, in sickness, and in pain?

"Our only true hope is in Jesus. Within Christendom, an organized, concerted effort in seeking the Lord is needed. If American Christians would fill stadiums like a college football team's faithful, or like NBA basketball fans fill a municipal arena, or Major League Baseball fans fill stadiums—crying out to God in prayer, repenting of our sins before Almighty God, petitioning Him for the solutions to social ills, crying out to Him for mercy on a society on the verge of destruction—perhaps He would send a reprieve of judgment to a nation fast spiraling toward an ever-widening abyss.

"Today, as judgment is mercifully delayed, God's people need to pray."

The speaker paused and looked at the congregation. "In closing. In the Old Testament Book of Nehemiah we read of a cup bearer who goes before King Artaxerxes and requests permission to leave Persia, modern-day Iran, and journey to the Jewish homeland of Judah to help rebuild the walls and gates of Jerusalem. A number of years have passed and the Jewish people, having returned from exile in Babylon, Iraq, still have not completed the work. The king grants the Old Testament prophet his request, and Nehemiah proceeds to lead the Israelites in rebuilding the walls and hanging the gates of the city, thereby establishing a necessary fortress to protect the people from their enemies. In miraculous fashion and timing, and with notable solidarity, the people complete the work, and the city is restored.

"The Bible, in Nehemiah 6 verses 15–16, eloquently and powerfully testifies to the astounding feat the Jewish nation had successfully accomplished. 'So the wall was completed on the twenty-fifth of the month Elul, in fifty-two days. And it came about when all our enemies heard of it, and all the nations surrounding us saw it, they lost their confidence; for they recognized that this work had been accomplished with the help of our God' (NASB).

"I'm reminded that in times past, a group of pastors in Mountain Fire organized the first of a series of prayer assemblies in the city. The herald's clarion call was to organize Christians in the community to come together to seek God's touch in their land. The parallel is obvious: while Nehemiah and the Jewish nation of Israel rebuilt the city of Jerusalem with bricks and mortar and timber, the people of Mountain Fire, New Mexico, would rebuild their city through prayer. Both efforts involved the hand of Almighty God, clearly and miraculously directing and blessing the work.

"Today, as citizens of the United States, we read with dismay of the struggle our country faces both at home and abroad. At home, we are diametrically opposed—spiritually, politically, philosophically. To the world at large, we're a paradox. While many still view the United States in terms of the American dream—a land of freedom, hope, and opportunity—many in the international community increasingly despise us and the hypocrisy we've come to represent. Is this resentment unfounded? Not entirely. On one hand, we're still the world's premier democracy— crying out against tyranny and other forms of injustice, giving of our resources to the less fortunate throughout the world, and aspiring to remain a voice of freedom to all those who cherish human dignity.

"On the other hand, we have become a nation anesthetized by its own luxury and comfort. History reveals that anytime a nation becomes as self-centered and self-seeking as the United States of America has become over the last generation, its demise soon follows.

"After enduring war protesters, drug abuse, and the 'me' generation of the sixties, followed by two decades of extreme political activism, two gulf wars, and the challenge of balancing families and work in an information-overload era, the average American wants to be left alone.

"Christians, too, are guilty of this apathy. A generation of ease and prosperity unknown to previous generations has made us self-centered and complacent. We expect to be prosperous, and yes, within the church itself, the word of faith and prosperity movements suggest there is something wrong with the person who is not prosperous. In other words, that individual must not possess an adequate faith. Sadly these movements focus much on self-fulfillment and oftentimes little on exhibiting the compassion and love of Jesus to a world deeply in need of His saving hand.

"But even at this critical time in our history—a crossroads, if you will, in which our survival as 'one nation under God' becomes less plausible with each passing decade—there is hope for the country that cries out to God for His mercy and grace. The psalmist says, 'Blessed is the nation whose God is the Lord.' Simply put, our fate and our future rest solely in the hands of Almighty God. To coin an old cliché, 'If ever there was a time to pray, it's now.'

"Little is known, and even less publicized by the mainstream media, of the impact that prayer has had on our country during times of crisis. Amazing stories of God's intervention in the affairs of this nation have long been known to those who believe in the power of prayer. An inspiring story of God's sovereignty and divine hand at work is documented in a book Pastor Sharon let me borrow not long ago. He said the book had been given to him by Alexander Joseph, a man of prayer that some of you knew well. Katherine Pollard Carter in *Hand on the Helm* shares Louise W. Eggleston's dramatic and eloquent story from *The How and Why of Prayer Groups* of the mysterious white cavalry that turned back the German infantry in World War I. The cavalry, invisible to the Allies, was led by a magnificent, white-robed leader whose presence brought terror and defeat to the German army.

"Others have written of divine intervention that miraculously turned the tide in critical battles with the Nazis during World War II. Many times throughout history when all seemed hopeless and defeat appeared imminent, our troops were delivered in remarkable, astonishing, and divine fashion.

"In 2 Chronicles 7:14, the Lord appeared to Solomon and said, 'If my people, which are called by my name, shall humble themselves, and pray, and seek my face, and turn from their wicked ways; then will I hear from heaven, and will forgive their sin, and will heal their land.'

"As a United States citizen, I'm grateful for our heritage, for the God-fearing men and women of faith who settled on Plymouth's shores, who sought a life of freedom in Christ. I'm ever mindful of the blessings God has bestowed on this land. As a Christian, I'm not ecumenical. I'm interdenominational but not interfaith. I believe in the triune God—Father, Son, and Holy Spirit—that Jesus came into this world, was born of a virgin, lived a life among men, performed miracles proving His deity, was crucified, dead, and buried, rose again on the third day, ascended into heaven, and will one day return in glory—all orthodox tenets of the Christian faith affirmed in Scripture and Christian liturgies since the time of Christ. I believe that Jesus is the creator of the universe and is, in fact, God Himself.

"I believe in His atoning work at Calvary—that He died for the sins of all who will put their faith in Him and trust Him with their lives. In the Old Testament Passover, a lamb's blood was sprinkled on the lintel and side panels of the doors to the Israelites' homes to protect the Jewish people from the wrath of God, which was to be poured out upon Israel's enemies. In the New Testament, the new covenant, the sacrificial lamb is Jesus Himself. The blood of Jesus is the covering of protection.

"Virtually every organization in the world has specific criteria for membership. One must believe, profess, acknowledge, or act in a certain manner to be included. Jesus said, 'I am the way, the truth, and the life: no man cometh unto the Father, but by me' (John 14:6). There is no pluralism or all-inclusiveness in this statement. With Christianity, to be a Christian—a follower of Christ—one must believe in Jesus.

"And so from the position of being first a Christian and secondly an American, I call upon every God-fearing pastor and layperson, male and female, young and old alike, to join together in community-wide prayer assemblies to pray for God's mercies upon the United States of America. I encourage you to hold prayer assemblies in your towns, cities, counties, and states for a prolonged and sustained period of time—that is, frequent prayer gatherings that are scheduled over a span of months, even years—to pray for God's mercies upon our country and to beseech the hand of God to move across our land.

"Perhaps yet, God will hear from heaven, and heal our land.

"Thank you so much for listening. May God bless each of you!"

Chapter Twenty-One

The service ended, and Clifton Rockwell looked at Nicole. "Would you give me fifteen minutes? I'm going to see if I can have a few minutes with the pastor. I don't know if he's available, but I'm going to ask. I have some thoughts I want to run by him."

"Sure, Clifton. I'll mingle around. This is such a beautiful church. I love the banners. I'll meet you in the lobby."

Clifton walked briskly toward the stage and called out to the speaker as he was walking down the steps from the podium.

"Reverend Phillips. Can I have a word with you?"

"Sure. How can I help you?" Reverend Phillips replied.

"Clifton Rockwell." Rockwell extended his hand. "Really appreciated your message. Just wanted to ask you a couple of questions if you have the time."

"Certainly. Should we sit down in the front row here?" Reverend Phillips turned and looked at two of the church elders who had approached the podium. "Bill, Ken, give me a few minutes, please."

The men sat down, and Rockwell began with a rapid-fire succession of challenges and objections: "We were founded on Christian principles. Some of the country's forefathers were deists, granted, but many were Christians. The Pilgrims and Puritans were Christian men and women of faith. Didn't God deliver the early settlers from a repressive Church of England? You say that God is going to judge the United States? Haven't American missionaries taken the gospel all over the world? Hasn't He blessed America for our global outreach work? Aren't we favored, aren't we His chosen? Isn't He going to give us time to turn this around, well, to repent, I should say?"

"Here's how I'm going to answer your question: with a couple of thoughts and then a question to you. Let's review the last one hundred years. In the 1920s we had Billy Sunday, in the thirties and forties, D. L. Moody. Billy Graham's first crusade was in 1947. David Wilkerson began preaching to gang members in New York City in 1958. All of these men of faith preached repentance and warned of judgment as the country fell deeper into sin and apostasy. At this juncture in our history, it's hard to imagine how much deeper into the pit of sin we could fall. So let me ask you, what would we use the additional time for? To be led by the Spirit of God and work faithfully to advance the gospel or to accumulate possessions and enjoy the luxuries and pleasures this world has to offer? Or even worse, to continue in sin?

"I don't say this to you to be judgmental," Reverend Phillips said. "I tell you this to provide perspective. The America, the 'Land of the Free' of the Pilgrims, Puritans, and our Founding Fathers, was a different country than the America we see today. The country of our forefathers taught the Bible to grade-school children. Today, the nation, and by nation I mean the ruling authorities. Government, academia, and the media, frequently promote views that teach *against* the Bible. All of that to say, we can't expect our godly heritage to save us as a nation any more than an individual can expect his godly parents' faith to save him or her.

"Let me ask you another question, respectfully. What do you do for a living?"

"I'm a district manager. I work for Artisan Building Supplies. I have a number of stores in New Mexico."

"I'm familiar with the company. I've been in a couple of your stores. So here's my thought. You're obviously very skilled in your trade or you wouldn't have been put in that position, right?"

"I've worked hard," Clifton replied.

"I would suggest you've done more than work hard. I would think you've become somewhat of an expert in your field. Still learning of course, we all are, but you've gained enough knowledge to put you at the top of the class, so to speak.

"Here's my question: How many American Christians are experts in the Word of God? How many American Christians read the Bible daily? How many American

Christians have read the entire Bible? How many professing believers store up Scripture in their hearts, memorizing verses for their own edification and also for a time when the Holy Spirit might lead them to recite a passage of Scripture in exhortation, admonishment, encouragement, or praise, or in sharing the gospel with an unbeliever?"

Rockwell was silent. He didn't know what to say. There was nothing more to say. In an instant, if he hadn't already known, it was now perfectly clear.

The speaker looked inquisitively at Rockwell. "Are you a Christian?" he asked.

"Yes," Rockwell replied weakly.

"Good. I'm glad to hear that." Reverend Phillips looked thoughtfully at Rockwell. "I want you to know something: I care deeply about our country. Following my final year in seminary, I took a lengthy road trip and drove through almost every state in the union. 'America the Beautiful' has long been one of my favorite hymns.

"My dad worked on oil rigs when I was a kid growing up. Except for a few years when we moved to Montana, and another few years when I was off to Bible school, I've lived in New Mexico all my life. I've spent my entire adult life watching a remarkable transformation take place in the United States. I'm now seventy-five years old. It's a different country today than the America I've known most of my life. Many good things have transpired, I agree with that . . ." Reverend Phillips paused, straightened up, and continued. "I'm just one voice. David Wilkerson spoke out against the debauchery in our nation and the judgment to come, but his warnings were largely unheeded by the masses. Speed forward forty to fifty years: the cloud of deception over America is staggering.

"All the best to you, Clifton, and may God bless you and your family. I need to run. I'm heading home tonight. I have a bit of a drive. I live north of here between Crownpoint and Farmington. I don't have good cell phone service, but someone at the church can get ahold of me if need be."

The last thing Reverend Phillips said was, "I care about our country, but I fear for our sin."

Clifton thanked the man and got up to leave. As he was walking toward the lobby to meet Nicole, his mind was racing—churning over nuances from the conversation with Reverend Phillips. He thought about the title *expert*. For his entire career he had worked to become knowledgeable, proficient, skilled, and, in his mind, *expert* at his trade. He was proud of the almost relentless ambition that had taken him from position to position over the course of his career. But there was no hiding from the fact that he was a novice when it came to Scripture.

It was as if Reverend Phillips had spoken privately to Nicole. His mind flashed to the conversation they had on the drive to Mountain Fire earlier that afternoon.

"How often do you read the Bible?" she said. "I know the answer. Not very often."

"How much time do you think I have?" he responded, exasperated by the question.

"You mean after giving your company sixty hours a week, watching conservative talk shows every night until bed, golfing on Saturday and sometimes on Sunday? Not very much, I guess," she replied sarcastically but then apologized.

"Forgive me, Clifton. It's just that I've taken second place in your life for our entire marriage. Your job has always come first. I should be second, but God should be first place in your life. In each of our lives!

"You're planning for twenty years down the road," Nicole told him. "I'm watching for the Lord's return." She then said, "I wish the Lord would come back tonight."

Rockwell was startled. She was hoping the Lord would return *tonight*? A procession of thoughts, compressed, buried, and hidden in a life of self and ambition overpowered him, blasting across his mind like a torrential rain washing away loose soil. What about his career goals? Everything he had worked so hard for. What was he supposed to do, put all that aside?

"Clifton, where does your identity lie? Are you a Christian? A Republican? A businessman? You sat on the plane with the woman running for office. Did you share the gospel with her?"

"No," he said grudgingly.

"Do you see the irony? You're discussing national problems but failing to provide the solution. There's only one solution. And that's what I want in my life, Clifton. More of God."

He knew she was right. The question now was how

did he recover? How did he dig out from such a life of self-absorption?

Hours later Clifton and Nicole Rockwell exited the church building, got in their car, followed a stream of lights to the interstate, and began the drive home.

"It was a powerful message," Clifton offered. "I'm trying to sort things out and come to a balance."

"I'm not sure what kind of balance there is to come to," Nicole replied. "You heard the preacher. All of this is a distraction. Judgment is coming to America.

"Don't worry," she continued. "God is in control. We just need to be in His will, not ours."

Clifton let out a deep sigh and nodded. The two were mostly silent as they drove through the darkened night to Albuquerque.

Stuart and Andréa Veronique were also at Faith Gospel Tabernacle when the speaker shared his message. She reluctantly attended the service after Stuart ran into Jack Broholm in town, who gave him a gentle nudge: "I know you guys are attending Abundant Blessings, but there's a guest speaker at Faith Gospel Tabernacle on Friday night. Our pastor has urged us to get the word out. I think it will be worth your while."

The service ended and Andréa Veronique left the sanctuary, tears streaming down her face.

She was clearly frustrated when they reached the car. The speaker's reference to the unborn early in the message had prevented her from concentrating on much of his sermon.

But the question "How long will God be patient?" and the words "hold back judgment" and the statement "a nation guilty of sixty million abortions" rang in her mind like tornado sirens piercing an Oklahoma night.

Stuart started the engine, but before beginning the drive home he looked at Andréa Veronique and asked, "You don't look good. Are you all right?"

"Don't talk to me," she snapped and then burst out crying. "I'm sorry, Stuart," she said between choked sobs. "I can't believe I said that. I can't believe I said that . . ."

"It's okay, it's okay," Stuart said, handing her his scarf. Andréa Veronique damped the silk scarf against her cheeks and then pressed the garment against her eyes. "I feel so much pressure. I don't know what to do. What are we going to do, Stuart? Please tell me. What are we going to do?"

Jack Broholm left the sanctuary and went straight to the small chapel on the far side of the church building. Jack closed the chapel door behind him, sat down for an instant but then changed positions and dropped to his knees, pressing his elbows against the chair. Four prayer intercessors had met in the second-floor upper room during the guest speaker's sermon, lifting him up in prayer and praying over the needs of the congregation. But the chapel had not been in use and the lights were off, leaving the room darkened other than a glimmer of light through the window from a nearby streetlight. "He was speaking directly to me, Lord," Jack whispered. How had he not understood sooner? How had it taken so long to register?

His thoughts were interrupted by the sound of a melody coming from an overhead speaker, a musical composition he was long ago acquainted with, the song lyrics heard many times before but this time being sung by an unfamiliar artist with the loveliest voice imaginable. Jack listened to the words, his spirit moved by the adoration and devotion of the songwriter, the meaning of the words penetrating his spirit and inspiring his faith, the music soothing his heart and mind like the comforting glow of a warm fire.

> "I'd rather have Jesus than silver or gold;
> I'd rather be His than have riches untold;
> I'd rather have Jesus than houses or lands.
> I'd rather be led by His nail pierced hand
>
> "Than to be the king of a vast domain
> Or be held in sin's dread sway.
> I'd rather have Jesus than anything
> This world affords today.
>
> "I'd rather have Jesus than men's applause;
> I'd rather be faithful to His dear cause;
> I'd rather have Jesus than worldwide fame.
> I'd rather be true to His holy name

"Than to be the king of a vast domain
Or be held in sin's dread sway.
I'd rather have Jesus than anything
This world affords today."

Just as the song ended, the chapel lights came on. Still on his knees, Jack turned to see a young man from the church staff walk abruptly through the chapel door.

"Oh, pardon me, Mr. Broholm. I didn't know anyone was here. There's an electrical issue that I didn't get to earlier today. I won't be working tomorrow. I was here for the service tonight and thought I'd take a quick look. I thought I'd listen to the playlist while I worked. Please excuse me. The repairs can wait until next week. I'll let you get back to your prayer time, Mr. Broholm."

"No, I'm leaving shortly. If you would give me five minutes, I'll be gone."

The young man stepped back through the doorway, reaching to the wall outside the chapel and turning out the lights. As the door closed, Jack called out. "Caleb, play that last song again, if you would please."

That night Jack fell asleep with the words playing over and over in his heart and mind:

"I'd rather have Jesus than silver or gold;
I'd rather be His than have riches untold . . .
Than to be the king of a vast domain
Or be held in sin's dread sway . . ."

That night Clifton Rockwell sat in the living room of their home and reflected on the service, Reverend Phillips' words, his career, his marriage, his Christian life, or, more accurately he thought, his failure to live a committed Christian life.

On New Year's Eve of the year he went forward at a Billy Graham crusade, Rockwell went to bed early but lay awake well past midnight into the small hours of the new year, overcome by a great conviction to share his faith with coworkers at the workplace of the job he held at the time. He felt God telling him to wear a "Jesus First" pin on his lapel and publicly proclaim his faith. His dad had given him the pin months before, but he hadn't put it on, placing it instead in an empty watch case tucked away in the corner of a bottom dresser drawer.

Rockwell wrestled with the conviction well into the night but fell asleep resolved to take a stand for his faith.

On his next scheduled shift, Rockwell began the new year wearing the pin at work. Initially his testimony was met with respect, but in the busyness of life it wasn't long after that he stopped attending a weekly Bible study group he'd been part of, and it wasn't long after that when he stopped wearing the pin. Step by step, little by little, compromise by compromise, however seemingly small, his workplace testimony eased off and was soon, to the casual observer, untethered from his work relationships.

As the years went by he never actually stopped *professing* to be a Christian, but he frequently didn't *live* like a Christian. He seldom discussed his faith with any real certitude. He rarely thought about sin, never about defeat of any sort. Brash, arrogant, aggressive, impatient, self-righteous, and condescending were all adjectives used to describe Rockwell at one time or another, but in his mind he was as good as the next guy, better than most, and on extremely confident days, which was much of the time, he was better than the best.

But tonight, his past sins were crashing down on him like a man shipwrecked in a sea of broken planks and tattered mast. Rockwell was going through a period of uncharacteristic introspection. He felt overwhelmed with regrets. He should have been a better husband, father, son—how could he have spoken so harshly to his parents, even as a young adult?

He thought of his great-aunt, Stella, and his great-grandfather, August Rockwell, family members who had gone on before him after leaving a godly heritage. During the funeral services, the eulogies were filled with tributes of exemplary living and victory. The preachers said things like, "Her faith never wavered" and "He fought the good fight." Rockwell knew that for much of his life, he had not fought the good fight.

What happened? he wondered. He had asked Jesus into his heart. How had he fallen so far from God's leading in his life? He knew the answer as soon as he asked the question: His Bible reading was irregular and infrequent. The weekly men's fellowship group was now years in the past. Church attendance was sporadic. He was engrossed in his management career, and his free time was engaged in a pursuit of self-gratification. He led an adult life dominated by self with material gain and personal satisfaction at the forefront, and now he was submerged in a sea of stormy waves, unable to navigate to safe waters.

He thought of the Scripture passages Nicole had read to him the night before:

"Then he called the crowd to him along with his disciples and said: 'Whoever wants to be my disciple must deny themselves and take up their cross and follow me. For whoever wants to save their life will lose it, but whoever loses their life for me and for the gospel will save it.' "
(Mark 8:34–35 NIV)

"God requires a full surrender, Clifton. He wants all of you," she said.

"I have another verse for you," she said. " 'May I never boast except in the cross of our Lord Jesus Christ, through which the world has been crucified to me, and I to the world' (Galatians 6:14 NIV).

"Clifton, don't you see that confidence without God is a snare?"

Rockwell was in a state of despair. He thought about the addictions and besetting sins in his life he had struggled with. The weight of the past pressed in upon him; the scourge of self, sin, and neglect overpowered him. For all of the confidence he normally felt, he was overcome by fear and regrets. A sense of abject failure and utter sinfulness engulfed him.

Chapter Twenty-Two

Sarai Levy could scarcely imagine the transformation her life had undergone the past month. A conversion and surrender to Yeshua Hamashiach, Jesus the Messiah, the one true God, Elohim, the God of the Torah, God of the old covenant and the New Testament, the Creator of heaven and earth who had revealed Himself to her! She found herself immersed in His love with a determined purpose to learn everything she could about this Savior she had neglected, until recently, her entire life.

And then being reunited with the man she always believed she was supposed to marry! What an extravagant blessing had been showered upon her! Sarai's mind was swirling with wonder.

Now she was seated in the front row of a historic stone building of asymmetrical limestone blocks— Jerusalem Stone—in the Old City of Jerusalem, as Benjamin Sharon approached the podium to begin his lecture on the statehood of Israel.

Today she was in the audience, tomorrow she would

be married. It would not be the wedding she had planned so many years before: a wedding to be celebrated by scores of family members and friends, numerous business associates of her father, a host of congregational and esteemed rabbinical colleagues of Rabbi Isaac Sharon, Benjamin's father, in all, a guest list in the hundreds gathered at a synagogue she had attended first when she was a child and then at times throughout the years until her father's death—a point in time that marked the beginning of what would become a gradual departure from the orthodoxy of her upbringing.

The lights were turned off in the theater, but beacons of light from several directions shone on the lectern in front of Benjamin. After a brief introduction from the host, Benjamin began speaking:

"The title of my talk today is 'Woe to Those Who Divide up the Land! Israel: The Land God Gave Abraham and Affirmed to Joshua.'

"The land that God promised Abraham's descendants in Genesis, that was reaffirmed to Moses in Scripture passages in Exodus and Leviticus, and reaffirmed again to Joshua in Joshua chapter 1 was far greater in geographical scope than the small sliver of land that represents modern-day Israel—which since its founding seventy years ago has been a thorn of contention among the nations of the world.

"For much of the modern-day history of Israel, the United States has been an unflinching ally, one of Israel's strongest and most prominent supporters. This support and friendship have largely maintained the test of time. From Israel becoming a nation in 1948, during and after the 1967 Six-Day War and the 1973 Yom Kippur War, through the shuttle diplomacy of Henry Kissinger, through the host of the Israeli-Palestinian Authority peace treaty diplomats—George Shultz, James Baker, Warren Christopher, Madeleine Albright, Colin Powell, Condoleezza Rice, Hillary Rodham Clinton, John Kerry; in the Trump administration Rex Tillerson and now today, Secretary of State Mike Pompeo—the United States has been a friend of Israel. From the PLO suicide bombings in the 1980s to the recent negotiations by representatives of the Trump administration, both the Democratic and Republican parties have pledged an allegiance to Israel, albeit not all administrations have maintained unwavering support for the boundaries of this Zionist nation.

"In Genesis 15:18, we read, 'That day *ADONAI* made a covenant with Avram: "I have given this land to your descendants—from the *Vadi* of Egypt to the great river, the Euphrates River" ' (CJB). Some scholars believe that the river of Egypt referenced here is the Nile River, but whether this is the Nile or a lesser river, it clearly encompassed parts of Egypt; the Euphrates River begins in Turkey and flows through Syria and Iraq.

"Two brief points I'd like to make as we continue. One: In 1970, Jordan expelled the PLO from Jordanian territory killing between ten and fifteen thousand Palestinians in the process. Prior to this massacre, Jordan had been a homeland to thousands of Palestinians. Point two: The nation of Israel encompasses approximately eighty-five hundred square miles, which, prior to Israel becoming a nation, had been heavily desert area. Through tremendous perseverance, hard work, and ingenuity, this area was developed into a fertile land. The combined land mass of Syria, Saudi Arabia, Lebanon, Iran, Iraq, Jordan, and Egypt is . . . hold your breath now—over 2.1 million square miles. The analogy is—in square miles, Israel is to the Mideast countries aforementioned as Vermont and Connecticut are to the balance of the United States. So here you have a relatively obscure little nation surrounded by countries that include some of the largest oil-producing nations in the world and, which in square miles, are close to 250 times the size of Israel. The whole picture connotes images of David and Goliath. When you consider that some of these regions have pledged the obliteration of Israel, how can one fault the survival instincts of a country that by no means can be looked upon in a rational manner as trying to conquer its neighbor's land? Secondly, why hasn't one of these countries offered the Palestinians a small tract of land? Certainly the capabilities are there.

"In Psalm 24:1 we read, 'The earth is the LORD's, and the fullness thereof.' Haggai chapter 2, verse 8 says, 'The silver is mine, and the gold is mine, saith the LORD of hosts.' In Psalm 50:10 we read, 'For every beast of the forest is mine, and the cattle upon a thousand hills.'

"God's ownership of everything is irrefutable. There is no law above the law of God Almighty. No local, state, national, or international law can supersede the declarations of God. In Joel chapter 3 the Lord declares, 'I will also gather all nations, and will bring them down into the valley of Jehoshaphat, and will plead with them there for my people and for my heritage Israel, whom they have scattered among the nations, and parted my land' (v. 2).

"Woe to those who divide up the land! It is critical that we maintain our support of Israel, unabashedly, unflinchingly, and remember the covenant that the God of Israel made with Abraham for his descendants, the children of Israel.

"Israel should hold to the established territories. She should not have given up Bethlehem, Jericho, or Gaza, and should not relinquish the West Bank or the Golan Heights, which are needed for Israel's security.

"As a Christian Zionist, I believe in the statehood of Israel. I believe in Yeshua, Jesus, the God of the Bible, the God of Abraham, Isaac, and Jacob."

That night at dinner, Benjamin and Sarai discussed their future plans together.

"I will be a devoted wife for as many remaining years as Yeshua has for us in this life." She paused and looked earnestly at Benjamin, the man she had pledged to marry so many years before and now, in the providence of Yeshua's perfect will and timing, had pledged to marry once again.

"Benjamin, I want you to know that my commitment to Yeshua was not conditional. When I finally understood who He was, and I surrendered my life to Him, it was a genuine surrender." Sarai looked down, carefully choosing her words. "What I'm trying to say is, I don't want you to think that my decision to follow Yeshua, to become His follower, was contingent on our being together, that it had anything to do with us. If I had found out there was someone else in your life or that you no longer carried these feelings, I would still have served Him.

"After my conversion, I told Him, 'I've neglected You long enough.' I asked Him to saturate me with His presence. I asked Him to permeate my soul with Himself, to shower me with oracles of truth.

"Benjamin, I have something very serious I need to tell you. I know I made light of our staying in my apartment with a view of Central Park. I felt Yeshua speaking to me. I think He told me I would soon be parting with much of my father's estate. He told me He would guide me and that you would help. I don't even know where to start in giving to Christian charities and endowments.

"I also read some verses from the Tanakh, from the Nevi'im." Sarai reached for her purse and pulled out a small journal. "I wrote these verses down and wanted to share them with you. May I read this to you?"

Benjamin looked approvingly at his bride. "Of course you may. Please do."

Sarai began reading:

> " 'Then you will call, and *ADONAI* will answer;
> you will cry, and he will say, "Here I am."
> If you will remove the yoke from among you,
> stop false accusation and slander,

generously offer food to the hungry
and meet the needs of the person in trouble;
then your light will rise in the darkness,
and your gloom become like noon.
ADONAI will always guide you;
he will satisfy your needs in the desert,
he will renew the strength in your limbs;
so that you will be like a watered garden,
like a spring whose water never fails.'
(Isaiah 58:9–11 CJB)

"Then I read verse ten from the New English Translation I discovered online, and the words jumped out at me.

" 'You must actively help the hungry
and feed the oppressed.
Then your light will dispel the darkness,
and your darkness will be transformed into noonday.'
(Isaiah 58:10 NET)

"And another verse I wrote down.

" 'He who is kind to the poor is lending to
ADONAI;
and he will repay him for his good deed.'
(Proverbs 19:17 CJB)

"One more, if I may." Sarai looked anxiously at Benjamin and then continued reading.

> " 'Who is a God like you,
> pardoning the sin and overlooking the crimes
> of the remnant of his heritage?
> He does not retain his anger forever,
> because he delights in grace.
> He will again have compassion on us,
> he will subdue our iniquities.
> You will throw all their sins
> into the depths of the sea.'
> (Micah 7:18–19 CJB)

"Benjamin, after all these years of unbelief, Yeshua has poured out His grace on me and pardoned my sins. His sacrifice is inconceivable to me. I'm so incredibly grateful. I know I can never repay Him, but I will serve Him.

"I'm giving Him everything. I won't miss anything I'm leaving behind."

The next morning, on the day of their wedding, Benjamin and Sarai walked along the beach of the Sea of Galilee not far from the park where they would stand and share their vows. Waves splashed playfully on their feet and ankles as they walked hand in hand, gazing at the sea, discussing the remarkable, momentous changes just ahead in their lives, sometimes reminiscing about times and events from many years before, cherishing their moment together, enjoying the sunshine and cool breeze of a glorious spring day.

The wedding had come together only days before. After all these years apart, they would not be planning a large ceremony in New York, complete with an impressive registry of family, friends, dignitaries, and noteworthy personalities. There were no plans for a large ceremony in Mountain Fire, joined by a number of Christian pastors, parishioners, and friends, who at this time would be acquainted with the groom only. Their reuniting was extraordinary, and given the unusual and remarkable circumstances surrounding their decision, it was decided that any large receptions or gatherings would come later. Instead, they would make their vows in a small, private ceremony in Israel by the Sea of Galilee, a special place of divine history, a place where Yeshua had walked.

"What an honor," Benjamin explained to Sarai, though no explanation was needed. Sarai, too, shared a love for the place of her forefathers and newfound King.

But there were last minute complications. Noncitizen foreigners in Israel do not simply announce they are getting married the prior week and expect a straightforward and uncomplicated process. They were initially told, "No, it can't be done." Plans were then changed. They would fly to Cyprus, marry at an Orthodox church, and then return to Tiberias for their honeymoon. In the eleventh hour their marriage license was granted. "This is nothing less than a miracle," the presiding official, a Jewish believer and minister from a Messianic church in Tiberias, shared with Benjamin and Sarai.

"Friends, chaver, chavera, we are gathered here today at Lake Tiberias, *Yam Kinneret* in Hebrew, known in the Old Testament as the Sea of Kinneret and the Sea of Chinnereth, a lake we know of in modern translations of the Bible as the Sea of Galilee, the place where Yeshua performed so many of His miracles.

"In Numbers 34:2 the Lord spoke to Moses and said, 'Command the children of Israel, and say unto them, When ye come into the land of Canaan; (this is the land that shall fall unto you for an inheritance, even the land of Canaan with the coasts thereof),' and then in verse 11 the Lord says, 'And the coast shall go down from Shepham to Riblah, on the east side of Ain; and the border shall descend, and shall reach unto the side of the sea of Chinnereth eastward.'

"In Joshua 13:27 we read, 'And in the valley, Betharam, and Bethnimrah, and Succoth, and Zaphon, the rest of the kingdom of Sihon king of Heshbon, Jordan and his border, even onto the edge of the sea of Chinnereth on the other side Jordan eastward' (KJV).

"So you see, friends, that the Sea of Galilee is a special place indeed. And it is here that we are gathered together for the marriage, *nissuin* in the Hebrew, of Benjamin Isaac Sharon and Sarai Rebekah Levy.

"We are standing in an area where Yeshua performed many wonderful miracles for the people.

"Look off in the distance to your left. This is where Yeshua walked on water and calmed the storm.

"I might add that Benjamin and Sarai would never compare their wedding to the divine and sacred miracles our Savior performed in new covenant biblical times, but they do believe that their wedding ceremony today is a miracle from Yeshua.

"Today, we will unite two Jewish believers in holy matrimony. Over the past few days, I had the honor of getting to know this brother and sister in Yeshua and hear the testimonies of how they came to know Yeshua as Messiah, and how, after many years apart, Yeshua brought them together, soon to be united as man and wife. I was inspired as well by a presentation that Benjamin shared in Jerusalem about the land, this land, that God promised our fathers. Benjamin Sharon, a Messianic Jewish pastor from the province, or I should say, the state of New Mexico in the United States, and Sarai Levy, a new-in-the-faith Jewish believer from New York City, have decided to hold this ceremony near the Sea of Galilee, in the midst of the place where Yeshua ministered and performed so many of His miracles. We know from the new covenant that Yeshua walked on water and calmed a storm and, in Bethsaida not far from where we stand, He fed five thousand men along with women and children from five loaves and two fish.

"I might point out to the handful of witnesses to this wedding ceremony that Pastor Sharon shepherds a flock of five hundred men and women and young people of diverse nationalities and backgrounds. Hispanic, or Latino, as some might say, Native Americans of the

Navajo tribe, some of the Zuni nationality, some from the local Arab population, several Jewish believers—yes, there are Jewish believers in the place called Mountain Fire, New Mexico, USA—and many Caucasian believers in Yeshua.

"Sarai Levy is a well-known philanthropist, I think that is a good word, known to many in the Jewish community in New York City.

"I tell you this to let you know that there is a large circle of family members and friends in the United States who will be very disappointed that this ceremony took place without them and who will say, 'Why did you get married in Israel with only a handful of acquaintances?' Well, friends, after hearing Benjamin and Sarai's testimony, I understand how they have come to see Yeshua's leading in their lives and how He has led them to the most sacred of ceremonies between a man and woman here in the land of Israel that both Benjamin and Sarai admire and treasure so much.

"Our lovely bride, by the way, is wearing the wedding dress she would have worn many years before when she and Benjamin first contemplated spending their lives together."

Pastor Chaim Dayan glanced at a creased page of notes, smiled at the joyful faces darting back and forth from Benjamin to Sarai, and said, "I might add that a large wedding reception is being planned at this very moment in Benjamin's hometown of Mountain Fire, New Mexico, and that all who want to attend are genuinely and graciously invited. The couple has shared with me that the invitation includes each of you."

A cheerful affirmation erupted among the small crowd, followed by hands clapping and the blowing of a shofar by a young man who had accompanied the minister.

"And now I will read from Scripture. There are a number of verses, selected by Benjamin and Sarai, I should add, verses I believe were divinely chosen for this special day, words put on their hearts by Yeshua, that I would like to share with you before we ask this couple to make their vows.

"In Genesis, the Word of our Lord tells us,

" 'God created humankind in His image, in the image of God He created him, male and female He created them.'
(Genesis 1:27 TLV)

"Yeshua tells us in the Gospel of Matthew,

" ' "Haven't you read?" He answered. "He who created them from the beginning 'made them male and female' and said, 'For this reason a man shall leave his father and mother and be joined to his wife, and the two shall become one flesh.' So they are no longer two, but one flesh. Therefore what God has joined together, let no man separate." '
(Matthew 19:4–6 TLV)

"Benjamin, in Proverbs we read,

" 'Who can find an aishes chayil (a woman of valor, an excellent wife *Prov 12:4*)? For her worth is far above rubies.
The lev of her ba'al (husband) doth securely trust in her, so that he shall have no lack of gain.'
(Mishle [Proverbs] 31:10–11 OJB)

"Sarai, in the new covenant of God's grace, Peter, under the inspiration of God's Holy Spirit, writes,

" 'For this is the way the holy women, who put their hope in God, used to beautify themselves long ago—being submitted to their own husbands just as Sarah obeyed Abraham, calling him lord. You have become her daughters by doing what is good and not fearing intimidation.'
(1 Peter 3:5–6 TLV)

"And Benjamin, I turn back to you to say that Peter goes on and says,

" 'In the same way, husbands, live with your wives in an understanding way. Though they are weaker partners, honor them as equal heirs of the grace of life. In this way, your prayers will not be hindered.'

(1 Peter 3:7 TLV)

"To each of you I emphasize that you are 'equal heirs of the grace of life' in Yeshua our Lord and King.

"Finally, to each of you, let love govern your lives together from this time forth. In the beauty and blessedness of 1 Corinthians 13, our Lord and Savior defines this love in the most eloquent of ways:

" 'If I had the gift of being able to speak in other languages without learning them and could speak in every language there is in all of heaven and earth, but didn't love others, I would only be making noise. If I had the gift of prophecy and knew all about what is going to happen in the future, knew everything about *everything*, but didn't love others, what good would it do? Even if I had the gift of faith so that I could speak to a mountain and make it move, I would still be worth nothing at all without love. If I gave everything I have to poor people, and if I were burned alive for preaching the Gospel but didn't love others, it would be of no value whatever.

" 'Love is very patient and kind, never jealous or envious, never boastful or proud, never haughty or selfish or rude. Love does not demand its own way. It is not irritable or touchy. It does not hold grudges and will hardly even notice when others do it wrong. It is never glad about injustice, but rejoices whenever truth wins out. If you love someone, you will be loyal to him no matter what the cost. You will always believe in him, always expect the best of him, and always stand your ground in defending him.

" 'All the special gifts and powers from God will someday come to an end, but love goes on forever. Someday prophecy and speaking in unknown languages and special knowledge—these gifts will disappear. Now we know so little, even with our special gifts, and the preaching of those most gifted is still so poor. But when we have been made perfect and complete, then the need for these inadequate special gifts will come to an end, and they will disappear.

" 'It's like this: when I was a child I spoke and thought and reasoned as a child does. But when I became a man my thoughts grew far beyond those of my childhood, and now I have put away the childish things. In the same way, we can see and understand only a little about God now, as if we were peering at his reflection in a poor mirror; but someday we are going to see him in his completeness, face-to-face. Now all that I know is hazy and blurred, but then I will see everything clearly, just as clearly as God sees into my heart right now.

" 'There are three things that remain—faith, hope, and love—and the greatest of these is love.' (1 Corinthians 13 TLB)

"Benjamin, do you take Sarai Rebekah Levy to be your lawfully wedded wife?"

"I do." Benjamin smiled at his bride.

"Sarai, do you take Benjamin Isaac Sharon to be your lawfully wedded husband?"

"I do, I do," Sarai said quietly, as Benjamin placed a golden ring on her finger and she, in turn, placed a golden ring on his.

"Benjamin and Sarai. Under the authority vested to me by the state, I now pronounce you man and wife."

Cheers erupted from the small gathering and once again the young man blew the shofar.

"And yes, you may kiss the bride."

Chapter Twenty-Three

Andréa Veronique was unusually quiet during dinner that evening. After Verity and Michala left the room, Stuart spoke first. "What's wrong, hon?" he asked gently.

Andréa looked down. "Stuart, there's something I need to tell you," she said softly. She hesitated, her words breaking momentarily. "I . . . I . . . don't know where to start. I can't believe we're about to have this conversation. I'm so ashamed . . ." Andréa began to weep. "Oh, Stuart, I'm so sorry . . ."

"Honey, what's wrong? Andréa, what is it? Tell me." Stuart stood up and walked briskly around the table, then moved a chair close to his wife and leaned toward her, placing his hands on her shoulders, his face inches from hers. Stuart looked alarmed. "*Please* tell me," he pleaded.

Andréa Veronique tried to compose herself, but the words came out falteringly, as if stumbling on an uneven trail. "When I was in college . . . I . . . I don't know how to say it. How should . . . how should I even begin? Stuart, I had an abortion!" she cried out. "Stuart, I had an abortion, I had an abortion, I had an abortion!" Andréa Veronique clutched at her hair, her face twisted in anguish. Tears welled up in her eyes as she looked up at Stuart, and then she began sobbing.

Stuart was confused, dumbfounded. He couldn't believe what he was hearing. "What are you saying? Andréa, what did you just say?" he exclaimed. "What did I just hear?" he said, but his words were drowned out by Andréa Veronique's crying as she sat in the chair, heaving forward, taking deep breaths between sobs. He stared at her blankly, his face frozen, horror-struck, and then he pushed himself up from the table and walked several steps into the living room. He placed his hands over his eyes and bowed his head in a state of bewilderment. Something about the moment wasn't real. He felt his equilibrium fading, and he steadied himself against the wall. He was in a bad dream, a nightmare detached from reality. This couldn't be his wife he had just heard. No, rather, he was on a battlefield with one hundred or one thousand weapons firing simultaneously while he ran for cover. He looked across the room at Andréa Veronique, who sat with her hands covering her face, sobbing. Stuart covered his ears and closed his eyes to drown out the sounds and sights of battle, but the prolonged fighting screamed through the piercing sounds and blinding flashes of light. Stuart took a deep breath and walked back to the table. Andréa Veronique sat in the chair, her hands now pressing on the top of her head, still crying, her body rocking back and forth as she lowered her hands and braced herself on the table, taking deep breaths between sobs.

"Why didn't you tell me?" Stuart said, his voice cracking. "All these years of marriage, two children together. Didn't I have a right to know?" he said pleadingly.

"Yes . . . you had . . . a right . . . to know," Andréa said, gasping as she said the words, unable to stop crying. "I should . . . have told you. I always meant to tell you . . . I felt like such a despicable person . . ." She stopped, took several deep breaths, and then began speaking again, slowly but evenly now. "I've never told anyone. I didn't think anyone would understand. I didn't think anyone would ever forgive me."

"When did this happen?" Stuart asked, shaking his head from side to side as he spoke.

"When I was eighteen. It was well before we started dating. Before we had even met. It was during my freshman year in college. I was seeing a guy. It wasn't even serious. We had gone to a club with a group of students, everyone was drinking . . . I drank far more than I should have . . ." Her voice trailed off. "Six weeks later I was sick and found out I was pregnant."

"He wanted you to get an abortion?"

"Yes, but I didn't need to be persuaded. I didn't want a child. Not at eighteen years old. Not as a single mother. All my plans and aspirations were suddenly disappearing before my eyes."

Andréa Veronique composed herself for a moment but

again burst into tears, sobbing as she said, "Stuart, I'm so sorry. I'm so sorry."

Jack Broholm recognized that suffering, loss, persecution, even death was common in the lives of Christian believers—in centuries past and still today. He was torn by the inhumane prison conditions affecting so many Christian believers worldwide. He understood there would be adversity and that even within extreme trials and hardship there was a need to persevere and overcome.

And yet how many who *say* they are living for Him would fall away in the final hour if faced with the reality of having to truly die for Him?

Do you love Him enough to die for Him? Do you love Him enough to live for Him? Reverend Phillips had touched on the same questions and misgivings he had wrestled with for weeks. The age-old questions of faith pierced through his mind like lightning bolts in a blackened, stormy night.

Paul wrote, under the anointing of the Holy Spirit, "For many walk, of whom I have told you often, and now tell you even weeping, *that they are* the enemies of the cross of Christ: whose end *is* destruction, whose god *is their* belly, and *whose* glory *is* in their shame—who set their mind on earthly things" (Philippians 3:18–19 NKJV).

"Lord God Almighty!" he cried aloud. "Don't let this ever be me—please, Lord!"

Broholm reflected on the amount of loss he could

incur and "live with," when he suddenly realized that even if he lost it all, he would still have the Lord. O my Lord! I would still have You! Thank You for holding my life in Your hands!

Jack had learned not to proceed with any important decision unless he and Natalie were in agreement. Earlier in their marriage, Jack proceeded with a business decision that Natalie had questioned. She was right. Financially, the decision had been costly. Jack learned a valuable lesson. As the years ensued he was mindful to always consult with her even if she didn't completely understand the nuances of a particular business proposition. She would take an advocate role, and her questions often added insight. Most importantly, their prayers together brought them into agreement.

On Monday morning after Jack had finished his Bible reading and devotions, and before beginning his workday, Jack shared his thoughts with her. "Please pray about this with me. I'm considering liquidating our stock portfolio and investing in church planting. There's not much of a return from an interest rate standpoint, but we'll be investing in eternity.

"I don't expect anyone else to agree. Most company profit sharing plans and 401(k) plans are invested in the market. I'm not saying that's wrong. But God has been speaking to me. We have far more than we need. I think the Lord is moving us in a different direction."

Jack had a sensitivity to sin. As a young boy he responded to an altar call following a movie presentation of

The Cross and the Switchblade. From his early childhood, he had prayed for discernment. Please don't let me be deceived. Help me to worship the true Jesus, the "image of the invisible God," the "exact representation of His nature," the Son in the Godhead, the Suffering Servant but also the eternal, all-powerful, omniscient God of creation. Don't let me ever attempt to conform the God of the Bible to fit my desires. Rather, help me to conform my life to His leading, for better or for worse.

Jack remembered the sermon on obedience that Benjamin preached some months back, a sermon on complete surrender. "Not our will, but His," he said in his message that day.

" 'Remember, too, that knowing what is right to do and then not doing it is sin' (James 4:17 TLB). We've all been there. We know what we should do, but we rationalize and justify, too often we delay doing what we know is right. That's a dangerous place to be, my friends," Benjamin said.

Two other Scripture passages had spoken to Jack that morning.

"Therefore we also, since we are surrounded by so great a cloud of witnesses, let us lay aside every weight, and the sin which so easily ensnares *us*, and let us run with endurance the race that is set before us, looking unto Jesus, the author and finisher of *our* faith, who for the joy that was set before Him endured the cross, despising the shame, and has sat

down at the right hand of the throne of God."
(Hebrews 12:1–2 NKJV)

"Keep your heart with all diligence,
For out of it *spring* the issues of life."
(Proverbs 4:23 NKJV)

"*Above all else, guard your affections.* For they
influence everything else in your life."
(Proverbs 4:23 TLB)

Natalie looked thoughtfully at her husband. "I have
been praying, Jack. I believe you've heard from the Lord."

Chapter Twenty-Four

Clifton made one last call before wrapping up his day.

"Broholm," the voice answered after one ring.

"Jack! Clifton Rockwell."

"Clifton, great to hear from you!"

"I hope I'm not bothering you. Listen, this isn't work related. I'm going to be in Mountain Fire tomorrow morning; I'll be there for the day. I was hoping we could spend some time together. Could I buy you lunch?"

The men met at noon at Rico's, a small Mexican diner not far from the Artisan Building Supplies store. For the next sixty minutes, Clifton talked about his marriage, his job, his career plans, and the speaker he and Nicole had heard at Faith Gospel Tabernacle.

"Thank you for inviting me to the service. In all honesty, even though I appreciated the invite, I probably wouldn't have gone. Nicole saw an ad in the journal and twisted my arm. I couldn't believe what I was hearing. I've been a conservative my entire adult life, but in all honesty, I wanted freedom for the sake of my own pursuits, not because I was sold out for God.

"I've been a Christian for a long time . . . believe it or not." Clifton looked down. "I had a rigid upbringing, a lot of dogma. Don't get me wrong, I have great parents, the best. But needless to say when I was a little older, old enough to get away with it, I rebelled. Speed forward to my career: Since I was a young manager, it's always been business first. Numbers over people. And in my personal life, ideals over sympathy. Sorry. Not proud of it. Just being honest."

Jack sat quietly, listening thoughtfully, prayerfully.

Clifton gazed out the window and shook his head. "I've let a lot of people down," he said, his voice choking out the words. "I need an accountability partner. I was hoping that . . . I'm hoping that might be you."

Jack smiled, chuckled, and placed his hand on Clifton's shoulder. "I'm old enough to be your dad, but that's okay. Absolutely, Clifton. I'm here for you. We can have lunch every other week when you're in town. Call me in between if you need to talk about something.

"Before you leave, can we pray together?" Jack asked.

"Sure. Yes . . . I would appreciate that."

Jack spent the next few minutes praying for Clifton, Nicole, their two sons, Clifton's job, and, specifically, for God's direction in Clifton's life. He ended his prayer saying, "Lord, thank You for the opportunity to pray with Clifton. Please help my friend. He, too, wants to do the right thing in life. Bless him with Your presence, please.

In Jesus' precious name, I pray, amen."

Jack sat quietly with his head bowed for a few moments and then looked up at Rockwell. "My wife and I have enough money," he said thoughtfully. "I don't know . . . maybe it's growing up in the United States, working endlessly, or so it seems, to improve our standard of living, but like Reverend Phillips said the other night, we always seem to want more."

"I understand," Clifton replied. "Believe me, I understand."

Clifton rested his hand on Jack's shoulder. "You don't know how much I appreciate you. Can I pray as well?"

Rockwell bowed his head, his hand still resting on Jack's shoulder. "Dear God. Help me to be the dedicated, committed Christian I'm supposed to be. Forgive me for being so worldly. It's embarrassing to think about. Nicole was right. Help me not to get ahead of You, Lord," Clifton prayed. "Help me to be in step with You, walking side by side," he continued, when he suddenly realized what he was saying. "No, that's not right, Lord. Help me to *follow* You. I've lived so much of my life with an us-against-them mindset. I'm not a very loving person. I don't really know how to change. I'm willing to go in a different direction, but I'm not sure how. I am willing, but I need help. Thank you for a wife who supports me even though I don't deserve that support. And God, thank you for Jack's friendship. He's a good mentor. Thank You for sending him. Amen.

"Thank you for praying," Clifton said. "I have a lot to

think about. Everything you said resonates. I get it." He paused for a moment. "I certainly hope I get it."

Rockwell took a deep breath and closed his eyes, slowly shaking his head from side to side before turning his gaze back to Jack. "I have a prayer request to mention, and forgive me if I'm overburdening you."

"You're not overburdening me in the least," Jack said.

Rockwell nodded and continued. "Pray for my two sons. Neither one is walking with God. I believe in accountability, but still, I blame myself for not being a better dad. You know, one of my boys once described me as 'a man with a relentless ambition.' My ego went through the roof when I heard him say that. Looking back, what an embarrassment. It's shameful that I wasn't a better example of a Christian father. Remember them in your prayers, please."

"They will be in my prayers every day. You have my commitment," Jack replied.

The men shook hands, and Clifton got in his car and left. Jack sat alone in the small banquet room and began to pray: "Please help me, Lord, to be the man You want me to be. As John the Baptist said, 'He must increase, but I must decrease.' "

Jack sat silently, reflecting on his time with Clifton Rockwell and thanking the Lord for the opportunity to pray with him. He then began to pray again, quietly, but audibly.

"Lord, first let me acknowledge Your mercy in my own life. In respect to material blessings, all I can say is thank you. These blessings haven't been given to me because I'm a holier man than the believer in Sudan who has little in respect to material possessions. They haven't been given to me because I have greater faith than the impoverished Christian in Rwanda. Blessings haven't been bestowed upon me because I work harder than the mother and child subsisting on rice in Laos. My health isn't stronger because I'm more deserving than the frail couple in Pakistan. My freedom has not come as a result of a break-the-chains type of faith, a faith stronger than that of Christian believers in China who have been imprisoned for their testimonies. No, Lord, the truth is that I'm not as holy as the believer in Sudan. I don't have greater faith than the impoverished believer in Rwanda. I don't work harder than the mother and child subsisting on rice in Laos, thankful for what might be their last meal. I do not have greater faith than my Christian brothers and sisters in Pakistan who are persecuted by family members, or Christians in China, many who are behind bars for their faith. Lord, I realize that I have these blessings, in large part, because I live in the United States of America. You allowed me to grow up in an upper-middle-class home. I was given a good education. Financial opportunities have abounded since my youth. Not because I'm better than anyone else and certainly not because I'm more deserving. Please give me a grateful heart. Help me to be humble. As I reflect on the blessings surrounding me, I ask you to help me to be a great giver. A great giver of the time and resources allotted to me. Please loosen the grip, the hold that any of my earthly treasures have on me. And with whatever sufficiency You've given me that might remain, all I can say is thank you."

Rockwell was dismayed by how much he had taken the Lord for granted. How could someone who made a profession of faith so many years before have lived so aimlessly for himself? How did he dig out from such a crater of neglect, a cavern as deep as a mineshaft? As he drove back to the store after his meeting with Jack, he thought about his conversation the night before with Nicole.

"I wish I could relive my life," he told her.

"It's not too late, Clifton. We just need to make a decision to trust and follow Him."

A few days later, Rockwell was back in Santa Fe doing inspections at the Artisan Building Supplies stores. As he drove home that evening, he thought about the conversation earlier in the afternoon with a college student he spoke with at one of the stores. "Some of the greatest scientific minds, scholars, and leaders throughout all of Western civilization have accepted Christianity as the ultimate truth. And you pride yourself on being an atheist?"

"I guess you could say that I've examined the evidence from more of a critical point of view than most so-called Christians. I see too many inconsistencies."

"Inconsistencies in what?"

The young man failed to answer but continued undeterred.

"And besides. There are too many hypocrites in the church."

"Let me share something with you," Rockwell said. "I started meeting with this guy, a business associate, a really strong man of faith. Very studied in the Bible. He shared with me recently that ten of the original disciples were martyred for their faith; many of the deaths were absolutely brutal. Let me back up. There were twelve original disciples of Jesus. One of the disciples, Judas, betrayed Jesus and then later hung himself. The apostle John was exiled to a Greek island where God moved on him to write the book of Revelation—the last book of the Bible. Jack, my friend, shared with me that many scholars believe John died of natural causes, although that's uncertain. But assuming that's the case, there are ten remaining disciples. All ten died horrific deaths for the sake of the gospel."

The young man looked at Rockwell, unsure how to respond. "What's your point?" he finally asked.

"These men followed Jesus for close to three years. They witnessed miracle after miracle. Amazing stories of people being healed, even raised from the dead. After Jesus was crucified and rose from the dead, each one of these men personally saw Him. They saw the resurrected Christ. Eventually, each one came under persecution and they all suffered horrific deaths for their beliefs and for spreading the gospel. The point is, do you think they would have gone to their graves and died a terrible death if the gospel story wasn't true?"

"I can't explain that," the young man muttered, his eyes darting to the left and right of Rockwell's uncharacteristically compassionate gaze.

"You know, we may not agree on this. But I care about you, I really do. I want you to know that what I believe is the truth. My wife and I are Christians. Not perfect people by any stretch. I'm a flawed messenger. More so than most. My wife, she's a lot stronger in the faith than I am, but what I mean is that we're believers. I want the best for you."

"I can tell you're sincere," the young man said. "You wouldn't have spent all this time with me in the aisle of your store if you didn't care."

"Would you mind if I prayed for you?" Clifton asked.

The young man looked surprised but then nodded his acceptance. Clifton laid his hand on the man's shoulder and prayed. It was an awkward prayer, but when he was done Clifton looked at the young man and saw tears welling up in his eyes.

"Reggie, right? Thanks for spending time with me. Here's my card. I'd love to talk to you again. I live in Albuquerque, but I'm in Santa Fe regularly."

Reggie's face lit up. "I live in Albuquerque too," he said excitedly. "I go to UNM!"

On the drive home that evening, Clifton had a pronounced realization of how much Nicole's prayers had meant. He had just prayed for a young man in the aisle of one of his stores with customers and employees an earshot away. That had never happened. His thoughts turned to his family. He was suddenly overwhelmed, again, by the lack of leadership he had provided Nicole, Danny, and Sam. Why did she even stay with me? he thought. How could he make it up to her? How could he undo years of not being there for his sons? For a moment he felt hopeless, but then he recalled a verse from the book of Joel that Jack had quoted when they last met. Rockwell remembered that the Scripture passage involved God restoring the years that the locust had eaten, and he wondered what application the verse had for him. "It's not too late," Jack told him. "God's not done with you yet."

At dinner that night, Clifton shared the events of the day with Nicole and Sam.

"I'm surprised myself," he said, "but things are going to be different."

Rockwell apologized to Sam, who said, "No worries, Dad. We're good." Sam excused himself, and Clifton was left alone with Nicole.

"He needs to see it in action," Nicole said softly.

"He will. You both will. Danny will," Clifton replied.

"Something else I'd like to discuss. I want to address the Dallas move. We need to pray about this. If God wants us to go, fine. With that said, I believe you'll know His leading, probably way before me. Jack shared a story with me . . . well, I won't go into it now, but I'm committed to not doing anything involving a move unless we're in complete agreement. And I think that if we seriously pray about it, God will make His will clear to us. I'm good with staying in Albuquerque. I'm good, in fact, with stepping down to a single store and getting off the road . . . no more travel, if that's what He wants."

"Are you serious? Really? You would take a demotion?"

"I look back on all the decisions I made without seeking God, all the decisions I made where you and I were not in agreement. I'm sorry, babe. I was wrong. I can't change the past, but I'm going to work to make things right in the future."

Rockwell fell asleep that night with a peace he hadn't felt for a very long time.

Chapter Twenty-Five

The following evening, Andréa Veronique walked into the bedroom toward the small desk in the corner where Stuart was grading papers for his class. "Stuart, can we talk for a minute? I have something important I need to tell you." Stuart turned and looked up at Andréa Veronique, who then sat down on the bed a short distance from the desk. "I had lunch today with Arthur Cousins. He handed me an envelope that felt like it was an inch thick."

Stuart nodded. "I'm listening . . . and then?"

Andréa Veronique took a deep breath and continued. "I gave it back to him. I didn't even open the envelope. I don't know how much was in it. I didn't ask. I told him I couldn't support his agenda. He told me I was making a big mistake."

Stuart looked thoughtfully at his wife. "Now what?"

"Well, my plan is, if you agree, to continue my candidacy. I'll be running on a pro-life ticket. If God wants me to get elected, He'll give me the necessary support. If not, it wasn't meant to be."

Stuart stood up and gently lifted Andréa Veronique from her sitting position on the bed. The two embraced, holding each other tightly, and then together they sat down on the bed. Stuart held Andréa Veronique's hands and looked approvingly at his wife. "Andréa, I couldn't be prouder of you. That was the decision I hoped you would make. As far as my income goes, I always feel one breath away from drowning, but I'll get a second job if need be. In the end, neither one of us felt right about this. I didn't want you to compromise your beliefs, my beliefs too."

"I was sure you would understand, but I didn't want to disappoint you," Andréa Veronique said softly. "I know how much you wanted a house. We both want a house." Her voice suddenly took on a rejuvenated tone, and she said excitedly, "It still may happen. If I win the race, our income will change."

Stuart's demeanor had gone from thoughtful to approving to compassionate to loving, but it now took on an eagerness as he looked earnestly at Andréa Veronique. "I have something I need to tell you."

"What, Stuart?" Andréa Veronique looked puzzled.

"I got a call from the bank today." Stuart paused just long enough to see his wife's eyes widen momentarily as she awaited his next words. "We got the loan! We can buy the house we looked at on Rolling Hills. It's small, but it meets our needs."

Andréa Veronique closed her eyes and lowered her head as if to pray. Tears streamed down her cheeks, creating white streaks of uneven lines over the reddish-colored makeup she had put on that morning. She looked up at Stuart and shook her head. "I knew God would see us through. Whether we got the loan or not, I was sure He would help us if we obeyed Him. I knew He would help us if we did the right thing."

"Yes," Stuart replied. "He will help us, I believe that. Something else that I didn't mention to you. I ran into a pastor this afternoon. A former pastor, actually. His name is Robert Thompson. He was at the school picking up one of his grandkids. He used to pastor Grace Covenant Presbyterian Church before he retired. He's still involved with the church; it's the one up the hill near the track, and he invited us to the service on Sunday. We need to find a church home. I don't think Abundant Blessings Word of Faith is a good fit for us. Faith Gospel Tabernacle is a good church, but I'm thinking something smaller would be better. I remember you telling me how much you appreciated singing from a hymnal and how much church orthodoxy meant to you growing up. Pastor Thompson said the service was very traditional.

"He also said he would be happy to meet with us over lunch at the church, at our house, wherever we'd like, and that he would do his best to answer any questions we might have about the Bible, Grace Covenant Presbyterian Church, the Sunday school program for the kids, and his own ministry work before he retired."

Stuart paused and continued circumspectly. "We chatted for about ten minutes. Very, very nice man. I told him that our encounter could not have been timelier, that we were both searching and had a lot of questions right now. He said there are no accidents with God and that God's timing is always perfect.

"What would you think of attending Grace Covenant on Sunday? The service is at 10:45. Actually, I took a liberty and kind of committed us. I told him we'd do our best to make it. Here's the card he gave me."

Andréa Veronique glanced at a cream-colored business card complete with phone number and address, but what caught her eye was the name and title prominently displayed in bold black letters.

Robert Thompson

Kingdom Ambassador

Andréa Veronique smiled at Stuart and handed back the card. "I would like that very much, Stuart. I can't wait to meet Pastor Thompson after the service on Sunday."

Robert Thompson had reached a place in life where he felt his main job was to press into the Lord, to worship Him, wait on Him, and let Him take care of everything else. He wasn't sure what remaining outreach work the Lord might have for him. The afternoon before, Robert had met a young man in the waiting area of a local middle school. A casual greeting turned into small talk, introductions, and before Robert knew it, he was inviting the man and his family to attend Grace Covenant Presbyterian

Church that Sunday.

As Robert drove home, a myriad of encounters spanning forty-plus years of ministry flooded his mind—memories of divine meetings that God had orchestrated, Robert often testified.

That Sunday following the service, Andréa Veronique, Stuart, and Robert Thompson sat in a small conference room at the Presbyterian church Robert had pastored for over twelve years.

"It's very evident to me that I'm not serving Him." Andréa Veronique's face grimaced. Tears welled up in her eyes.

"There's no disguising it. It's clear I'm not where I should be spiritually.

"I asked Him to be my Savior when I was a child. I grew up believing I was saved. I don't even know what that means anymore. I've tried to be a good person. I've made mistakes like everyone else, but everyone else hasn't done what I've done. I've never forgiven myself. Why would anyone forgive me? How could He forgive me? I've lived with this guilt for so long. There are no reparations . . . I know I can never undo what I've done. I've asked God to forgive me. I told Him I was sorry, but how could He ever forgive me?"

"I'm encouraged that you're not justifying what you did. If you were, I'm afraid my counsel would be in vain. But I feel compelled to add that none of us can justify our sins. We're all guilty before God until the blood of Jesus cleanses us."

"No, I'm not justifying what I did. I know it was wrong. I have regrets every day of my life."

"Allow me to read some Scripture passages to you." Robert picked up the New American Standard Bible that he had placed on the conference table. The black leather cover was worn from years of use. The corners were bent, with faded letters and lines of wear creased across the face, but it was an irreplaceable Bible that had been a spiritual treasure from the Lord since Robert's first pastoral calling more than forty years before.

Robert opened the Bible to the book of Romans and began reading. "Romans 5:8 says, 'But God demonstrates His own love toward us, in that while we were yet sinners, Christ died for us.' "

Robert looked at the young couple and said, "God didn't wait until we were perfect people, which, by the way, will never be the case in this life. He died for us while we were still sinful people. Do each of you believe that?"

"Yes, I believe that. I would never doubt what the Bible says," Andréa Veronique said.

"Yes," Stuart said.

Robert turned the pages to 1 John 1:9 and began reading again. " 'If we confess our sins, He is faithful and righteous to forgive us our sins and to cleanse us from all unrighteousness.'

"David tells us in the Psalms that, 'As far as the east is from the west, So far has He removed our transgressions from us' (Psalm 103:12 NASB)."

Robert set the Bible on the table and looked kindly at the young couple. "Andréa Veronique, what you did was very serious. But you've acknowledged your sin. The God who created the universe is the God of redemption, the God who sent His only begotten Son to die for our sins."

Andréa Veronique and Stuart nodded. "We do believe that," Andréa Veronique said.

An hour passed. Robert shared God's plan of salvation, discussed water baptism, answered questions from both Andréa Veronique and Stuart, and read additional passages of Scripture from the Bible.

"I don't want to sound prideful in any way when I say that I've counseled many married couples who were facing very serious challenges of one type or another," Robert said. "My experience tells me that the two of you will need more instruction and guidance than one meeting can provide. I'd like to offer my services to you. I'm willing to meet with you biweekly. Stuart, with your job, Andréa Veronique, with your campaign work, with each of your obligations as parents, you both have a lot going on. I think every other week will suffice."

"We appreciate that offer very much. We really do, Pastor Thompson. We can't afford counseling right now," Andréa Veronique said. "But thank you so much."

"There won't be a fee. I wouldn't dream of accepting anything. This is a ministry the Lord gave to me. Just hours ago, actually." Robert smiled and reached across the table. "Give me your hands. May I pray for you before we leave?"

Stuart and Andréa Veronique nodded eagerly. "You're so kind," Andréa Veronique said.

"Thank you, Pastor Thompson," Stuart said.

Jack Broholm could not remember a happier time. Years before at a Pentecostal revival service, Jack had seen what he would later affectionately describe as "the saintliest looking little old lady" dancing in the aisle of the church, all the while proclaiming, "God is on His throne, glory to God! God is exalted, glory to God!"—though on a personal level he wasn't sure what it meant to dance in the Spirit.

But today, he was willing to try. Jack lifted his arms toward heaven and spun happily through the room. "You have been so good to me, Lord!" he cried out as he moved back and forth, side to side, all the while exclaiming, "Thank You, Lord! Thank You for Your goodness! Praise the blessed name of Jesus!"

Whatever self-consciousness he would have normally experienced was thrown out the window, although it certainly helped that there was no one present to watch. However much his movements lacked in graceful form, he more than compensated with gleeful rejoicing.

A burden had been lifted, a burden weighing one hundred times greater than all the red candlesticks on a trading chart could ever weigh—assuming and understanding the heaviness that so often comes with monetary loss. But Jack's burden was far greater; his concern was having a grateful and giving heart in every circumstance, regardless of the cost. He had sought God's will, and God had graciously revealed the next steps in his life. Those steps were to love Him, serve Him, obey Him, and prepare for whatever plans He might have for him in these uncertain times.

Jack's movements ceased, but he remained standing, arms uplifted. "If You take it all away from me today, I will still love You," he prayed aloud. Jack had a newfound goal, however distant it seemed: he was striving to reach a place of fulfillment where he could say, "Not that I speak in regard to need, for I have learned in whatever state I am, to be content" (Philippians 4:11 NKJV).

The sun shone brightly through the second-floor window, lighting up the desktop and brightening the symmetrically spotted books, papers, pens, bookmarkers, and small portrait of the Thompson family gathered in a park at a picnic outing years before.

Robert sat thoughtfully at his desk, reflecting on his life. There had never been enough time, and now this season too was coming to a close. There was no reason to believe, given the pattern of the past forty-plus years, that the next phase would unveil a different set of circumstances. Only a lightened door, now slightly ajar, suggested any notion that varied results would somehow redeem the challenging years.

Some men divide their life into stages, platforms, acts in a play. Robert divided the years into lives, the lives into seasons, the seasons into chapters, each chapter a segment in time awakened by faces, events, places, and memories, some of which were happy, but most, it seemed, filled with sadness; always striving to arrive someplace, but to a destination vague and undefined with shortcomings and imperfections glaring largely at the forefront, preventing or diminishing the achievements that might have otherwise been satisfying.

Robert knew his calling. There had never been any ambiguity as far as pastoring the flocks the Lord had entrusted to his care. He had faithfully preached the gospel, obediently served in missions work, compassionately served his parishioners, been a faithful, dedicated, and committed husband and father, but he had been unable to rest. There was always something more to be done. The results were never final. The work was never complete.

Robert sat quietly, gazing at the rays of sunshine crisscrossing the family portrait but seeing nothing as his mind raced deep within the thoughts that had perplexed him for so many months now. Lord, how do we reconcile the death of a dream? he thought. You place us here to work and, within the scope of that work, we invariably develop goals—worthy goals oftentimes, goals necessary for the success of our endeavors. You put before us a work and along with that work the desire to achieve results and attain accomplishments that coincide with our efforts. As we pursue these goals, we dream of larger accomplishments and sometimes a vision sets in of loftier yet achievements. Sometimes the dream exceeds our normal sphere of talents, and yet, unmistakably, the abilities and talents and ingenuity come together in a triumph and celebration of effort that works to the fulfillment of our cause—or, as in some cases, the anguish of dreams unfulfilled. And, as Robert feared, dreams perhaps unsanctioned by Him. Robert knew that God alone was the author of man's talents.

Deep in Robert Thompson's spirit, deep within his soul in that meeting place of the Most High, Robert sensed the Lord speaking to him in that still, small moment: The achievements were never intended to be your achievements. The work was always Mine; the goals were always Mine; the results were always Mine; the battle was always Mine; the victory was always Mine. Your part was to embrace that work—the goals, the results, the dreams, and yes, the battle, knowing that you labor for the King, not for yourself; not a humanistic pursuit, not a pursuit of self-fulfillment but the work of a soldier in a cause not of his own making, but of allegiance to the ultimate leader and general, the King of kings! The one true God, the King of Glory in a war far greater in scope than the soldier's vision of how the battle should unfold.

Robert thought of the Scripture passage from Isaiah:

> "The people whom I formed for Myself,
> Will declare My praise."
> (Isaiah 43:21 NASB)

"Thank You, Lord," Robert prayed quietly. "Whatever time I have left in this world, let my life be sanctified for

You, *not for me, but for You.* All of my dreams I give to You. Help my talents to be used for Your glory. Let my remaining years be of service to You for Your honor."

Ever since he could remember, Robert had spent his life *doing.* Now he felt God telling him it was time to rest.

Lying on the right-side corner of his desk, still wrapped in brown paper, was a beautiful woodgrain plaque that Robert had ordered from a local stationery store. Robert removed the paper, walked to the wall opposite his desk, and carefully replaced the plaque that had hung on a half dozen office walls over the past three decades, gingerly and ever so slightly shifting the new mahogany plate from side to side, up and down, ensuring it was tightened snugly on the nail. The message had always been missing something, a fourth and final line describing a place of rest that Robert had taught about, preached on, testified to, but too often in his pursuit of accomplishment and success, failed to abide in.

Robert looked at the plaque and smiled.

NEVER GIVE UP
ALWAYS ENDURE TO THE END
ALWAYS WALK TO THE EDGE OF THE RED SEA
OUR GOD SAVES!

Robert heard a soft voice from behind. "That was never in doubt," Miriam said, gently wrapping her arms around his chest, leaning her head on his shoulder.

"No, it was never in doubt," he said softly.

Benjamin approached the podium and looked at the small audience gathered at the Lutheran Church of the Redeemer near the Church of the Holy Sepulchre in Jerusalem. "Please join me in prayer.

"Lord Jesus, Yeshua, thank You for the cross. Thank You for the agony and the sorrow You endured in the garden of Gethsemane on the Mount of Olives. Thank You for the brutality You endured at the hands of the Roman soldiers in Pilate's Praetorium. Thank You for the exceeding pain You suffered being nailed to the tree, hung on the cross, Your precious body broken, Your precious blood poured out for the sins of the world, for the sins of all who will believe, for my sins, Lord. Thank You for the emotional pain You experienced, I believe, seeing Your loved ones as You hung on the cross being mocked and ridiculed by evil men.

"But O dear God, Lord Jesus: Master, Savior, King; Rabbi, Teacher, Friend; Arm of the Lord; Blessed and Only Covenant; Ancient of Days; Redeemer.

"O Christ Jesus, Messiah: the Way, the Truth, the Life; Wonderful Counselor, Mighty God, Everlasting Father, Prince of Peace.

"O Lord Jesus, Yeshua: Strength of Israel; Shiloh, Scepter, Star; Son of David; Son of Man;

Son of God.

"O Lord Jesus, Yeshua: Lamb of God; Lion of the Tribe of Judah; Bread of Life; Living Water; Light of the World.

"O dear God, Lord Jesus, King of Kings and Lord of Lords! I know that You are a risen, soon coming Lord, Savior, and King! Death could not hold You! The grave could not contain You! You rose again on the third day just as You prophesied! You left the grave clothes lying in the tomb! The stone was rolled away!

"You appeared first to Mary Magdalene near the tomb. You appeared to two men on the road to Emmaus. Two of Your followers were making the seven-mile journey from Jerusalem to the village of Emmaus and You walked with them, and beginning with Moses and through the prophets, You explained the Scriptures about Yourself to them. You appeared to Your disciples. You appeared to Peter. In the Gospel of John we read that You appeared to ten of Your disciples who were meeting behind closed doors for fear of the Jews, and You breathed on them and said, 'Receive the Holy Spirit.' Thomas wasn't present at that meeting, but eight days later You appeared to the disciples again. Thomas had doubted after hearing of Your appearance, but now he exclaimed, 'My Lord and my God!'

"Paul writes that You appeared to over five hundred of the brethren at once, and You appeared to

Your brother James, who later went on to become, under You, the head of the church in Jerusalem.

"And then You ascended into heaven and sat down at the right hand of the Father from whence You will come to judge the quick and the dead.

"Lord Jesus, Yeshua, thank You for the cross!

"And friends—chaver, chavera—this is the message of the cross: that God Incarnate, Jesus, came into this world, was born of a virgin, lived a life among men, preached the coming of the kingdom of God, healed the sick, cast out tormenting spirits—demons— from people, raised the dead, forgave sins, but then allowed Himself to be crucified, hung on a cross, mocked and ridiculed by evil men, His body broken, His blood poured out for the sins of all who would put their faith and trust in Him.

"The triune God, Father, Son, and Holy Spirit, decreed *from the very foundation of the world* that Jesus, as part of the Trinity, as God's only begotten Son, would go to the cross as God's Sacrificial Lamb and pour out His blood for the sins of all who would believe in Him.

"Now two thousand years after the death and resurrection of Yeshua, God's message to mankind is *still*, there is redemption by the blood of Jesus at the cross."

Benjamin looked at the congregation. "Chaverim, friends. As our lives go by, shouldn't we be so much more mindful of the cross?

"Isaiah the prophet said,

'Seek *ADONAI* while He may be found,
call on Him while He is near.
Let the wicked forsake his way,
and the unrighteous one his thoughts,
let him return to *ADONAI*, so He may have
compassion on him, and to our God,
for He will abundantly pardon.'
(Isaiah 55:6–7 TLV)

"We've all sinned. We all need His forgiveness. I urge you to put your faith and trust in Him today. Confess your sinfulness, ask Him into your heart, and surrender your life to Him.

"*But please, listen closely to me*. Your prayer needs to be sincere. You must be willing to follow Him unconditionally, no matter what the cost."

Benjamin motioned for the small gathering to rise and then began singing, a cappella, lifting his tenor voice in worship as the voices of the small assembly blended joyfully, reverentially in unison.

"When I survey the wondrous cross
on which the Prince of glory died,
my richest gain I count but loss,
and pour contempt on all my pride.

"The Bible says, 'For all the promises of God in Him *are* Yes, and in Him Amen, to the glory of God through us' (2 Corinthians 1:20 NKJV).

"What a glorious God we serve, amen?"

Benjamin left the podium and sat down next to Sarai.

"That was beautiful, Benjamin," Sarai whispered.

"All praise to the Father, to Yeshua, to the Holy Spirit, the Lord, the giver of life. Thank You, Lord Jesus, Yeshua. Thank You for Your great sacrifice on the cross."

Benjamin sat quietly as he bowed his head and closed his eyes. "What a glorious God we serve," he whispered.

Amen and amen.

> "Even though the fig trees are all destroyed,
> and there is neither blossom left nor fruit;
> though the olive crops all fail, and the fields
> lie barren; even if the flocks die in the fields
> and the cattle barns are empty, yet I will
> rejoice in the Lord; I will be happy in the
> God of my salvation."
> (Habakkuk 3:17–18 TLB)

The End

"Some trust in chariots, and some in horses:
but we will remember the name of the LORD
our God."

(Psalm 20:7)

Appendix

Within the storyline of *Riches and Prosperity*, multiple Scripture passages are quoted or referenced. In some instances, Scripture quotations are accompanied by notations listing the Bible translation, book of the Bible, chapter number, and verse number(s). In other instances, notations are not made. Dialogue in the story in which a character references a Scripture passage, recites part of a verse, or paraphrases a portion of Scripture are examples of this. In addition, some familiar verses may not be listed. Also, please note that some references below may include only part of the Scripture verse. The author encourages the readers to continue their studies and read each passage in its entirety.

For the benefit of the reader, the following appendix lists the chapter and verse for a number of Scripture passages or paraphrases of Scripture in which reference detail is not provided in the text.

Chapter One:

"Cause me to hear thy lovingkindness in the morning; for in thee do I trust: cause me to know the way wherein I should walk; for I lift up my soul unto thee." (Psalm 143:8)

"Pray without ceasing." (1 Thessalonians 5:17)

"But in every thing by prayer and supplication with thanksgiving let your requests be made known unto God." (Philippians 4:6: verse begins, "Be careful for nothing;)

"The effectual fervent prayer of a righteous man availeth much." (James 5:16: verse begins, "Confess your faults one to another, and pray one for another, that ye may be healed.")

"The book of Revelation describes the prayers of God's people as golden vials filled with incense." (Reference from Revelation 5:8)

"The Bible also tells us that we're to be doers not just hearers of the Word." (Reference from James 1:22)

"Jesus told His disciples that the fields are white unto harvest." (Paraphrase from John 4:35)

"And then Jesus said that we're to be perfect even as our Father in heaven is perfect." (Reference taken from Matthew 5:48)

"Jesus is my righteousness." (Paraphrase from 1 Corinthians 1:30; paraphrase from 2 Corinthians 5:21)

"For all have sinned, and come short of the glory of God." (Romans 3:23)

Chapter Seven:
"I have coveted no one's silver or gold or apparel." (Acts 20:33 NKJV)

Chapter Twelve:
"Whose goings forth have been from of old, from everlasting." (Micah 5:2: verse begins, "But thou, Beth-lehem Ephratah, though thou be little among the thousands of Judah, yet out of thee shall he come forth unto me that is to be ruler in Israel . . .")

Chapter Fifteen:
"Jesus said, 'Abide in me, and I in you.' " (John 15:4)

"In James we read that life is like a vapor, a mist. Here today and then gone." (Reference from James 4:14)

"His mercies are 'new every morning' . . . 'great is His faithfulness.' " (References from Lamentations 3:23)

"We cling to the biblical promise that our sins have been thrown out as far as the east is from the west." (Reference from Psalm 103:12)

"Before the flood, men lived to be hundreds of years old. The Bible tells us that Noah lived to be nine hundred and fifty years old. His father, Lamech, died at the age of seven hundred and seventy-seven. What a blessed number that is! His father, Methuselah, lived to be nine hundred and sixty-nine." (Reference from Genesis 9:29; 5:31; 5:27)

"We're to 'redeem the time.'" (Reference taken from Ephesians 5:16)

Chapter Nineteen:
"The lust of the flesh, and the lust of the eyes, and the pride of life." (1 John 2:16)

"A peculiar people." (1 Peter 2:9)

"Declaring the praises of Him who called us out of darkness into His marvelous light." (Paraphrase from 1 Peter 2:9)

"The servant is not greater than his lord. If they have persecuted me, they will also persecute you." (John 15:20)

"In this world ye will have tribulation." (Paraphrase from John 16:33)

"Guard our hearts and minds in Christ Jesus." (Paraphrase from Philippians 4:7)

Chapter Twenty:
"Apple of God's eye." (Reference taken/paraphrase from Zechariah 2:8)

Chapter Twenty-Three:
"Image of the invisible God." (Colossians 1:15)

"The exact representation of His nature." (Hebrews 1:3 NASB)

Chapter Twenty-Four:

"As John the Baptist said, 'He must increase, but I must decrease.' " (John 3:30)

"For a moment he felt hopeless, but then he recalled a verse from the book of Joel that Jack had quoted when they last met. Rockwell remembered that the Scripture passage involved God restoring the years that the locust had eaten, and he wondered what application that verse had for him." (The verse referenced is from Joel 2:25)

About the Author

R.A. Stokes lived in western New Mexico for a number of years and, for a time, was privileged to have a ministry involving prayer and evangelism. Mr. Stokes desires, in these last days before the Lord's return, to see the body of Christ—all those who are washed in the blood of Jesus—turn to God with revived hearts, awaiting that awesome day of the Lord, the return of our great Savior, Lord, and King, Jesus Christ!

Mr. Stokes believes that Jesus Christ is man's only hope for a lost and dying world. In Acts chapter 16 we read of the prison jailer asking Paul and Silas, "Sirs, what must I do to be saved?" (v. 30). Today, the cry of man, "What must I do to be saved?" is answered powerfully with the words, "Believe on the Lord Jesus Christ, and you will be saved, you and your household" (Acts 16:31 NKJV).

Jesus is a God of perfect justice and righteousness, but He is also a God of love, mercy, and forgiveness for those who will turn to Him in repentance and faith.

Riches and Prosperity will be an encouragement to prayer intercessors and other ministers of the gospel as well as to those seeking hope in a world in need of the mercy, grace, and redemption that only Jesus can give.

www.ingramcontent.com/pod-product-compliance
Lightning Source LLC
Chambersburg PA
CBHW071239300726

48975CB00002B/481